COURAGE IS NOT GIVEN

Courage Is Not Given

By

DRAYTON MAYRANT

APPLETON-CENTURY-CROFTS, INC.

New York

This book is for

UNCLE BILL

CONTENTS

COURAGE IS NOT GIVEN

Part One

THE GOOD LITTLE LEAVES

The blade of Père Joany's pruning knife was wet with the sap of the vines. Pale tendrils and leaf fragments stuck to it, and he wiped them off with his kerchief. The good little leaves, he thought to himself, they are overlooked for the grapes. Yet without the leaves to breathe and drink there could be no harvest. They are workers who toil to make bud become flower and flower swell to fruit. They are beautiful too, the small busy leaves with their delicate hues and their intricate shapes.

Félice-Marie, he remembered, had always loved the leaves. That was why they had named their daughter "Feuille." He sighed as he thought of Félice-Marie. He had been without her for seven years now. He was glad that Feuille resembled her, with the deep blue eyes and light brown hair of the true Gallic type. Ever since her mother's death she had kept his house like a woman. His own eyes brightened at the thought of her, and the bubbling soup in the *pot-au-feu*. Such anticipation was more pleasant than brooding on the religious wars still flaring through the Cévennes. He had hoped the trouble was over, but the king's soldiers had returned to hunt down the last of the peasant leaders. He had advised his cousin the captain to leave the country. He, Père Joany, refused to take part in the fighting. He was middle-aged, a peaceful grower of grapes, with a motherless daughter for whom he must work and find a good husband.

As he came within sight of the farmhouse he saw her at its door. Stockily built and not tall as were most of the mountain girls, she was a spot of bright color in her full red skirt and white apron. She ran to meet him, her wooden shoes clattering on the hard ground.

"You are home early today, Papa. I am glad." She slipped a hand in his. "I have been watching the sunset, and hoping that you would come."

He smiled down into her mobile face, with its upturned nose and generous mouth. Her only beauty was the vivid blue of her eyes that sparkled between thick dark lashes. Her hair was braided and coiled like a matron's, but little ends had escaped and curled around her neck and ears, like the young tendrils of the grapevines he had been pruning.

"Why do you watch the sun go down?" Père Joany asked. "To me its going is always sad."

He knew that it was because of that close of day seven years ago when Félice-Marie had left them and gone with the sunset. But he did not say the words to her daughter.

Feuille shook her head.

"It will come again. If it did not go, Papa, you would never come home to rest and sleep. You would work on in the vineyard as long as you had light to see. I am grateful to the sun for making you come in so that I may give you your hot supper."

I, too, am grateful, he thought, as he squeezed the small, capable hand. I am grateful for the daughterly love and the womanly care she gives me. Perhaps I am grateful most of all for the courage of youth which can face the sunset saying "It will come again."

She looked up at him wistfully.

"Besides, when I look at the sunset I picture against it the tall houses of the great city where Uncle Tonpain lives. I see the Gironde like a reddened lake, and upon it masts of the ships which carry wine from our grapes to England in his big wine casks."

"Some day you shall go," he told her. "I have promised you

that, and I have promised your mother's brother to take you to see him."

He had been delaying the trip until the country was once more at peace. A journey in a farm cart was difficult enough, without being stopped on the way to be searched by the king's guards. But some day he would take her to visit the wine exporter. Since her mother's death he had lived solely for her and the vineyard.

In the kitchen, which was lighted only by the open fire, he pulled his stool up to the table and reached for the bowl that Feuille had filled. Savory smoke rose from it, and the thick china was so hot it burned his hard fingers. She was dipping her own soup from the black pot that stood on the fire from year end to year end and was replenished daily. He and Feuille dropped into it whatever they got from the garden: small hard potatoes, carrots or beets or herbs. Also they picked from the roadsides anything edible, such as wild parsley and wild asparagus shoots. On Sunday and at midweek they dined on potted hare or a fat hen. For he was a prosperous vine grower, although his vineyard was small. He had a barn with a cow and an old Percheron draft horse, a hutch of brown rabbits, and a neat kitchen garden.

They faced each other, drinking the soup and eating thick slices of coarse dark bread. The reflection from the leaping flames danced along festoons of pearly-skinned onions and strings of dried peppers. The stone floor was scrubbed as clean as the table from which they ate. His Feuille would make some man a good wife, but he would then lose her. Had she been a boy, it would not have been so bad; for a boy brought his wife to his father's farmhouse. But soon Feuille would go with some boy to the home of that boy's parents, while he, Joany, remained alone with the grapes and the memories. His thoughts were so intent upon the matter that he did not hear her repeating "Papa!"

It must be a good boy, he told himself, an honest and kind boy. The son of Videau shows white in his eye, like a horse that kicks and bites. Although Videau has by far more land, I would prefer young François Gouttes. His father and Achille Videau have both hinted at a marriage. But there is no hurry, and I shall insist that when she takes a husband my Feuille have a kind man. Kindness of heart and honesty are worth more than all the vineyards. Then, too, I would like her to stay near me and not to leave the Cévennes. Except for the deeds of some hotheads, the mountains are quiet and safe. By the sea men and women are restless, and her path does not lie that way. Some day I will take her to Bordeaux to see my brother-in-law Tonpain. Then I will bring her back—my dear one and my only—to live her life in the safety and the quietude of the mountains.

"Papa," she said, "I have spoken three times. Are you troubled about the grapes?"

"Not about grapes. I was thinking of you. What did you say, little cabbage?"

"I said that this morning Monsieur Gouttes came by to see you. He said that the matter was important and that he would return this evening."

He looked at her intently, but she was unaware of the sharp little sorrow that her message had caused him. He saw that she had no idea why Père Gouttes was coming to see him. She was rinsing the soup bowls and setting the bread back in its box. He watched her moving—quietly but confidently and quickly. Félice-Marie, he recalled, had been gentler and more dependent. But at seven years of age Feuille had become the woman of his house, and for that reason had been obliged to grow self-reliant. A woman who was protected could remain dependent and gentle, but one who had to fend for herself had a choice of only two ways. She could either be crushed and set aside, or she could harden herself and fight her way through. He had the Frenchman's thrifty respect for the woman who did a woman's part, but he wished for his only daughter protection and happiness. He wished her to have her own home and to move briskly in it, upon happy tasks for her husband and children.

She brought her basket of mending, and seated herself beside him on a low three-legged stool in the fan of firelight. He reached out a hand and put it on hers.

"No work this evening, my Feuille. Go to your room and smooth your hair and put on your mother's lace kerchief."

With his torn woolen sock in her free hand, she looked up in surprise.

"Monsieur Gouttes will not see me, so why should I dress for him? As soon as I hear his footstep I will run off to bed."

"I wish Monsieur Gouttes to see you, and to see you at your best. You will open the door for him, and will stay with us until I tell you to go."

Her eyes widened until they were round azure pools of astonishment.

"But why, Papa? I have always gone to my room when your friends came to see you."

His fingers tightened on her hand.

"Because, my little green leaf, this time Monsieur Gouttes will ask my permission for you to marry his son François."

No other man in all the Cévennes would have let his daughter be present while he discussed her marriage with a prospective father-in-law. But Père Joany knew just what he was doing. He wished to observe Feuille's reaction to the whole affair and to see whether or not the boy in question pleased her. He also wished Monsieur Gouttes to see that his son would be getting a girl who had dignity and was at ease with her elders, as well as one who was thrifty and competent in her work.

In the kerchief of Valenciennes lace she looked more like her mother. It softened her square little face and framed her full, childish throat. She opened the door for Monsieur Gouttes and dropped him a quick little curtsy. Her grandmother Joany had been a woman of breeding and had taught her granddaughter many things before she died.

Joany watched as Gouttes stopped in surprise, then put a hand on the blond-brown hair. He was a good man, and his life too centered around his only child.

"What have we here?" he asked. "Is it the little one become a fine demoiselle with a lace kerchief? Just yesterday she and my Franz were children with their pet rabbits. Today he is taller than I, and she has all the graces of a woman."

Joany was pleased with the compliment but understood just what it prefaced, and he made a mental note that the marriage should not be hurried. His Feuille was just fourteen. He would keep her another year.

She was smiling at Gouttes and closing the door behind him. For the first time in her simple hard-working life she sensed herself the focus of interest for grown-up people. It pleased her but did not excite her. She had always taken it for granted that some day she would marry a son of one of her father's friends. She had always accepted the fact that she would live on in the mountains she loved, but upon another farm in the house of her husband. There was less excitement in that thought than there was in the novelty of a journey. All French girls were affianced early and married young, but few girls from among her friends traveled to a city and saw its ships and its wharves. She seated herself upon her stool at a little distance from the two men. Gouttes looked at her and nodded his satisfaction.

"She is a good girl, no? And my Franz is an honest boy. He will be good to her—and he will get all I have when I am gone."

"She is a good girl," said Joany, "and your François is an honest boy. The dot that I give her will not be too small." He sighed. "But I shall miss her."

"Ah! You will miss her? But she will be near you, my friend. You will come often to see her, and to see me. Upon those visits I shall perhaps persuade you that the white wine I make so like a wine of Provence is better than the red which you call your near-Bordeaux. There will always be welcome for you *chez Gouttes,* my old one."

Even the challenge to his wine did not divert Joany. He sighed again, and it troubled Gouttes. Most men were glad to get a daughter affianced well.

"A woman must have a husband," he said. "She must have a home of her own and must not wander from it. Otherwise there comes trouble; for the world is full of danger and the good God, knowing it, meant women to stay at home. My wife and I like your daughter. Do you find my boy to your taste?"

"He suits me," said Joany briefly; "but I am not marrying him. Let us ask Feuille if he is to her taste."

Again Monsieur Gouttes was not as much surprised as another man might have been. He too considered his child's happiness as well as material things. He thought more of Joany because of this deference to a daughter whom he hoped to have as daughter-in-law. He turned to her with twinkling eyes.

"How do you find it, Mademoiselle? Will you have my Franz for fiancé and his papa for papa-in-law?"

She looked at him gravely and she spoke with dignity. "I would like you for my father-in-law, Monsieur."

"And Franz—would you like him too?"

She flushed and nodded slowly.

"He has always been good to me."

"He will be good to you always. Are you content to give him your promise and to come one day to live your life at the farm of Gouttes?"

"I am content to promise, Monsieur. But—there is one thing—"

She stopped and looked pleadingly at her father.

"What is it?" he asked her.

"It is that you promised, long ago, to take me to Bordeaux to see my Uncle Tonpain."

Monsieur Gouttes burst into affectionate laughter.

"We have here a woman who travels! Is it not so? And afterward, when you are married, you will sit by the fire and tell Papa and Maman Gouttes of all the wonderful things that you saw on your journey?"

She nodded shyly but happily at him. For the first time since his arrival Gouttes saw Joany smile.

"You shall see Bordeaux, my daughter. Now you may say good night to Monsieur Gouttes and leave us. Since you are content with his Franz he and I can finish the matter."

From her bed up in the loft Feuille could still hear the sound of their voices. They would arrange all things, she knew; but her thoughts went to young Franz. . . .

He was a dark tall boy, just a year older than herself. They had played together from childhood, for the Gouttes farm was nearby. She remembered that once when her rabbits had burrowed free and she had wept because they were lost in the wild rocky terrain, Franz had hunted the slopes until he caught the last one of them, then he had made the rabbit house escape-proof for her. She had been only nine or ten years old, and the rabbits now on the farm were by many generations removed from the fugitives. But she still loved them and cared for them, although she no longer played with them.

There were other and more recent pictures of Franz. He always came to stand by her side at the secret Huguenot gatherings in homes or in caves of the mountains. Other girls smiled at him, but he looked only at her, Feuille. . . . And when he did so she blushed and was glad to remember that she was wearing her mother's lace kerchief.

She had folded that kerchief from Valence and put it away with care. She would probably wear it when she was married, for she knew that her mother had worn it at her own wedding. Perhaps she would have a white bridal dress. But that was a great deal to hope for. At any rate she would go to Bordeaux and see how the girls of a city were dressed.

The voices of her father and of Monsieur Gouttes grew more faint. She forgot what they were discussing as she thought drowsily of Bordeaux. There would be girls in fine dresses . . . tall houses . . . wharf sheds where the wine waited for shipment in the casks called "pipes". . . .

The rhythm of sleep was in her ears like a distant sound of

rolling. She dreamed of her Uncle Tonpain's casks rolling aboard the Channel ships. . . .

Down in the kitchen Monsieur Gouttes had risen to say good night. He was well satisfied with the result of his visit. His old friend had finally promised that Feuille should marry Franz, although he insisted upon delay until she was fifteen. They had made plans for the two young people they loved, and had lived again in the planning. They had drunk each a cup of Joany's red wine to a long peaceful life for their children: to a quiet life of hard work and temperate living, and godliness by the creed of the French Huguenots.

What can be better, they asked each other, than to live on in the house where one's fathers have lived and to raise sons and daughters to live there after one?

"Eh?" said Gouttes. "But the time passes, and you and I rise before daybreak."

Joany nodded. Together they moved toward the door with its heavy bolt. Before they reached it they stopped—for they heard the sound of running footsteps. . . .

Footsteps loud on the stony ground—and growing nearer and louder. . . .

The two men looked at each other. They were still not far from the terror which had stalked the Cévennes from 1702 to 1705. It had come this way to many farms. It had come out of the night, with the noise of running feet and of hands that beat on a door.

Someone was trying to open it now, but the wooden bar held it fast. Through its crack came the harsh gasping of over-worked lungs that fought for breath.

Joany spoke quickly but low. "Who goes?" he demanded.

A man's hoarse whisper came back to them. He paused to gasp between words.

"It is I—your cousin. I ask shelter. The Royalist—soldiers—are hunting me."

His words ceased, but they heard his breath still come and go with a whistling sound. The two men within looked at each other, and each saw that the brown face of the other had gone pale. Gouttes' lips parted for speech, but the voice without implored: *"Hide me—I ask you in the name of a tie of blood and a bond of faith! Open your door to me, Joany—for sake of the Protestants' God!"*

The disturbance had awakened Feuille. She sat up and rubbed her eyes, thinking at first that it was time to get up and start her morning work. She still dreamed of Bordeaux and the casks, but they were bumping and thumping now. They sounded to her like feet running outside the house.

She jumped up and ran to the small window cut just below the eaves. It was directly above the door, and she heard what the man was saying.

His words brought her wide awake. She had never seen this cousin, but she had heard of him. He was known through the mountains as a captain of Camisards. She had heard her father and Monsieur Gouttes discuss the Camisards and say that they were not exclusively Huguenot, but included other sects which the king and the Church of Rome proscribed as heresies. But they were all Protestants being persecuted for their beliefs, and this man who led them was her kinsman.

When she heard her father admit him she went to the top of the ladder that led from the kitchen to her room high under the roof. She descended a few steps and perched upon a rung out of sight from below and yet within hearing. Monsieur Gouttes was speaking.

"You are wrong to come here, and what is worse you are foolish. This is the first place where the king's soldiers will seek you."

"I know," said that hoarse new voice. "But what would you do, I ask you, if you ran with death on your heels like dogs on a fox's tail?"

Feuille heard the door being closed and the bar set in its slot. She heard her father ask: "How far behind you are the Royalists?"

"I gave them the slip at Saint Affrique. Friends were hiding me there. That was three days ago, and I hoped they had lost me. But they have enough soldiers to encircle the district. I am caught within that cordon, and I tell you there is but one chance for me."

Even before her father spoke Feuille knew what that one chance was. In her childhood she had played in the cave beneath the Joany farm, but she knew that it could now serve a more practical purpose. Its outlet was narrow, a mere slit in the rock, not far from her rabbit cage.

"The friends who helped me and passed me along," she heard the voice continuing, "kept themselves informed and warned me when the enemy came within ten miles of me. I was then at the farm of Saint Esprit, and I fled as soon as night fell. They cannot reach this place before tomorrow, because they are stopping to search every house on the way."

Père Joany said calmly: "You must be in the cave before tomorrow's day breaks."

Gouttes warned him sharply: "You risk not only your life but your property and your child, when you give shelter to a leader of Camisards."

"Then I must risk all three. I cannot give up to death a man of my own blood who is being hunted down because of his religion."

"His religion is not ours. It smells of heresy. It comes of hysteria which makes men and women fall into fits and imagine they see celestial visions and hear the voices of prophets."

"The odor of heresy, my friend, is a strange and elusive scent. It clings to the sabot of any man whom the king and the priests do not favor. When once the hounds of the Royalists have been given a sniff of that shoe, they are off on the trail of its wearer, neither knowing nor caring whether he be guilty or innocent."

"I do not understand you," said Gouttes. "I warn you for your own good. You took no part in the Wars of the Camisards. With my own ears I heard you deplore the killing of the Abbé du Chayla."

The Camisard's voice was passionate as he broke into the discussion.

"How can you deplore the removal of a torturer? It was du Chayla who brought 'the boot' to the Cévennes! I ask you, have you ever seen a victim's leg and foot after they have been forced into that instrument and squeezed? I—I have seen—I tell you! I have seen white splinters of bone sticking through the bloody pulp of flesh which resembles red grapes crushed in the wine press!"

"The Abbé was a monster," Joany agreed. "But in my life I have never yet seen two wrongs that made one right."

"His death saved many other men of our mountains from that agony—an agony inflicted merely because they chose to worship as they thought right."

"I know," said Joany wearily. "I have said that I will hide you."

He was thinking: Trouble has come to me, although I refused to go to it. For generations my fathers have kept the Protestant faith. They have been quiet men who endured and who tried not to strike back. But they have kept what they had a right to keep, in spite of hardship and persecution and torture. I, myself, am a quiet man and a man no longer young. I had hoped that danger would stay afar—at least until I had reared my child. But she is the child of Huguenots. That is her legacy: a dower far more important than her dot as a bride. Although I consider this kinsman ill-advised and violent, I cannot refuse succor when asked in the name of any man's religion.

Gouttes sighed in resignation. "Since I cannot stop you, I will assist you, my old one. He must be given water and food if he is to last in the cave. The quicker we get him and his provisions in hiding, the safer it will be both for him and for us."

Feuille spoke aloud from her perch above their heads.

"There are cheeses already in the cave. I keep them there to ripen, because underground it never gets colder or warmer. I made them myself, and I hope you will find them good, Monsieur my cousin."

Her father gave a short cry of distress. He had meant her to know nothing of what went on. She was too young for the dreadful responsibility. If it ended in disaster she, at least, might be spared if her ignorance of it was convincing.

Monsieur Gouttes was more practical. He had tried to stop his friend. Now that he saw Joany was going through with it, he realized it was best to make a thorough job.

"It is a true daughter of Huguenots that you have here!" he exclaimed. "She will do her part and she will keep her silence."

Feuille did not hear him. She had run back up the ladder and was dressing hastily in her warmest clothes. She was going over in her mind what food she had for the fugitive. There was a new loaf of bread, a generous peasant loaf longer than her arm. It was fortunate that yesterday she had done her baking. She would give him a string of onions and a big bunch of carrots. Her father and Monsieur Gouttes could provide him with wine and water. Along with the cheeses, she thought, he can live a long time on all that, in case the king's soldiers keep us from taking him more.

She ran down the ladder into a kitchen almost as dark as her unlighted sleeping room. The stranger was a darker shape crouched over the few sparks of the fire. Monsieur Gouttes had hastily banked it. Too much light could be dangerous. There must be nothing this night to call the attention of any passer-by to the Joany farm.

Feuille did not stop for greetings. She went straight to the chimney, climbed upon a bench and took down a long string of onions.

The man stood up and stared at her, and she faced him as she climbed down. She saw he was not as tall as either her father or Monsieur Gouttes, and he was so thin that his clothes hung emptily on his frame.

"I think you are hungry already," she said. "But we can give you a plenty."

"It is not the food for him which troubles me," said Gouttes. "What troubles me is to find something which will disguise the entrance to the cave."

He turned to Joany. "Precisely how high is it?"

Joany frowned. "Three feet and a half. A man bends double to enter it."

"But it is narrow," Feuille said. "I recall that when Franz caught my big rabbit—"

Her father checked her. "We have no time to talk now of rabbits."

"I meant, Papa, that after the big rabbit dug his way out of the hutch and Franz brought him back to me, Franz built for him another room on the top of the cage. Since the cage has a wooden roof, he cannot dig his way out. And building that room made the rabbit hutch stand higher than my head, so that if we move it against the cave mouth it will hide completely the entrance to the cave."

When the king's soldiers arrived next day Joany was again pruning his vines. Feuille was with him. He could not risk letting her out of his sight now. Until the danger was past he must keep her close and be sure that nobody talked with her when he was not present. He knew she was practical and brave and intelligent. But she was after all still a child, and she might give the secret away before she realized that she was doing so.

She was working with a small pointed hoe, mounding soil at the vine roots and chopping the few weeds that dared spring up. It was an accustomed task and she liked to do it. She was graceful yet businesslike as she swayed her small strong body until her red skirt billowed with every stroke.

The soldiers were only eight men led by a corporal. They came slowly down the opposite slope from the farm of Videau. Feuille's heart was jumping. It seemed to kick her chest the same way the big rabbit kicked her when she tried to hold him. But she continued hoeing as her father told her to do.

"Do not stop until I appear to see them, little one. Then remember what I have told you. Keep silent; and if they question you pretend you are too afraid to speak."

He had no confidence in her skill at deceit. She had always been crystal clear and honest in word and deed. Even if she forced her lips to deny what would be asked her, he told himself that a questioner would read the truth in her eyes.

He straightened up as the squad came to a spot where he must perceive them. Then he stood, shading his eyes with a hand and staring at their approach. He was aware of his daughter beside him, leaning on her hoe and gazing with parted lips.

The corporal was a short squat man with a stomach that pushed his tunic far out. He squinted into the sunset but did not look unkind as he shouted: "Attention! Long live the king!" "Long live the king," replied Joany.

He stared without expression at the nine men in dirty, disordered uniform. From behind that unintelligent look he was observing them closely. From which one, he wondered, would the danger come? They looked weary and bored. Yet one among them might have the ferret instinct to make more than a routine search. Even more likely, one of them would be the type to try to force advances upon a fourteen-year-old girl.

"It is forbidden," the corporal said, "to give aid to the king's enemies."

He tried to scowl; but having long since lost all his teeth, he only succeeded in drawing back his lips and showing bare gums and a few blackened stumps.

"Yes?" replied Joany in a purposely stupid tone.

But his brain was racing to set every observance in place. I have nothing to fear from this one, he thought, so long as I do not provoke him. If I obey him and appear to have no sense, he will merely look around my farm and go on to the next one. He will look at a rabbit hutch set against a wall of rock; but he will not think to have it moved and examine the wall behind it.

"We seek a rebel and miscreant, an inciter of heretics. He bears the same name you bear. You are the vine grower, Joany?"

Joany relaxed his face muscles and allowed his expression to show the fear that he felt.

"I am the old one called Père Joany. You find me among my vines, corporal. I am a man of peace, and my neighbors will tell you that I refused to take part in the mountain rebellion."

"The farmer Gouttes has just told me so. It is true, however, that you have a kinsman who not only took part in but led that rebellion?"

Joany took off his kerchief and wiped his sweating face. At this point, he thought, it is natural to show distress. He stammered as he spoke.

"It is true that I have a cousin. During the wars in the Cévennes I forbade him my house. When I saw him three years ago I thought he had ceased all violence. I am a man of peace and I will have no traffic with firebrands. All I ask is to work my vines and care for my motherless daughter."

The corporal looked at Feuille. She was staring up at him, with her face rounded by the dark blue kerchief tied under her chin and her eyes round and brilliantly blue between their short thick lashes. His expression softened, and Joany was clever enough to notice and take quick advantage.

"When a man must be both father and mother to his only child, he has no time for rebellion, Monsieur the corporal."

A soldier grounded his musket butt. Another spat. They shuffled their feet and scratched themselves. They were wondering what they were going to get for that evening's meal, instead of thinking about the Camisard they hunted.

"It is true," said the corporal. "And yet this man is your cousin."

"The good God made him my cousin, Monsieur the corporal." Joany added fervently: "I would not have chosen him!"

The corporal realized the justice of the remark and he was impressed by the sincerity of its tone. He could not know the reason which inspired Joany's fervor.

"Nevertheless we must search both your house and your land. My men and I have a hard task. We walk from dawn to dark, and we never know when we will eat."

Feuille's eyes seemed to grow bigger and even bluer. She was a young girl, but she did a woman's work. In its doing she had not failed to learn that men grow gentler and kinder when they are fed. She broke her father's injunction of silence.

"Are you hungry, Monsieur the corporal?"

She turned to her father.

"Papa, the *pot-au-feu* is full tonight. Shall I run to the house and make supper ready for the good corporal and his soldiers?"

Joany looked down into the blue innocence of her eyes and wondered if every woman-child was born with her share of the serpent's guile. The soldiers had snapped to attention. Although the king's men, they had no objection to supping with Protestants provided the soup was rich and hot and the cheese ripe and tasty. They looked eagerly after the flying red skirt, as Feuille made good her offer to run to the house.

Her father turned from watching her too. He reassured himself. Nothing better than this could have happened. Had I made the offer they might have thought that I was trying to bribe them. She has won them over by her innocence and kindness of heart. Yet even I, her father, am not sure whether it is her innocence or her guile.

The corporal rubbed his stomach. "I too have a daughter," he said. "Mine is little joy to me. She resembles her mother, which is why I stay in the army. But it leaps to the eye that this one is a comfort to you, *mon vieux*."

The muscles of Père Joany's heart relaxed like those of his face. No Frenchman says "my old one" to a man he intends to injure. So long as he stayed in this humor the fat corporal would not be difficult to deal with.

The sun was a red ball above the roof which sheltered Feuille's attic room. Joany threw out an arm and pointed in that direction.

"There is a barn beyond the house, and we keep poultry and rabbits. You will wish to look while you still have light. Shall I go with you, my corporal?"

He was thinking: They will hurry because of the fading day,

and they will hurry even more because of the soup Feuille offered.

"It is useless," said the corporal. He made an expansive gesture. "But we must search, I tell you, because we must search. What else would you have?" he demanded.

"Nothing," said Joany, walking with him toward the Percheron's stable.

The corporal waved his soldiers on.

"It is useless, as I said before. But do your duty, my children."

One of his "children" was going toward the rabbit hutch. Père Joany's heart stood still as he saw it. The man was a gangling Provençal with a face like a bearded baby. He came to a stop before the structure that hid the cave mouth, and he bent over until his eyes were on a level with its second story.

"See the little brown rabbits," he cried. "When I was a small child in Provence, I had just such rabbits, I tell you, my corporal!"

His corporal appeared highly pleased at his reminiscences. Joany wondered if the others heard his heart beating.

"Always my rabbits were docile," the long-legged soldier went on. "Other boys told me a rabbit would bite. I would like to establish that fact. It is the reason I always offer a finger to them."

As he spoke he stuck a long dirty finger between the slats of the upper cage. The bad-tempered buck rabbit, without hesitation, seized it between his long curved teeth and bit it to the bone. With a howl of anguish the man jerked it away. Joany saw the top-heavy house rock for a moment on its base, then settle back against the wall of the cave.

The corporal laughed heartily.

"Since the fact is established," he said, "let us go into the farmhouse and sup with this good man, my children."

That supper was a nightmare to Joany. The soldiers sprawled in the kitchen, laughing and joking with each other but not behaving badly. They treated Feuille like a small mother, speaking politely to her and complimenting the food. She seemed at ease and unafraid as she went among them, ladling more soup into their bowls and dividing among them the loaf she had baked that morning to replace the one given her cousin.

Trying to hide his uneasiness, Joany talked with the corporal.

"You find my red *vin ordinaire* not too bad for the palate?"

"It is the best wine of the country I have tasted along my way. And you, my comrade, are the best man I have found in the Cévennes. The others are like their mountains: rough and as hard as stone."

They are deep too as their caves, Joany was thinking. He was glad that the corporal's mind stayed aboveground with the stones. Justice made him speak up for the mountaineers.

"It takes a hard man to break a hard soil. Although I do not share either their faith or their quarrels, I tell you that you can find much good in the Cévennes."

"It may be. But nothing so good as your red wine or the cheese that you make."

The corporal broke a large portion, and smacked his lips over it.

"This is ripened to perfection. I myself am a gourmet upon the subject of cheeses. My mother's brother is a priest, and he loves them to passion. In fact I have accused him of going into the priesthood because he preferred poultry and fish and cheese to red meat."

Joany smiled faintly and inquired: "So?"

"My uncle, who is my godfather too, answered by saying that he would have got more godly results had he baptized the family goat instead of baptizing me. Ah, but my uncle likes his joke. You should see him, my old one!"

"I would like to see this merry priest. Where does he live?"

"His house is at Montauban, but he is seldom in it. It is his task to scour the country for heretics. When he is at leisure my uncle can laugh at a joke, but when he is on duty he is a different man. Have you not observed that men who eat meat are less dangerous than those who fast and scourge themselves?"

"I have not observed," said Joany.

His heart was beating faster. He told himself that whether or not the cheese-eating priest was dangerous, the conversation was verging upon danger.

"Here, my daughter," he called aloud. "Bring more cheese for the corporal."

The man broke another piece and examined and smelled it.

"This, for example, has been kept in an even temperature. It has been guarded from dampness yet not allowed to dry out. My uncle the priest once told me that it was difficult to find aboveground a place to ripen cheeses."

Feuille was at his elbow with the big soup ladle. She tilted it and filled his bowl to the brim.

Joany tried to speak carelessly. His throat felt dry as chalk.

"Did you not see the cheeses on the roof beams of the child's room when you searched it just now, Monsieur the corporal?"

"I saw them there. It is hard to believe that such excellent flavor can be produced by ripening in the house."

"Beneath the roof it is cool and moist," Feuille told him eagerly. She had forgotten danger and was enjoying herself. "When I climbed last time to turn them," she assured the corporal, "I told my papa that the cheeses lived in a different climate from ours below."

"It is amazing," the corporal said. "And I—I thought I knew cheeses!"

Perhaps he knows more than cheeses, Joany told himself. Perhaps he knows all, and is playing with me as Feuille's kitten plays with a mouse.

But supper went on, and the corporal roared again with laughter when his attention was drawn to his soldier's bandaged hand. Feuille had given the man a scrap of linen to wind around it and stop the bleeding.

"You will stick no more fingers at rabbits, my brave Provençal! A rabbit is abstemious. It lives upon grass and carrots. Such harsh discipline, as I have just told my friend, causes bad temper more surely than does eating red meat."

At last the ordeal came to an end. Joany shut his door after them and looked around his disordered kitchen. His shelves of food were stripped bare and his floor tracked with clay and mud. Feuille was already preparing to scrub it.

But the soldiers had not stolen his stock or destroyed his property, as they had done at so many other farms. Most important of all, they had not moved Feuille's rabbit hutch. Perhaps the buck rabbit had done him a favor when it bit the inquisitive Provençal and amused his officer. Yet he, Joany, had sensed danger in the corporal's talk.

The fugitive must be spirited away. That decision emerged clearly from a jumble of thoughts and fears. He must be passed on, as the Camisards were always passed. One farm could not be expected to keep him and take the whole risk. The Gouttes were Huguenots, like the Joanys. But most of the other neighbors called themselves "Children of God" and had taken active part in fighting for that religion. The men of those families should be the ones under obligation to take over their leader and get him out to safety.

Joany slept fitfully. Early the next morning he left Feuille at work and on watch and started for the farm of Lerac. It lay just over the slope and was a vineyard like his own. But the father and two grown sons had been accustomed when the call came to put the long shirt of the Camisards over what little armor they had and go out in the night to defend some neighbor's home.

He found Gil Lerac in the nearer orchard and told him the story of the preceding night.

Lerac's black eyes glittered in his gypsy face. There came over it the wild and exalted expression of those who claimed that visions appeared to them and entitled them to prophesy.

He wiped his knife on his smock and sheathed it in his belt.

"While I prune in my orchard," he said, "a greater pruning is needed. God is calling us to go forth and prune the evil from His world."

Joany tried to calm him and bring him back to the subject.

"Can you not remove your leader, now that the soldiers have gone?"

"They have not gone far. Their commander knows that he has the man he seeks surrounded. Why should we let them close in on us? We should strike this very night!"

"How do you know they have not gone far?" Joany asked.

"I was on the Camisard patrol last night, and I waited in your barn and followed the squad when it left your house." His eyes flamed again. "I wished then to strike and kill them to a man, but the others forbade it!"

"It would have done no good. Others would have come in their place. Tell me what they did when they left my farm."

"Within a few miles they met other squads. The cordon is drawing in and tightening on its prey."

"Who is their commander? He must have information."

Lerac gave a bark of grim laughter.

"There are no informers in the Cévennes. We cannot afford to let them live. Where this officer gets his information I cannot say. I only know that he is a colonel of horse whose cheeks are loose and blue and hang down like the jowls of a bloodhound. His baying is far worse than his bite, and he is not the man to be feared."

Lerac paused and looked westward, where the king's soldiers had gone, and his face took on the lines it assumed when he put on the fighting shirt of the Camisards.

"The man to be feared and the real leader of this search is a priest from Montauban. He devotes his life to the hunting of those he calls heretics. I have seen him and I remember his mouth. It is small and narrow, and his teeth protrude from it as sharp and curved as the teeth of a rabbit."

While Père Joany kept watch, Lerac crawled into the cave to tell the hidden man of the latest developments and to plan with him the next move.

The rabbits were excited by the disturbance of their house. The little ones cowered so close to their mother that the lower cage seemed occupied by a single heap of brown fur. Above them the buck thumped on their roof with his long hind legs, then lay crouched with flattened ears and a red spark in his eyes.

Feuille was doing her housework, and as she worked she sang:

> *"On the bridge of Avignon*
> *We dance around and around...."*

She has had little dancing in her life, her father told himself. As soon as I am free of this suspense, I will keep my promise and take her to Bordeaux.

The thought struck him of a sudden. Why not take her at once? Surely, if I am away from my farm I cannot be held responsible for a hunted man who comes and hides in its cave. The very fact that I go away will bear silent witness that I am not afraid for it to be searched. On the other hand, departure can do my kinsman no harm. He has been given provisions, and he will be safer if the place appears deserted.

When Lerac came out of the cave he listened and agreed.

"It will be best for you and for him. If you go he can stay in the cave."

He glanced from the hillside where the vineyard lay clean and trim to the small house and its outbuildings.

"I can come over before dawn of every day and feed your stock before I start my own work. It will give me an excuse both to see if the soldiers return and to keep an eye on *him.*"

"There will be only the rabbits and hens and the cow."

Joany paused while his eyes followed the rows of the vineyard he loved.

"I have finished my pruning. The vines will be resting for weeks."

He stabbed his stable fork in the ground, cupped his hands to his mouth and shouted: *"Feuille!"*

She came running, flushed and breathless.

"What is it, Papa? I was afraid the soldiers—"

She paused to greet Lerac.

"Goodday, Monsieur Gil."

Her father told her: "Our good friend here has offered to feed the stock and watch the farm while you and I make a journey we have often planned."

"To Bordeaux?" she cried.

Her eyes sparkled like sapphires turned in a ray of light. She clapped her hands.

But she is almost pretty, Joany was thinking. My little one has charm. I thought her too stocky and chubby. Her mother was more delicate. But this one has beauty of her own: beauty of red cheeks and blue eyes and vivacity of manner.

Lerac was looking down at her with a frown on his leathery face.

"It is well for you to take her away," he said. "I will harness the horse while you get ready. If you start now and the beast trots, you can sleep at Millau tonight."

Feuille danced until her sabots clattered like castanets.

"Monsieur the Fat One will trot well. He is big and strong."

"Go then," Lerac told her, "and get what you wish to take, while I see to Monsieur the Fat One."

As she turned and sped toward the house he added grimly to Joany: "The Royalists, when they hunt heretics, make no distinction between fat and thin—or between fighting men of the Camisards and innocent women and children."

While Lerac watered and cleaned the fat horse and put it between the shafts of the cart, he was preoccupied with thoughts of the man in the cave. He wished that the captain had not been obliged to come here to claim sanctuary; for he, Lerac, also had a family for whom he was apprehensive in spite of his wish to fight. Yet, where else should a Camisard come except to the caves of the Cévennes? Men whom he had led in battle would never refuse to help him. It was hard luck for Joany that this particular cave happened to be on his land at just the place and time it was needed. But the Huguenots were strong of heart and tough of fiber, and they would die rather than betray another Protestant. Good luck and bad luck and life and death. What will you have? he mused.... At any rate it is good luck that Père Joany and the girl are about to escape it all and start for Bordeaux.

In the house Feuille laughed and sang as she packed her small traveling box. Her father heard her and told himself that he was doing right. The hidden man can in no way be endangered by our departure, he thought. If the worst befalls and he is found, his punishment will be no more severe. It may be that they would then believe he got in the cave after I left. As for Lerac, he is clever although violent, and he knows how to fight this warfare. He will do all that should be done, and will guard my vineyard besides.

His thoughts returned to the vineyard, for next to Feuille he loved it best. The little green leaves would wait. They stood to him for perfect peace, and he prayed silently: May this way I am taking lead us away from all trouble. When we return along it, please God let us return to the peace of the vineyard and the good little leaves!

Feuille called to him gaily: "Papa, I am ready! Can I help you?"

"No, chérie; I am ready too. And Monsieur Gil has the cart at the door."

She ran out ahead of him and climbed into it. Lerac was stowing her box under the seat when he suddenly straightened and looked westward. Joany froze in his tracks. He too heard it now: the pounding of many horses' hoofs in a gallop. The Percheron raised his head on his thick neck and whinnied aloud.

Over the west slope and down upon the house there poured a troop of cavalry. At their head rode an officer with the face of a mournful hound. At his side galloped a black-frocked priest upon a handsome mule.

And as he saw the farm cart the priest spurred his mount in the lead. He thundered down upon them like a dark-winged Fury, shouting his triumph and giving his commands.

"Seize them! For they confess their guilt by trying to escape. Colonel Charolles, dismount your men and start a search for the cave."

Part Two

THE WINE CASK

In those few seconds of uproar Lerac made his escape. The troopers who threw themselves from their horses surrounded a two-wheeled cart in which a young girl sat, and an elderly farmer who soothed an excited horse.

The priest was still screaming orders which the colonel echoed in deeper tones, which were in turn relayed by an underofficer.

"Go seek the cave, you imbeciles! Two men can guard the prisoners. Take them into the house, and remove this cart from my way."

A trooper took the bridle of the frightened Percheron. Another gestured with his saber to the farmhouse door.

"Inside, farmer!"

He turned to Feuille, who sat white-faced and enormous-eyed. She waited for no words but jumped down and stood by her father. He caught her hand and drew her along by his side. As they entered the door he looked down at her face and found her gazing up at him. He raised his right hand and drew two fingers across his lips.

In silence they stood by the hearth while the trooper lounged at the door. Feuille's cheeks were still colorless, and her lips were parted with fear as she stared from the guard to her father. Joany was haggard, and his heart was a stone in his breast. He was frantic to know just what was occurring outside. How could they fail to find the Camisard? If they found him, how could there be hope for any sentence other than death for the man who gave him sanctuary?

But the fact that Lerac had got away under the very nose of the pack gave him a faint hope that his cousin might too be gone.

Joany's first anxiety was for his child and himself. He would be grateful if the fugitive escaped; but he would be even more grateful if the fugitive was not found on his farm.

Feuille whispered: "Papa, how did the priest—"

He stopped her with a shake of his head. He too was wondering why the priest seemed so certain that there was a cave on the farm. Could there be informers among the Cévenols, in spite of Lerac's savage denial?

At any rate he must in some way convey to Feuille the command that she pretend ignorance and say nothing at all when questioned. His brain was racing in his head like a dog in a turnspit cage. He took a few steps toward the cavalryman.

"Monsieur the trooper, will you not allow my daughter to go to her room? Whatever it is that your officers seek, she has no knowledge of it."

He turned his head there, to glance warningly at Feuille.

"Even if they question her, she can have nothing to say. As you see, she is a young girl—and frightened—and innocent."

The man eyed Feuille with a leering grin.

"I see that she is a young girl, and I can see her fright. As for her innocence—"

His indecency was checked by a cry behind him.

"Out of my way, unregenerate one! You were set here to guard criminals, not to indulge in sinful thought about a daughter of heresy."

The trooper cringed, then straightened like a ramrod and presented arms. The priest ignored him and raged at Colonel Charolles who followed.

"You are unable to train your men. That is the reason we have no success."

The colonel's head drooped, and his bluish jowls drooped with it.

"I do my best, but the task is hard. Men have natural instincts."

"Men—and women too"—the priest's small eyes glared at Feuille—"have instincts of original sin which must be eradicated. That is my task, and I do not shrink from its doing. In punishing a body to accomplish that end, I know that I am saving an immortal soul."

His voice rose almost to a squeal, and as he turned upon Charolles, Joany could see his rodent profile. It was convex like its Roman nose, and its small mouth was full of projecting teeth.

The colonel cowered like a whipped hound.

"Yes! Yes! Of a surety, your Reverence."

"Assist me then by sending that lustful son of Satan outside. Order the prisoners to stand where the light falls on their faces."

The colonel obeyed, and Joany drew Feuille into the light from the door. The rabbit priest had seated himself on the bench near the fireplace.

"You call yourself Père Joany?" he demanded.

Joany faced him, beret-like cap held in one hand and Feuille's small cold hand in the other.

"I am Père Joany, Monsieur the priest."

"You are then owner of this house and farm?"

"It belonged to my grandfather and to his grandfather before him. I am a cultivator of vines, as they were. But I had finished my pruning and was about to start with my child to visit my brother-in-law in Bordeaux."

"*You* say you were leaving to visit your brother-in-law. *I* say you were fleeing in order to escape the consequences of giving aid to a man proscribed by State and Church."

Joany gave himself a few seconds to gather his wits by merely staring back and letting his mouth hang open. He did not yet know whether or not the Camisard had been caught in his cave.

"I tell you I do not understand. I have done nothing wrong, Monsieur. My wife's brother in Bordeaux wrote me a letter two years ago. He is a wine exporter and a man of education. I have his letter still, and I can show it to you. In it he asks me to bring his sister's daughter to see him."

"And my father promised that he would," Feuille added in her sweet young-womanly voice.

"Be silent, spawn of heretics!" their inquisitor shrilled at her.

Joany clasped her hand tighter and drew her closer to him. He saw that he must fight for her with every weapon his brain could find: repetition of innocence, pretense of stupidity, quick thinking and remorseless lying.

"Lying will not save you," the priest said, as if reading his mind. "I can fit you to a boot which will make you speak truth."

"I have already told you the truth. I do not even know of what you accuse me."

"There is a cave beneath your farm?"

"There is a cave, Monsieur. As you must know, there are caves all through the Cévennes."

"I know that there are; and I know that these caves are used to hide malefactors. What is more, I know that you hid one of the worst in your cave."

"The caves belong to God, Monsieur. This one is not mine. It reaches so far that part of it lies under another man's vineyard."

"Although you disclaim it," said the priest, "you seem to know all about it. Also, its only entrance lies upon your land."

"Why should I not know about it? As a boy I played in it. As a man I put it only to innocent and practical use."

"Why then did you disguise its entrance so that it was not found by the fools who first made a search? I have the misfortune to have a nephew who is an idiot. He did not find it although it was underneath his nose. Yet the facts were so plain that in questioning him I discovered at once that you had a hidden cave."

Joany did not know what to say, so he tried to look as if he too were an idiot.

"Merely from my nephew's talk I knew that you had a cave. So I brought the colonel this time, with his troop of cavalry."

He spoke scornfully as he glanced at the table where the colonel had relapsed upon a bench. That officer was exactly as Lerac had described him. His loose, unshaven jowls hung down, and the outer corners of his eyes sagged and showed bloodshot membrane like the eyes of an old hound.

"But the colonel has done little more than did my idiot nephew. Your cave has been found, and in it is evidence that a fugitive has been hiding."

So Lerac got him out, Joany thought. It must have been in those seconds when the troop rode down the slope from the west, when the farmhouse had hidden the cave from their sight, a hundred yards to the east. But, he told himself, it does me little good if there is left evidence enough to convict me.

He pleaded: "Monsieur, how can you be sure that anyone really hid in the cave? The boys of the mountains play in these caves—as I myself used to do."

"Boys would not have taken provisions. Food is too scarce in this country. In your cave we found bread and wine and onions—*and cheese.*"

Joany cried out in what he hoped sounded like outraged protest at theft: "Have the young wretches been eating my supply of cheese for the year? I put the cave, as I told you, to a harmless and practical use. I ripen my cheeses in it."

He saw the lips above the curved teeth draw back in a smile. There was pleasure in the high, squeaking voice.

"So you confess that you ripen your cheeses underground? If you do so in innocence, why did you try to fool the imbecile who is my nephew that you ripened them on the roof beams of your loft?"

"There are cheeses on my roof beams now, Monsieur the priest," said Joany. "They spend a certain time in the cave and a certain time indoors. I did not lie to the corporal. We talked of many things. There was no time to relate to him the whole process of cheese-making. Besides—I ask the pardon of Monsieur the colonel here—but it is known that soldiers are fond of stealing cheeses."

The colonel agreed gloomily: "They steal not only cheeses. They steal everything they can lay their hands upon. There is never a day when I am not drowned in complaints from the peasants."

The shrill voice rose more shrilly. In it was a note of rising eagerness which chilled Joany's warm blood.

"Do not try to turn me aside from the subject, farmer! It is a subject of importance to me—and of even more importance to you, I assure you. It is useless to deny either that you hid the cave mouth with a rabbit cage or that you lied about the making of cheeses. Those two offenses by themselves convict you of intent to keep the king's men from finding what was in the cave."

"Monsieur, I am a poor man. I have known a lifetime of hunger. I tell you I feared the soldiers would steal my year's crop of cheese if they found it."

"I say you are lying, Joany! I say that you feared the king's men would find a notorious Camisard—a kinsman so close that he bears the same name you do—hidden by you in the cave. I say that you would have accomplished your evil work except for me and my knowledge of cheeses."

He stopped and licked his lips as if savoring both the taste of cheese and of his victim's deathblow.

"I say that you would have done so except for the fact that I realized from the corporal's story that such cheese as he ate here must be ripened in a cave."

So it went on into the night. A fire was kindled in the big chimney place. Joany tried to explain and deny, but the high voice interrupted and overrode him.

He felt Feuille's body sagging against him, and he heard her trying to choke back her hiccoughing sobs.

"Monsieur," he begged, "whatever it is that you accuse me of having done, surely you are not accusing a young girl of fourteen years. I pray you to let her leave us. She is weary and terrified and should be asleep in her bed."

"I do not accuse her—yet. Her time has not yet come, and I am still questioning you. She may go, because her whimpering annoys me. But I bid you keep in mind that a full and frank confession may both lessen your own punishment and save her."

Joany led her gently across and into the shadows around the foot of the ladder that went up to her room.

"Go, my daughter," he whispered. "God will watch over us both. Go—and sleep. Try to think that all may be well in the morning."

She held onto his hand with both her hands.

"Papa, I am afraid! The priest with teeth like a rabbit frightens me, because he really *enjoys* tormenting you."

He tried to hush her, in terror lest the two behind him should hear. Glancing over his shoulder he saw the priest had risen from his bench and was leaning over the colonel. The colonel, who had fallen fast asleep, started violently and then nodded as he listened to the priest's low instructions.

It gave Joany a moment to comfort Feuille.

"You are not afraid of rabbits," he scoffed. "From childhood you have handled and fed them, and you know how to lift the vicious ones by their ears so they cannot bite."

She was distracted by his pretense at lightness and by the thought of the animals she loved.

"They may be hungry now. I can see by the starlight to go and feed them."

"It is not necessary. They can wait until morning."

He pushed her again toward the ladder.

"Go, and sleep. But—" he dropped his voice even lower— "before you sleep, pray on your knees to the God of the Huguenots to keep you from all harm."

She still sobbed as she embraced him.

"But I am afraid for *you*, Papa!"

He held her close as he tried to recall all that might give them help.

"Anyone and everyone can be afraid, my Feuille. Only a few can be brave, and I wish you to be one of those few. There was once a good pastor who talked to us at a meeting, and I have never forgotten a story that he told us."

He was not clever with words, and he groped now to find the right ones.

"He told us a story about a great Huguenot. This man was a poet and soldier, and he knew persecution. He knew what it meant to be tortured until he broke under suffering. He knew that courage is not a thing given like a piece of cheese. He said, 'It is something that God lends.' I forget the words, little cabbage. But I charge you that when God lends it to you, you must hold it tight with both hands."

"I will try, Papa," she promised—and then she let go of him.

When he faced the red light again the priest had returned to his bench. The colonel sat upright. He had been given his orders and was taking over once more. He raised his voice almost to a shout.

"Do not waste my time, farmer! I am no corporal whom you can trick. I am a colonel of cavalry who serves his king. In the name of His Majesty, I command you to confess the crime you have committed."

"I have committed no crime, Monsieur the colonel. Neither my king nor my God would wish me to lie."

"The king has declared himself the Lieutenant of God. His wishes are God's wishes, and he has commanded that no man give shelter to a Camisard."

"I know that, Monsieur the colonel. But I am innocent. Neither my king nor my God would accuse a man wrongfully."

The priest cried loudly and shrilly: "You both blaspheme and speak treason! Your attempt at departure convicts you, for you were fleeing from arrest. We know that you are a Protestant, of that cursed sect called 'Huguenot.'"

"All Camisards, Monsieur the priest, are not Huguenots. Their wars are waged by several dissenting sects. Neither I

nor my Huguenot neighbors took any part in them. Although
the Edict of Nantes has long been revoked, we are supposed
to be allowed to keep our faith so long as we do not practice
it in public."

"All rights were denied Protestants by the Revocation."

"I know that, Monsieur the priest. But many priests have
been kind to us and interpreted its terms liberally. My fathers
have been Protestant for a hundred and fifty years. They were
quiet men and they always kept the peace."

"No Huguenot keeps the peace. Their heads are hard and
their blows are hard. It is true that some priests have been
weak enough to allow them to live in their heresy. From that
very weakness sprang the wars of the Cévennes, and for that
reason I was sent to deal with the matter. You claim you are
not a Camisard, but I have certain proof that you are in sympathy with them and have given aid to one."

He paused.

"I give you one last chance. I warn you that it will help
you to make full confession that you hid this man and to give
me the names of the other Camisards who brought him to
you."

Joany said: "I am innocent. I would lie in the sight of God
and bear false witness against my neighbor if I told you any
man brought a Camisard to my farm."

In the firelight the eyes above the curved profile looked red.
The priest rose and his cassock hung straight, showing him
tall and thin.

"Since this man is obdurate and refuses to accept the help
offered him, I can no longer be gentle in my methods. Let us
waste no more of your time or mine, Colonel Charolles. You
may order your soldiers to bring him to me at Montauban for
the real inquiry."

Joany stood slightly stooped in his peasant smock and
watched them leave. He stood alone in his own kitchen, but
the world had caved beneath his feet.

Two days ago, he was thinking, I was happy pruning my
vines. Will I ever return from this inquiry to prune them

again? What of my child? Without me she will be alone in the world.

He started toward the ladder and called her name softly. "Silence!" shouted an angry voice.

The corporal stepped through the door. He blustered loudly: "Say no word! You are under arrest."

He looked back over his shoulder and out into the night. From it came men's voices and the sound of horses' feet. As they grew more distant he turned his head back, met Joany's eyes and whispered: "Be quiet until they have gone! For I have something to tell you."

When Feuille turned away from that last embrace with her father, she intended to do as he told her and go up the ladder to her sleeping room. But she was excited and frightened, and wider awake than she had ever been. She cast a look upward —then stopped with a foot on the lowest tread.

How could she face the darkness and cold and fear in the attic alone? Her whole body was shaking as if with a chill. How could she bear to lie awake in her bed, knowing that in the kitchen below the man with teeth like a rabbit was threatening her father?

She had no human being except her father to whom to turn in distress. The uncle in Bordeaux was still only a name to her. In spite of her terror of soldiers and priest, she wished to stay with her father and to know what was happening to him. She tried to calm herself by praying, as he had told her, that all would be well when the red sun came up again. She tried to think of accustomed tasks that she would soon be doing. Only the rabbits came to her mind in the long minute she stood there. Perhaps the rabbits were hungry and waiting for her to come.

She turned from the scene by the fire and from the dark ladder, and she stole out through the door where the corporal was stationed on guard. She did not blame him for this reappearance of inquisition and she was not afraid of him.

When he saw her and said, "Holà, little mademoiselle," she remembered his former visit and the pleasant excitement of supper with soldiers in the kitchen.

He was relieved to see her, for he had been thinking about her. He knew just what was going on in the farmhouse, and he knew just as surely what would be its outcome. He had been forced before this to serve the fanatic who was the only parent he had ever known, but whom he had been taught in childhood to call "uncle."

"Holà, small maker of cheeses," he said. "Where are you going at this time of night?"

"To feed my rabbits," she told him.

She was glad to stop and exchange friendly words with him. He was big and kind and she sensed his sympathy. For his part, he wished while they talked that she was going farther than the rabbit hutch. He scratched his head and tried to think. He had as yet been given no orders concerning her. He knew that the two men Gouttes and Lerac were somewhere around the place. Gouttes had come up and asked him how his friend Joany was faring. Only men who were real friends of Joany would have dared come.

He wished to help the girl, and he wondered how to do it. Attention would surely be drawn to her when her father's formal arrest was made. But if, before that arrest was made and orders were given about her, she simply disappeared as the Camisard had disappeared. . . .

His uncle would give him a tongue lashing and consign him to hellfire. But that would be all they could do to him since they had not told him to detain her when they ordered his squad to follow the cavalry back to the farm and guard it.

He called to the nearest soldier, who leaned against a chestnut trunk nearby.

"Attention, you half-German border pig! Make yourself useful for once by taking my place at the door. Let no one enter or depart without the colonel's consent."

The man yawned and lounged toward him, and the corporal followed Feuille.

He followed her around the barn, and the starlight showed him her small figure going directly toward the rabbit house. At once two men came out of the barn door ahead and followed her without looking back at him. He followed them and caught up with all three as they stopped by the mouth of the cave. It was now open. The rabbit hutch stood against the rock wall alongside of it.

Gil Lerac cursed savagely as he turned and saw the soldier. But Gouttes lifted a hand.

"Wait," he advised. "I do not think this is a man we need fear. When he searched my place I found him reasonable."

Lerac's voice was still savage.

"He wears the Royalist uniform. I know a hound by its bay, and one does not look for reason in hounds."

The corporal was angered. Only his interest in Feuille kept him from giving this Lerac something to remember him by. Fortunately for him he did not try to do so. It occurred to him that the dark face contorted by hatred looked like the face of a bandit in the *maquis*. But he did not guess that the sinewy hand on the belt of the loose smock was gripping a pruning knife as sharp as the knife of any bandit.

Gouttes, anxious to keep the peace, was repeating: "I tell you the corporal was kind. A man must do his duty."

"Precisely," said the corporal. "I must carry out my orders." He looked at Lerac with disfavor. "But I am no hound, and I do not make war on young girls."

Lerac's belligerent voice rose, but Gouttes touched his shoulder in warning. He feared the younger man's violence and recklessness, which had brought him back to the scene of his narrow escape with the Camisard captain. He knew that Lerac must have Captain Nicolas Joany hidden somewhere dangerously nearby, and he did not wish Lerac to antagonize a trooper and perhaps start the search off again. Nothing could now be done for Père Joany, but with the aid of a friendly guard something might be done for Feuille. So Gouttes spoke politely to the stout underofficer.

"Monsieur the corporal," he said, "this young lady is engaged to marry my son. Surely a man of your discretion and sympathy will not insist upon detaining her?"

The corporal treasured a compliment, for he very seldom got one. Moreover his heart was truly kind and was troubled about Feuille. He spoke slowly.

"As yet I have been given no orders concerning her."

"Then," said Gouttes, "you will not object if she visits her parents-in-law-to-be until this—this matter has been concluded?"

"I would not object," the corporal acquiesced. He added cautiously: "Neither would I give my permission."

"It is understood, for you are a man of intelligence. You would not, for example, even know where Joany's daughter could be found."

"It is understood," said the corporal.

Gouttes turned to Feuille who stood in the starlight gazing at them.

"Your father would wish you, my dear, to come now to Maman and Papa Gouttes."

It came upon her then in a wave of realization.

"No!" she cried. "My father needs me, and I must not leave him!"

She turned to run back to the farmhouse, but Lerac was swifter than she. He overtook her and scooped her up in his thin hard arms.

"It is fortunate she is small," he said. "Let us take her to your good wife."

No one had ever before laid hands on Feuille, and Lerac found that he grasped a young tigress. But he held her until he set her down in the kitchen of the Gouttes farmhouse. Madame Gouttes at once threw warm arms around her, and Feuille wept on her breast.

"I must go back to my father! Monsieur Gil had no right to take me away!"

"My darling—chérie—he did it for the best. I tell you that it is your father's wish."

"My father wishes me with him! What will he do without me? Who will cook his food? Who will look after the cow and the hens and the rabbits?"

"I will," said Franz. "I will go every day and look after them and feed them."

"Attention—all," said Papa Gouttes. "She is old enough to know the truth. Do you not realize, Feuille, that the Royalists are arresting your father?"

She wept more wildly. "I feared that they were! I wish to be arrested with him!"

"You must not. Listen to me! You must remain free in order to try to help him."

Her practical mind seized upon that. She raised her face and gazed at him through a waterfall of tears.

"How can I help him? Will you tell me what to do?"

Lerac gave Gouttes a look which said, You have talked yourself into this position and you can now extricate yourself without my help. Then the Camisard turned his back and departed without words.

Gouttes understood, but he reassured himself that prevarication was justified.

"You have an uncle in Bordeaux who is a man of importance. We will do what we can to send you there, and you can tell him the story."

He knew in his heart that no Huguenot had influence to intervene; but he also knew that girls as young as Feuille had been imprisoned and tortured and executed. He told himself that Joany would approve the untruth, and that the God they both worshiped would at least forgive it.

Her eyes were blazing blue through her tears, like bits of the sky through clouds.

"I will start tonight and walk to Bordeaux—the way the gypsies walk."

"If the Royalists find you they will arrest you. We must send you by secret and roundabout ways."

Health and youth finally sent her to sleep with that comfort, but Monsieur and Madame Gouttes talked until day broke.

"You know it is hopeless, my husband. Let us marry her to Franz at once and make her Feuille Gouttes instead of Feuille Joany."

"That would not save her. We are too close to her home, and we are known as Huguenots. Besides, only the hope of getting help from her uncle for her father is keeping her from going to her father now."

Lerac returned next day and agreed. He had been allowed by the corporal to see and speak with Joany before the prisoner was taken away the night before. Lerac's opinion of the squat soldier had changed.

"The man is no bloodhound, although he wears the king's uniform. When I went into the kitchen I heard him telling Joany that his daughter was safe with you."

"Gladly would I keep her here," said Gouttes. "She is affianced to my son, and my wife has always wanted a daughter."

"You cannot keep her. Joany knows that, and for that reason he sends you this message. 'Ask my good friend Gouttes,' he told me before they took him away, 'to send my child by what means he can to her uncle the wine merchant Tonpain in Bordeaux.'"

"It is what I was planning to do," said Gouttes. "It must be done at once—but how can we do it?"

"I have already made inquiries. The family Dupont have been trying for years to get to Toulouse to visit grandparents who are old and ill. They have a boy of Feuille's size and a girl who is younger."

"Toulouse is on the road to Montauban."

"All the better. The king's men will not look for her in that direction. And I have a married sister living in Toulouse. She will take the girl in and hide her until she can be sent by one of the river boats down to Bordeaux."

Gouttes sighed, but he knew that the thing must be done.

"There will be five in a farm cart?"

"No; and this is the best of it. Lack of money has delayed the trip from year to year. I have just been to Dupont and told him I needed help with the fruit trees, and offered to take his son Nicole to work for six months. What I pay will enable them to make the journey, and Feuille can go in Nicole's place."

"You have arranged it well, and you have been generous."

"No—only practical. Also I took the horse and the cow as soon as the soldiers left last night. I knew that the farm and all upon it would be confiscated as soon as Joany was condemned. I have already sold both animals, and I have here the money for Feuille."

Gouttes sighed. "Then there is nothing to be done except start her safely on her way?"

"There are two things to be done," said Gil Lerac. He turned his dark face away and his fingers played with his pruning knife. In the day it never left his hand or his belt, and at night he slept with it within reach. Its razor blade had many times done pruning foreign to grapevines.

"There are two things to be done," he repeated. "Now to start the girl at once, for the Duponts are on their way here. Afterward to exact payment of as many lives as we can when the king's men return to hunt her down in the mountains."

This was a very different journey from the happy journey Feuille had expected to make with her father. The cart creaked, and the old horse had to be lashed to make him go. Madame Dupont was sharp of tongue, and her husband seldom spoke. Jeanneton was a fat selfish thirteen-year-old who took up more than her share of room and who resented the older but smaller girl.

"You are ugly with your eyes all red from crying," she told Feuille. "Why are you going with us in my brother's place?"

Feuille, sitting on straw in the tail of the cart, still wept and did not reply. Both she and Madame Gouttes had wept at the departure. The farm of Gouttes was so like her own home that she could have been less unhappy there than anywhere else. Maman and Papa Gouttes loved her, and Franz wooed her shyly. He, like his mother, had suggested marriage at once. But Papa Gouttes had shaken his head, and Feuille had told Franz: "I cannot marry you until I have gone to Bordeaux and got my mother's brother to save my father."

"I will wait for you," the boy had said as he handed her bundle into the cart. "And you must not worry about the rabbits. I will go now and bring the whole hutch to our farm, and I will take care of them for you, my *bonne amie*."

As Dupont beat the horse and the crooked wheels groaned, the three at the door had called good-by. That was all the comfort Feuille had to help her now. Jeanneton's eyes were sharp on her face, as if to bore into her mind.

"Franz Gouttes will not wait for you," she gloated. "Yvonne LeBlanc and Henriette Dufours are both prettier than you are. When you come back from Toulouse you will find him married to one of them, and then you will have to be *vieille fille*."

When Feuille still did not answer she added: "And he will eat all your rabbits. He is probably skinning one now for his mother to cook."

Unable to provoke her victim even by that, the fat girl pushed her roughly.

"Move over farther! I want to lie down and sleep."

So day after day went by, with silence broken only by Madame Dupont's scolding and Jeanneton's slaps and pushes. They stopped at no inns; they slept in the fields. The mountains were left far behind them and the flat land was strange to Feuille. She was lonely and unhappy and neglected, but she told herself she could bear anything in order to help her father. She tried to forget the misery of the present by dreaming of Bordeaux and picturing a kind strong man who would welcome her and take up her cause. She saw her Uncle Tonpain in righteous indignation demanding of someone higher than Joany's captors that Joany be at once set free.

Jeanneton brought her back from the dream by an agonizing pinch. Feuille's self-control gave way and she boxed the fat girl's ears hard.

At once bedlam broke out in the tail of the cart. The two girls rolled in the straw, kicking and biting and striking.

Madame Dupont cried shrilly: "She is a wicked one! I tell you, species of a donkey, that she is beating your daughter!"

Dupont allowed his thin horse to stop while he turned his head to look. What he saw appeared to please him, and he smiled for the first time since they had started. Feuille was sitting on Jeanneton's stomach and gripping Jeanneton's hair with both hands.

"It is a thing I have often wished to do myself," he told his wife. "The little one is a true Huguenot. They hit as hard as they pray."

After that Jeanneton kept to her own side of the cart. But Feuille had learned something from the encounter. She had learned that in order to overcome unkindness and roughness one need only be more unkind and rough. It was a shortsighted method, and it was foreign to all her previous training. But through no fault of her own she was leaving gentleness and love and childhood behind her, and the new method was to serve her well in time of need.

At Toulouse Lerac's sister took her in, although her husband protested.

"We have no children of our own, and she will be noticed at once. France is at war, and visitors are supposed to report at the barracks. Besides, this witch hunt of Protestants has created a lucrative trade. Its rewards cause us to be betrayed by renegades of our own faith as well as by Roman Catholics."

Madame Tarbeaux was as frightened as he was, but she stood her ground.

"We cannot turn away a young girl, and one as small as a child. I will tell any who see her that she is my brother Gil's youngest daughter come to visit us from the Cévennes."

"According to Gil's message they are hunting her there. People in Toulouse will put two and two together and will know just who she is. I tell you we must send her on at once to Bordeaux."

"Go then to the wharves and inquire for boats," Madame Tarbeaux cried distractedly. "As you know, there are Protestant captains who are willing to take fugitives."

Tarbeaux went, and Feuille stood by with quivering lips. The dreaded word *fugitive* had been spoken aloud of her. She knew that Monsieur Gil's relatives did not want her, that they were actually afraid to keep her, and that she was being hunted as the Camisards were hunted from cave to cave. The effort of keeping back hot tears made her scowl unpleasantly. She did not appear attractive to her unwilling hosts, as they racked their brains for means to get rid of her. Madame Tarbeaux hustled her up to the top of the tall narrow house and shut her into a windowless cubicle by the chimney.

"I will bring you food," she said; "but you must stay hidden here."

For several days Feuille remained in darkness and suspense. If she had known the road to Bordeaux, she would have run away and tried to go there afoot. She thought of Franz feeding the rabbits and of the warmly-sweet smell that came from the grapes at noonday when the sun shone hard upon them. Above all, she thought of and longed for her father. Only the belief that she could save him upheld her in those days.

Meanwhile Tarbeaux was spending his every free moment at the water front. On the fourth day the bargelike freight boat of the Huguenot Guillaume Marigny was warped into dock. Her skipper-owner was a calm determined man, one of many who feared no risk in the name of their religion. He listened without comment to Tarbeaux's excited words.

"I sail as soon as I load. Bring the girl aboard at—"

"No," cried Tarbeaux. "I dare not take her through the streets!"

Captain Marigny looked at him with unspoken scorn.

"Then I will go to your house for her as soon as night has fallen."

Feuille liked and trusted him at first sight. Together they walked through the dark streets, his big hand guiding her with a reassuring grip on her elbow. At the head of the narrow alley which led to the wharf a gendarme stood like a ghost in the river mist.

"Who goes?" he demanded. "Eh! Is it you, my captain?"

"It is I," said Marigny, "with my daughter Alouette. Say good evening, my little lark, to Monsieur the handsome policeman."

He tapped the ugly young man upon a damp uniformed chest.

"He grows so handsome that I no longer dare bring your older sister Charlotte to Toulouse. That is why you, Alouette, had the good luck to come with me this time. They station him as a rule beneath the big lamp in the square; but tonight his charms are wasted in a water-front lane."

The gendarme beamed at them both and spoke confidingly.

"It is well that I am here and that I know you and your daughters. For a hunt is on in the city for a heretic girl. It is said she fled here from the Cévennes after murdering several Royalists."

"Do not let her murder you, my friend; for that would break too many hearts."

"Eh! I am far too clever for that. I am always on the alert. You will bring Charlotte next time with you, instead of this so-small lark?"

"Who knows? My wife may tell me that it is the turn of Louise or of Anne-Yvette. But I will tell my eldest daughter that a handsome gendarme inquired for her."

They went aboard, and Feuille remained on the river boat until it docked at Bordeaux. Its captain was made of different stuff from Lerac's brother-in-law. Danger made him more efficient instead of stampeding him, and this was not the first time that he had risked his life to run a fellow Protestant to safety.

His kindness restored Feuille's trust in human beings. She lost her fear and was happy for the several weeks of the voyage. Several times they had to turn back to carry cargo downriver again. But they never went as far south as Toulouse, and the boat was not searched at any place where they called. By the time it reached Bordeaux, her thinned face had filled out again and her eyes were bright with expectancy.

"I shall miss you, small cabbage," he told her. "If my good wife saw you she would keep you for her own instead of letting Tonpain have you—and that in spite of the fact that we already have five daughters."

She had been staring eagerly at the city they approached. It looked even larger than Toulouse, which was the largest town she had seen. Its wharves were far larger and more numerous, and the river appeared to her as wide as a sea. Of Toulouse she had terrible memories, but Bordeaux was lovely to her. The sun was setting beyond its skyline, as she had pictured it when she planned the trip with her father. The sky was red and the dock water through which they moved was red. She raised her eyes to the captain's face and spoke with a grave politeness.

"I shall miss you, *Monsieur le capitaine*. I thank you for bringing me, and I would like to see Madame your wife. But I must hurry to my uncle's house. As you know, he is going to help me make them set my father free."

Marigny looked away and frowned. He knew that her errand was hopeless, and he could not risk taking her to Tonpain's house and walking into a trap.

"You must stay aboard, little one, until I send him a message."

She did not protest, but he saw disappointment cloud her eager look. He told her to go to bed and started on his way.

The wine exporter and his wife gave him welcome and warm thanks. They were anxious to get the child at once, and they insisted upon returning with him to the boat.

"Have you heard any news from Montauban?" he asked them. "You must be careful of what you say to her. She has come all this long way in expectation that her uncle will be able to save her father."

Madame Tonpain burst into tears.

"Has she then not been told?"

"She has been told nothing since she left the Cévennes. I ask you again what news you have heard from Montauban."

Tonpain said heavily: "We have heard, and we were expecting my niece. She is an orphan now, for her father has been condemned and put to death."

Feuille's grief was a terrible thing. Père Joany had truly been both father and mother to her. In spite of hardship and fear she had been certain that she could save him if she reached Tonpain. That certainty had lighted her long hard road like a lantern. Although her uncle and aunt were kind, they were strangers to her.

Life with them was luxurious compared to her life on the farm. She had never before seen such a fine house nor eaten such varied and delicious food. Madame Tonpain prepared pastries and sweets, which she had longed for years to do for children of her own. She bought blue silk and made a dress far lovelier than the simple white one for which Feuille had hoped. She gave the girl a room next her own, a room with a big window from which she could see the Garonne. She knitted a warm blue cover for the little bed, and she hung an oval mirror on the wall.

"Look in it while you brush your hair, *mignonne*. It is soft and as yellow-brown as the grape leaves in autumn."

She touched it gently, twining a lock around one of her fingers.

It was the first mirror Feuille had ever seen. She had dressed without benefit of mirrors in her dim, chilly attic room. But she longed with a desperate longing to be back in that place and that time. She longed to be starting her day's work, which was heavy work for a girl of her age, cooking the soup and baking the bread, scrubbing and tidying the house, feeding the rabbits and milking the cow and helping to hoe in the vineyard. At each day's end when the sunset reddened the river's broad flood, her body as well as her heart ached to see her father returning.

She batted her thick dark lashes hard to keep the tears from starting again. When she wept, kindhearted Madame Tonpain broke down and wept with her. Through her sadness, Feuille felt the warm touch of affection and sympathy. She was not only grateful, she knew that she owed a return. Père Joany had been unlearned and had not taught her from books. But he had taught her by word and deed the laws by which he lived: justice and truth and gratitude and human kindness.

Gradually her gratitude warmed into affection for the aunt and uncle who did so much for her. To their joy the day came when her cheeks were rose-red and she laughed again.

"My husband," said Madame Tonpain proudly, "our daughter must not grow up unlearned. Today I will begin to teach her to read and write. For your part, you shall take her to the warehouse and wharf and explain to her the business of shipping wine."

Feuille had not realized that her aunt could read and write. So far as she knew that was an accomplishment limited to the wealthy and important. In her wildest dreams she had never hoped to attain it; but seeing it now within her reach she worked eagerly to learn.

When she was not studying or helping her aunt with housework, Tonpain took her to his business office with him. At first she merely sat on a high stool by his side and observed all that went on at the wharf. Soon she was able to do small tasks for him: to carry messages from one clerk to another, to count and check the casks of wine as they came in from the vineyards.

The dusky water-front sheds where those barrels waited for shipment were to her a wonderland. Listening to the grape growers when they came to make their sales, she learned the names of the famous châteaux which gave their stamp to the

vineyards: *Ausone* and *Yquem, Clos Margaux, Latour Domaine
et Premier Cru,* and *Haut Brion.* She learned how long the
wine of Bordeaux should be kept in its casks before being
decanted. She learned how it differed from Spanish or Portu-
guese wines. She heard and sympathized with the demands of
local grape growers that the name "Bordeaux" should be
limited to their product. She learned far more than she had
dreamed of learning when she planned to go with her father
to the seaport and see the wine pipes of her uncle go rolling
aboard the schooners.

These great barrels had for Feuille the fascination of everything that was linked to her father's life and work. When
there was no ship moored at the Tonpain wharf and the sheds
were full of empty open casks, she moved among them, counting them and peering to see that they were clean. Sometimes
she hummed or sang, listening to the hollow sound which
came back from the rounded sides. She helped the old con-
cierge sweep the floor, brushing dust and broken glass through
a trap door where a short ladder led to the river below. But
above all she liked to stand at her uncle's side on loading days,
watching the great barrels roar across the wharf and down the
ramps to the hold of a ship.

The English captains of those wine ships came to know her
and made much of her. Among them was a Cornishman by the
name of Evan Jeffery, who skippered his own small schooner,
the *Lass of Lizard Point.* Whenever in port he was entertained
at the Tonpain home, and he brought Feuille small gifts and
tried to teach her English. She found its words harsh on her
tongue.

"It is not pretty, and it is harder than French."

He laughed as he told her in fluent French with a broad
West Country accent: "It is no harder for you than was learning your tongue for me."

"Pay attention to him, my niece," said Tonpain. "All learning is of great value, for one does not know when one may
need it. It is even possible that some day you may visit
England."

Feuille's eyes widened, for the Channel seemed to her an ocean. She remembered that Papa Gouttes had said God meant women to stay at home. But she practiced the foreign speech both with Captain Jeffery and with her uncle when the sailor was not in port. By the time she had been a year with the Tonpains she could read and write French and speak a little English.

They were proud of her attainments and loved her like an own child, and she had learned to be happy with them. After she and Madame Tonpain had cleared the table of the night's meal, Tonpain would set two candles in slim brass holders upon it. He would bring out sometimes the Protestant Bible, sometimes a volume of the old Provençal poets, and sometimes the letters of Théodore Agrippa d'Aubigné, that great Huguenot who was both soldier and poet.

"Read to us, little niece," he would say.

And one night Feuille read aloud to them:

> "Courage is something that God does not
> give, but lends at His own discretion."

She stopped short. Her uncle and aunt heard her draw in her breath sharply and saw the pain in her eyes.

"What is it, mignonne?" Madame Tonpain asked anxiously.

"It is that on the last night I saw him, I think my father was trying to tell me this."

Bordeaux was at this date beginning an era of progress. It sprawled upon the Garonne's west bank: a rough semicircle of low white houses, with its many church spires soaring skyward from them. Feuille was now at home in it. She loved its wide streets and its river views. She had learned to wear with grace as well as pleasure the pretty dresses Madame Tonpain made. Thanks to her aunt she had made friends among the young people of its large Protestant colony.

Tonpain, as a wealthy merchant and a citizen of importance,

had so far been exempt from persecution. Like other Protestants of Bordeaux he practiced his religion without parading it. Although the Edict of Nantes had been revoked thirty years before, the Royalists were not unaware that the Huguenot Church still lived. As a political party the Huguenots had been destroyed by trials such as those of the Burning Court, massacres like that of Saint Bartholomew's Day, and the planned tortures of the Dragonnades. But the clean stalwart religion had come to the land to stay. Its small secret meetings were at this time not unlike earlier meetings held in the catacombs. The great Roman Catholic Florimond de Raemond described it, "as though Christianity had in it returned to its first innocence."

With her aunt and uncle Feuille attended those meetings, held in Huguenot homes or in hidden chapels. Their informal and austere services reminded her of less frequent meetings in the Cévennes. Here, as there, the pastor was not frocked. He wore an inconspicuous black coat, cut short with long sleeves, and a black ribbon edged narrowly with white. Somewhere about him or in a small basket or box he carried the tasseled cap to be worn while officiating.

But the Protestants of Bordeaux were grateful to be able to hold services, although secretly. At other places along the coast fishing boats put out on Sabbath Days. Once at sea, their crews became priest and congregation; and the communion for which they risked their lives was solemnly held in cold, damp, swaying holds.

The Cornishman Jeffery, being a militant Protestant and a Low Churchman, attended services with the Tonpains when he was in port. The four had returned one stormy afternoon from chapel, and the two men sat talking in the warm redcurtained room. Feuille, helping her aunt cook supper and lay the table, heard their conversation as she went in and out.

Her uncle was saying: "I will go to the wharf with you after the meal. There is no need for hurry. You have a competent mate to finish the loading, and the tide does not turn for three hours yet."

Feuille set the bread knife on the round board by the loaf.

"Let me go along," she begged. "I love to hear the last hatch slam shut and the mooring hawsers creak on the stanchions as you clear the *Lass of Lizard Point*."

Before either man could reply, all three heard the noise in the kitchen.

A door had crashed open and Madame Tonpain had cried out. The city clerk Riberac appeared in the archway between the two rooms. He was a small stooped man, a friend and fellow Huguenot who had kneeled with them that day. Now the shawl on his head had slipped back, his thin hair was dripping with rain, and his face was white with alarm.

"A company of Royalists has arrived at the city barracks. Half of them have been sent to your warehouse, and the others are now on their way to this house."

The two men had leapt to their feet. Over Riberac's shoulder they saw Madame Tonpain's agonized face.

The clerk went on: "I tell you there is no time to be lost! They are only a few blocks behind me. As I returned from church I saw a crowd around the barracks, and the last of the soldiers were filing into its door. I followed them in, telling the men in the guard room that I must go to my desk to find a tax report. As I ruffled my papers I listened and heard the commander tell the sergeant of gendarmes that they were sent to search the home and the property of the merchant Tonpain for a heretic girl."

Captain Jeffery said: "I will take Feuille to Blaise's dock and get one of his rowboats. When I once get her aboard my ship she will be on English ground."

Tonpain struck his forehead with the back of his hand; but high-strung Madame Tonpain kept her head. She ran to a closet and caught up a warm cloak. As she threw it around Feuille she clasped the girl closely.

"Take her through the kitchen gardens," she told Jeffery. "Take her quickly! We will do all we can to delay them."

She hugged the girl more closely. "*Au revoir, mignonne!* It is only *au revoir!*"

Feuille had not yet said a word, but Jeffery felt her trembling as he caught her arm and guided her like a marionette. In less than twenty minutes they had pushed off and Jeffery was rowing silently along the dark water front.

But as they came within sight of Tonpain's wharf where his ship was moored, he saw that both the *Lass of Lizard Point* and the warehouse were alight with lanterns and torches. He realized that it would be impossible to board his schooner without betrayal by that illumination. Soldiers were silhouetted all along the ramp down which his sailors were rolling the pipes of wine.

The Cornishman shipped his oars, caught hold on a dock pile, and slid his boat under the dock. Icy rain dripped down on them from cracks between the boards above. Across a hundred yards of wharf frontage he heard a voice of authority ring out.

"Remain on guard there by the loading ramp," it shouted. "The warehouse has been searched, and I am sending squads up and down river to search adjacent wharves."

Jeffery whispered to Feuille: "Is there not a ladder and a trap door under the warehouse?"

She tried to steady her voice. "Yes. It is halfway between the shore and the wharfhead."

Jeffery began to work his boat from pile to pile.

"They are coming to search this wharf," he told her; "so we cannot remain under it. Since they have already searched the warehouse, our best chance is to get into it and hide. From there I will find some way to get you aboard my ship."

The tramp of feet resounded above as he led the small boat along. Its passage made no sound, and it moved on dark water in darkness. When they neared the foot of the ladder he saw that it was unguarded. He tied the boat's painter to a rung, ascended and lifted the trap.

The great warehouse was dark and still. He could barely distinguish the empty casks lying row upon row. He whispered to Feuille to follow him, reached down and drew her up. As he did so the door of the trap slipped from his hand and banged itself shut.

At once there was a shout outside and the noise of running feet. Jeffery whispered urgently: "Hide in the nearest barrel!"

As Feuille slipped into it he seized a round barrelhead and a wooden mallet nearby, covered the wine pipe and drove the head into place. As he did so the door was flung open and soldiers crowded in. He went to meet them, with mallet in hand and with desperation in his brain.

"What are you doing upon this wharf while an English sea captain is busy loading his cargo?"

An underofficer stepped to meet him.

"We are searching, by the king's orders, for a girl who has been proscribed. Why are *you* here if you are captain of the ship? Your cargo is aboard and your hatches are being closed."

It gave Jeffery the idea. He raised his voice in an oath.

"Cargo aboard?" he yelled. "Somebody will feel my mate's cat-o'-nine-tails! The lazy lubbers always overlook a few casks. That is what I came to investigate, and I found here one sealed and ready to load."

He tilted the wine pipe which held Feuille and began to roll it slowly toward the ramp.

"Bosun," he yelled, "your loading crew is again short a cask! Everyone of these French pipes holds a hundred and twenty-six gallons. Get it aboard—or else one of you will have a sore backside tonight!"

As he kicked it toward them and shouted, the Royalist guards stood back, and the wine cask thundered along the wharf and down the ramp into the ship.

Part Three

SILK THROSTERS LANE

During those days which his schooner cleared the Bay of Biscay, bucked her way around the Breton capes and drove into the Channel currents, Jeffery tried to think of what would be best for the young girl in his care. In spite of her terror she has no idea of what is ahead for her, he thought. He knew the hardships because he had seen the French refugees in England. With the Revocation of the Edict of Nantes, Louis the lieutenant of God and the lover of Maintenon had driven from France four hundred thousand valuable and industrious citizens. Most went to England and Holland; some of them crossed the seas. England gave them shelter when they came as this girl was coming. Parliament voted funds for their relief; collections were taken up in churches and by public subscription for them. Wherever they went they paid their way by the skill they carried with them. But wherever they went they were a displaced people, hungry with nostalgia for a Frenchman's only home. And because they had more skill in craftsmanship and were willing to work harder and live more economically than the English craftsmen, the latter looked upon them with jealousy and dislike.

Thinking about it, the Cornishman made up his mind to take his friend's niece to his own home, a farm between Land's End and Truro. He told her about the cottage on its windy Cornish acres.

"My father is still able-bodied and farms the place. My wife and four children help him. They will be good to you."

He saw her winking back the tears as she tried to smile up at him.

"I will stay with them until my uncle comes for me. When you sail back to Bordeaux you can tell him where to find me."

He knew that her uncle could never come for her. Huguenots were forbidden to leave France under penalty of confiscation of property and pain of death.

Quiet and pale, she went with him to the offices of his agents. There Mr. Phillips, the senior partner, had news for him. "Phillips & Jarvey have made their first contact with wine importers in the New World. It is an opportunity for us, and it means advancement for you, Captain Jeffery. You have a stout craft, although she is small, and you keep her shipshape. For that reason you and she have been chosen to carry our first cargo of Bordeaux wines to the firm of Weiss & Anvers in the small but growing seaport of New York. Twenty-four hours are all I can give you to clear your papers and put to sea again."

As they went out into the street, Feuille said: "Captain Evan, I must stay in London."

"Why?" he asked her, startled. "You agreed to go to my farm."

"I would go there if you were going back to Bordeaux. But I dare not write my uncle and tell him where I am. On the voyage here you warned me that if I did so the letters might be intercepted. You also told me that all who came to England to find Huguenot friends and relatives went to the Church in Threadneedle Street. My aunt said it was only *au revoir*, and my uncle will surely come for me soon. When he comes I must be in London to meet him."

Jeffery was perplexed. He could not bear to tell her that her uncle was probably in prison.

"We can leave a message with the pastor at Threadneedle Church—a message saying where you are."

She shook her head. "I must be here when my uncle comes."

England was strange to her, and she could not risk putting the long unknown miles between herself and the rendezvous she expected to keep. Jeffery's arguments were in vain. He was finally obliged to take her to Threadneedle Street.

There the busy, troubled pastor who interviewed her in her own tongue tried conscientiously to find out all about her and to decide for what work she was fitted.

"There are three classes of employment: farm workers, household servants, and apprentices of the trades."

"I wish to stay in the city," she told him. "What are the trades to which I might be apprenticed?"

"The French silk makers always need apprentices, and a woman has there as good a chance as a man. Would you go to the Silk Throsters Lane and learn the craft of weaving?"

She nodded. "I would, Monsieur the pastor."

"It is a hard life, the hardest a refugee can choose. But it has advantages over domestic service. You will be assigned to a house where other weavers stay, and the woman of that house will lodge you and feed you. She will take in payment a percentage of what you earn every week."

As he spoke he looked searchingly into the small determined face.

"Your name and address will be written here in the books of Threadneedle Church, for any relative seeking you, to see. But, my daughter, are you strong enough for this labor you are undertaking? The hours are long and the work cruelly hard."

"I am strong, Monsieur the pastor, and older than I look."

He looked after her sadly as Jeffery took her away. He knew all about the weavers of Silk Throsters Lane. Most of them worked fourteen to sixteen hours out of the twenty-four. But that was not unusual for time and place, and he himself kept just as long a working day.

"Miss Peddar will go to the inn for you this afternoon," he called after her. "She is the worker who places the girls, and she will take you to the house where you are to live."

So Feuille and Jeffery had only a short time for their farewells. He gave her what warning and caution he would have given his own daughters in her place. He told her to keep in

touch with him through Mr. Phillips at the office of Phillips &
Jarvey. He charged her to go to the pastor in any emergency.
Then, before Miss Peddar arrived, he lettered a small card
carefully and held it out to her, advising her to keep it. As she
took it from him she read in his neat printing her name and
the place of her birth: FEUILLE JOANY—CÉVENNES.

As she hurried along by Miss Peddar's side through miles of
cobbles and mud and bad smells, Feuille noticed that the
streets grew shabbier. Silk Throsters Lane was dark and un-
paved and narrow, and its houses slouched like drunken slat-
terns. Miss Peddar stopped before one of them and rapped on
its door.

A woman who looked like an ogress opened it, filling its
frame. Her hair had slipped from its knot in greasy strands
around her face, and she clutched together with both fat hands
the loose gray wrapper she wore. She fawned upon Miss
Peddar.

"I was not expecting you, dearie, and you've caught me at
disadvantage. All night long I've been in pain with the tooth-
ache, and that's the reason I'm not yet dressed. If you smell
anything on my breath it's the painkiller I put on the tooth."

Feuille wrinkled her nose at a scent which carried her back
to the wine sheds. The fat woman was backing and beckoning
them to follow.

"Come in, Miss Peddar dearie, and make yourself at home.
I see you've brought me another girl." Her bleared eyes fastened on Feuille. "I'll be a mother to her, as I am to the others
you sent me. Daisy Ray is at work in the shops, but the little
one claims she is sick. It may be she's only lazy and I'm too
kind to her."

"Let me see her, Mrs. Riggs," Miss Peddar demanded.

Mrs. Riggs guided them past a closed door, and then opened
another door on the narrow corridor. The room had only one
window, and it took Feuille's eyes a few seconds to find the

bed and its occupant. Then she distinguished the splash of bright hair and the small white face.

"Moping," said Mrs. Riggs in a tone of resignation. "It's moping she is on this bright day. Sit up and say good afternoon to your benefactor, Flurrit."

The girl raised herself wearily and stared at them with expressionless dark eyes set in the most exquisite face that Feuille had ever seen. She tried not to cough as she whispered: "*Bon jour, Mademoiselle.*"

Mrs. Riggs waved her fat hands and her wrapper parted. She grasped and drew it together, and her voice was resentful.

"I spend my life looking after the girls you send me, and it's a proper trial they are. That Daisy Ray is a bold piece, and this one is not good for much."

"You are paid to look after them," Miss Peddar reminded her as the two women left the room.

Feuille was going toward the bed, and the big eyes were watching her.

"What is your name? And where in France was your home?"

Out of the eyes' dark blankness agony came alive.

"I—I don't remember. The château was on a river . . . and Madame let me play with the ducks on its bank. . . ."

Feuille wondered how old she was; for the child had aroused all her protective instincts. Also it was joy to know that her roommate spoke French. Fleurette held up a battered but once beautiful doll, with white hair dressed high on its head.

"Boum-Boum gave it to me," she volunteered. "Madame my governess told me never to let it go, but when I told Alf that, he took it away from me. I cried until Mrs. Riggs made him give it back. But"—she showed the torn side to Feuille—"he had broken it."

"I'll mend it for you," said Feuille. "Who is Boum-Boum? And who is Alf?"

She already hated Alf because he tormented this child. The other name interested her; for she, like other French children, had called a clown "Boum-Boum."

"Boum-Boum is my big brother," said Fleurette, and she

began to weep silent but desolate tears. "He is my brother—and I love him. But I don't know where he is—or where Maman is."

Feuille sat on the bed and put an arm around her.

"Don't cry! They will come for you. My uncle is going to come for me."

She choked on the words as she wondered how long this younger girl had already been waiting for someone to come.

"Some day they will come. Why do you call your brother Boum-Boum?"

"It is because one Shrovetide a carnival came to the village. They made their camp by the château gates, and my brother took me to see them. I did not call him Boum-Boum then. I called him—"

Her eyes grew wide and afraid, and again they filled with tears. Feuille realized that they were really blue, but such a deep blue that they could appear black.

"I—I cannot remember what I called my brother!"

"But you remember that you called him Boum-Boum. Tell me why you called him that."

"He took me to see the carnival, just he and I together. Neither Maman nor Madame my governess went with us. I laughed aloud and clapped my hands when I saw the carrousel and the performing dogs and the riders on horseback. So afterward my brother did the same tricks to amuse me. While his horse was galloping, he would fling himself from its back to the back of another galloping horse. He would make two stable men hold a great ring of burning paper, and he would jump his horse through that circle of fire. Then we would all laugh and applaud—the servants in the stable yard, and Maman and my governess and I where we sat on a balcony. We would call for 'Monsieur Boum-Boum,' and he would rein his horse up and bow—and then turn a somersault and land on his feet on the ground."

She was beginning to sob again.

"I called him Boum-Boum and I loved him best of all. But I have lost him—and Maman—and—"

The door flew open and Feuille glimpsed a tall slim figure as it plunged in. A voice screamed in English: "You bastard, Alf! If you're after Fleurette again—"

Voice ceased and figure halted as Feuille turned. The same shaft of light from the door which revealed her to the new-comer showed Feuille a grown girl, slender but well developed, with a mass of dark curly hair.

As they stared at each other Fleurette spoke. "It isn't Alf, Désirée. It's another girl, and she's kind to me."

Désirée caught Feuille by both elbows, held her arms out from her sides and turned her around for inspection. She lapsed into French. "You're small but you look tough. You'll have to be."

Feuille gazed up into the hard handsome young face. The eyes were black and flashing, and gold rings hung from the ears. The voice was passionately earnest.

"You poor little thing, you don't know what you're in for. But so long as I'm here I'll stand up for you and Fleurette."

A vast shadow blotted the light from the door. Mrs. Riggs stood there. By now she was unsteady. She balanced herself with both hands on the frame and spoke reprovingly.

"Did I hear you call my Alfie's name, you Daisy-whatever-you-are? I'll have you know he's an honest boy, so don't put temptation before him. When he marries he'll have a good English lass, not a French tinker with rings in her ears."

Désirée leapt for her like a cat, but the fat woman moved quickly. The girl did not pursue her; she slammed the bed-room door. But before she did so she slipped again into English.

"Your Alfie's a son-of-a-bitch," she shrieked, "and you're the right mother for him!"

Before dawn the next day Désirée and Fleurette and Feuille set out for the weaving sheds. Feuille was accustomed to early rising for work, but not to the cold smoky fog and slatternly

city daybreak. Although she could not yet distinguish figures,
she heard voices and footsteps and doors that opened and
closed. The silk makers of the Throsters Lane were done with
the short night allowed them and were hurrying back to the
long day of toil at the looms.

Fleurette insisted that she was well again. But Feuille was
recalling that every time she had awakened in the low bed
where the three of them slept, she had heard the younger girl
coughing. While they dressed Fleurette had hidden the doll
under the bed quilt.

"If Alfie finds it he'll break it again, just to make me cry."

"If he does," vowed Désirée, "I'll make *him* cry!"

The weaving sheds were not far away. Their proximity had
given the narrow byway its name. Feuille saw them sprawling,
long and low and uneven, with candlelight outlining their
narrow entrances. From every direction workers were pouring
toward them: men and women and children who exchanged
greetings in French. Fleurette left them at the first shop, but
Désirée took Feuille on with her.

"Fleurette is able to do nothing harder than wind the warp
on the frame. If you can work the treadles as I do, you will
always be sure of a job and you'll get better pay."

So for that day and the next and for three hundred days to
come, Feuille pumped the treadles that drove the shuttles
across the looms. Désirée was right. There was always a job
for those who were tough and strong. The weaker ones were
demoted to winding or tying or counting. But Feuille made up
her mind that she would not give up. In those first days and
first weeks pain crawled from the soles of her feet through the
bones of her ankles and tendons of her legs. It stiffened her
hips and settled like sores in her back and her abdomen. In
spite of it she set her teeth and went on, aching in every
muscle and with feet that felt burned. She padded her shoes
with old paper and rags of cloth, and gradually her over-
strained body adjusted itself. She was always weary, but the
pain had dulled. She came of working people and was not
afraid of work. She wished to win approval from Désirée, who

had recommended her for the hardest but highest-paid task. Above all things she wished to make her living in London, so as to remain there until her uncle could find her.

She liked and respected Désirée, in spite of the older girl's rough ways and speech. Désirée made it plain, at the weaving sheds and at the Riggs house, that the two younger girls were under her protection. She had at first bargained fiercely with the English overseer in regard to Feuille. The man was unwise enough to argue with her.

"If we shorten the term of apprenticeship the standard of our work will drop. Do you not know that the nobility of Italy refuse to buy any except English silk stockings?"

"*English* silk stockings?" she jeered at him.

She swept the room with a gesture of her hand, but without breaking the rhythm of the heavy treadles which her long legs pedaled for fourteen hours a day.

"Here are no English except yourself, slave driver! Your silk is spun and your stockings made by French Huguenot workers. You clumsy English cannot do it so delicately, and yet you get the credit for it."

She called him a name in French which made the French-women cry "*Chut*" and the Frenchmen laugh with delight. She dared defy him as none of the others did. As Feuille listened she realized the wisdom of Désirée's boldness. She understood that a girl whose work was more than satisfactory could dare what a poorer worker could not. In that moment she made up her mind to make herself indispensable by straining body and brain at her task, but at the same time to stand up for her rights. So at the end of the first month she faced the overseer boldly.

"You know that I do better work than most who have finished their time of apprenticeship. Unless you pay me what I earn I shall go to Threadneedle Street and ask the pastor to find me fairer treatment. He told me to come to him if anything went wrong."

The man glanced about him; then his small eyes came back to her face.

"If you tell no one," he whispered, "I will change the date of your apprenticeship and begin to pay you—but only a small sum. Few accomplish in a day what you and the gypsy girl do."

But hard work and small pay were not her only problems. Upon her second night at the house Feuille had met Alfie. In the long smoky twilight the girls had returned from their day's work hungry, for Mrs. Riggs' greasy paper of food had made them a scanty noon meal. While Feuille ate boiled beef and tallowy suet pudding, she thought of her aunt's veal fricassee with mushrooms and white wine sauce. Every time Mrs. Riggs approached she brought with her the sour-sweet smell which had assailed Feuille's nose on the doorstep. But the woman was not unkind and the supper was sufficient. Désirée ate fast and finished first, then she turned on her landlady.

"We cannot sleep three in a bed. Fleurette should have a cot to herself. You have one upstairs and I want it."

Mrs. Riggs wiped her mouth with the back of her hand.

"The cot is in Alfie's room, dearie. He's accustomed to bring home a chum now and then for the night. I don't know what he'd say about giving it up."

Désirée looked her in the eyes as she inquired: "But don't you know what Peddar will say if I tell her how many bucketfuls of beer you fetch from the tavern every day?"

The fat face crumpled. "Would you ruin my business, dearie?"

Désirée kept scornful silence. Feuille watched. Fleurette went on eating, very slowly and daintily, as if she did not even hear.

Désirée rose from the table. "Where's Alf now?" she demanded.

"He's working late, dearie. He hasn't yet come home."

"You know well enough he's at a cock fight, or laying up with some floozie by the docks. I'm going to get the cot. You can tell him *I* took it."

She turned to Feuille. "Bring a candle and come with me."

Feuille followed upstairs and into an attic room. She held the light while Désirée lifted one of two narrow cots as easily as if she had been lifting a broomstick. Mrs. Riggs stood with a troubled face and watched as they came downstairs.

"Get me a blanket and quilt," Désirée ordered; "and send Alfie to me if he makes trouble about it."

He rapped on the bolted door later, and Désirée opened it, facing him with hands on her hips. Feuille saw a large young man, coarsely handsome and with shifty eyes. He smelled of beer like his mother, and he was in high good humor.

"Give us a look at the new girl," he wheedled. "Ma says you've swiped my bed for her."

Désirée looked from the cot to him.

"We need it more than your drunk friends do. Anything to say about it?"

He winked broadly. "Only that the new girl could have had me along with it."

"Hush your dirty mouth," Désirée stormed at him. "I've told you not to talk that way before young girls."

Fleurette was lying upon the cot with the doll in her arms and with her dark blue eyes black with fright. Feuille stood near her and stared at Alf, her own eyes defiantly blue. Désirée gestured toward them.

"You scared them."

He was staring at Feuille. "She doesn't look as if she'd scare easily. What's your name, sweetheart?"

She tried not to stammer. "Feuille Joany."

He roared with delight and slapped his hips with both hands.

"Spell it for me, blue eyes. I can't speak frog language. I'd come closer and be friendly, except that Daisy'll break my head if I put a foot in the room."

"It's well for you that you remember that," she told him.

She turned and picked up from the bench where Feuille's extra clothes lay the name card that Captain Jeffery had printed so carefully. She held it under Alf Riggs' nose with its lettering: FEUILLE JOANY—CÉVENNES.

"Maybe you can read, you ox, if you can't hear or understand. Read this and get out! All three of us are tired."

He stared for a second and then went into convulsions of laughter.

"*Fool Johnny Sevens,*" he roared. "*Your name is Johnny Sevens!*"

F or day after day and week after week and then month after month, Feuille Joany worked in the weaving sheds. Gradually the skin upon the soles of her feet hardened, and the hot pain like a scald no longer made her limp. Gradually her growing body accepted the strain. She was strong and sturdy and young, and with all her heart she tried to hold onto courage. I must remember, she warned herself, that it is something God only lends. If I do not use it as He means it to be used, He may take it away and leave me a coward forever.

By the end of six months she had become one of the most efficient weavers of Silk Throsters Lane. But in spite of the cruel task the wages were pitiful, and at the end of every week Mrs. Riggs took most of them. For the period of apprenticeship she had boarded Feuille on credit; now she demanded interest on the money owing for that.

"I've had to borrow, dearie, in order to keep you. Mother Riggs is good to her girls. If you don't believe it, ask some of the others about the places they stay."

Feuille asked; and the replies led her to believe that she and Désirée and Fleurette were better off than average in the matter of lodging. Even when under the influence of beer, Mrs. Riggs fed them and cleaned their room and changed and washed their bed covering. Alf swaggered in and out with his tough companions; but beyond impertinent remarks he did not trouble them. Désirée walked out on Saturday nights and on Sundays with him or with one of his friends.

"Fleurette is happier since you came," she told Feuille. "She is always content with you, so I can leave."

Fleurette seemed more cheerful, but the cough still shook her night and day. She and the doll occupied the cot. Since her restless tossing in the same bed no longer awakened the other two, they slept soundly and imagined that she was also sleeping.

Feuille had mended the doll's torn side, and had for a half-penny purchased at the sheds a defective half yard of yellow silk with which to make it a dress.

"It is a birthday present for you, Fleurette. When is your birthday, and how old are you?"

But the child only shook her head and busied herself dressing the doll.

"Let us play then that you will be fourteen tomorrow. For tomorrow is my birthday, and I shall be sixteen."

She was trying not to recall her last birthday in Bordeaux: the cake her aunt had made, the new dress, the bottle of *Château Yquem* her uncle had opened to drink her health. She had aged far more than a year in the twelve months past. More than one of Alf Riggs' friends looked upon her with favor, and Alf frequently invited her to walk. But she compared them with young Franz Gouttes and shook her head. All her emotions of love found outlet in longing for her aunt and uncle and in mothering fragile Fleurette.

She and Désirée still tried to find out the family name of the younger girl. But some memory block had stopped conscious recollection. When they asked her she replied piteously: "Madame my governess always called me Fleurette. She dressed me in a smock that belonged to the stableman's daughter Émilie, and she told me to call her Gran'mère and never to tell my real name."

"Her governess brought her to London," Désirée explained to Feuille. "They were probably escaping from France when she warned Fleurette not to tell her name."

"What became of Madame your governess?" Feuille asked.

"She died. I can remember that. While she was ill the pastor came, and after she died he sent me here. I loved Madame. I loved Maman and Boum-Boum even more."

"Did they come to London with you and Madame?"

"No, they went another way." She paused to think, and her

face was distressed. "Boum-Boum told me that they must go by another road, but he promised he would find me."

She began to weep, and Feuille comforted her. Désirée shrugged her shoulders. Both recognized the Huguenots' pattern of escape: division of a family and flight in different directions. The governess had succeeded in playing her role of a peasant woman traveling with a grandchild. But no one could say whether or not the mother and brother had been as fortunate.

Feuille thought then of the lists at the Church in Threadneedle Street, where she went every Sunday to attend service and to ask if there had come any news of the Tonpains. She described Fleurette to the pastor.

"I recall the child," he said; "but I fear she is one of the lost ones. By the time I was summoned the governess was unconscious. All I could do was tell Miss Peddar to place the child."

"Were there no letters, Monsieur? Were there no ornaments which might identify her? I think, from what she tells, that her people were rich and important."

He shook his head sadly. "Rich and poor are alike when they flee from death. If these people were prominent, they had all the more reason to discard anything which could call attention to them. All this little one could tell us was that her governess called her Fleurette.

"It was a strange case," he added. "There was no money either. Miss Peddar searched the lodging, and the child's and the woman's clothes."

Feuille made her departure in disappointment. When she had stood before the pastor upon arrival, she had been almost as helpless as Fleurette; but she was learning self-reliance in a hard school. From Threadneedle Street she went on to make her fortnightly inquiry at the offices of Phillips & Jarvey. Mr. Phillips told her not to worry because the *Lass* was overdue. He told her that Captain Jeffery might be delaying to find a return cargo from some other colonial port. She went back to Silk Throsters Lane to find Fleurette and the doll at the window.

"We were watching for you. Désirée has gone out with Alf."

Feuille said coaxingly: "Fleurette, is that doll all you brought with you from your home?"

Fleurette glanced fearfully around, then leaned and whispered: "I brought Boum-Boum's snuffbox. But don't tell Alfie, or he'll take it and break it too."

Feuille's heart was beating fast. "Will you show it to me?"

Fleurette put a hand into the bertha-like neckline of her coarse work dress and drew out a small object wrapped in a torn lace handkerchief. She looked trustfully at Feuille as she put it in her hands.

"Nobody else except Boum-Boum knows that I have it. He used to let me play with it and listen to its song. I was crying when he kissed me good-by, and he slipped it into my hand and told me to keep it until he came."

Feuille unwrapped it slowly, in spite of her excitement. It was one of the new musical snuffboxes popular in England and France. Fleurette's brother, she realized, had evidently been a young man of fashion. But as she turned the pretty thing between her fingers, she also realized why he had let Fleurette keep it. It was made of gold and studded with small turquoises. But there was no crest upon it, not even initials to hint at who was the brother Fleurette called Boum-Boum.

Feuille sighed with disappointment as she touched its tiny spring. The lid flew up at once, but that revealed nothing more. Out into dirty Silk Throsters Lane tinkled the little dancing notes attributed to a French king and known as *Amaryllis*.

Time after time, as the months went by, when the little snuffbox lilted *Amaryllis* Fleurette seemed to be on the verge of some recollection. But although Feuille tried to help her remember, the sick girl was never able to recall her name.

Désirée said: "It's because she was frightened in her escape.

When the governess told her never to speak her real name, it frightened her so that it closed her memory as well as her lips."

Feuille could understand that. She lived again, when she thought of it, the shuddering coldness of heart as well as body during the hour in the rowboat with Jeffery. Again she felt his mallet blows vibrate the cask as he drove its head into place and imprisoned her. Her arms and legs again stiffened and extended to brace her body and protect it from a beating while the barrel revolved giddily along the quai and came to rest with a thud in the hold of the schooner. She remembered it; but she tried not to recall it, in order to avoid grieving which she knew to be vain. She braced her mind against it as she had braced her body, and she fought for courage while Fleurette gave up. It was a hard fight as the months went by with no word from the Tonpains or Jeffery.

When they showed Désirée the snuffbox she examined it, whistled and commented: "Don't ever let Riggs see it. It would buy a barrel of beer." She frowned as she added: "I've often wondered where she gets the money for beer, and how Alf can pay for the rum he drinks and the flashy clothes he wears."

Then she shot the bolt of the door and began to dance to the gay yet stately score of Louis the Thirteenth.

Feuille and Fleurette watched her in admiration. Feuille had never seen a minuet stepped, so she accepted improvisations. Fleurette was pleased but uncertain.

"Boum-Boum used to dance that dance. But he did not spin around or kick over his head, as you do."

Désirée flung herself full-length on the bed.

"It's a court dance, and I'm sure he danced it without kicking. But then he didn't *get kicked* when he was small, as I did."

Feuille and Fleurette chorused: "Who kicked you?"

"Jalón kicked me. When I think of him, the places he kicked still hurt." Her wide mouth twisted into a crooked red line and her voice went husky with yearning. "While I'm working the treadles I think of Jalón. It helps to pass the long day—to think of what I'd like to do. . . . I'd like to come up on him unawares with a sharp wooden spindle in my hand. I like to think whether to drive it in that soft place at the base of his brown neck or straight into his belly underneath his red sash."

Her head was thrown back and her eyes luminous. Feuille saw her long fingers contract convulsively.

"Or if I once got a strong silk line twisted around his neck . . . I'm strong enough to strangle him . . . slowly. . . ."

Fleurette asked in her light, sweet voice: "Who was Jalón?"

"He was a gypsy from Spain. That is all I know of him. He used to come to the house at Port Vendres. I remember the house—old and dark and overhanging the water. For weeks and for months he would stay away, and then he would walk in. I hated him, and was afraid of him too."

She lifted her chin and laughed very softly.

"I hate him still, but I'm not afraid of him now."

Feuille understood the tones of her voice as clearly as her words. But to Fleurette it was only an interesting story. She begged: "Why did he come? Why were you afraid?"

"He came to see Marguerite, and he was angry when he found me with her. I was only a small child—dark and scrawny and thin—and Marguerite hid me when she knew he was coming. But if he found me he would curse and kick me out of the door. Marguerite tried to stop him. She was always kind to me. She made me call her Sister, but I think she was my mother."

Feuille knew how far south was Port Vendres.

"How did you get to England?" she asked. "Were you and Marguerite and Jalón Protestants, and were you driven out by the Royalists?"

"Protestants?" echoed Désirée. Her voice was faintly surprised. "I had then never even heard of Protestants. Jalón was a Romany, and Marguerite went to a Catholic church. She was very devout and never missed a Mass. She took me with her and taught me to tell my beads and to make confession. When she went away with Jalón she did not forget me. She left a message with the Sisters at the Convent, and they came for me and put me in the Orphanage of the Faithful at Perpignan."

"Did you like the orphanage?" Fleurette inquired.

"As much as I would have liked living in prison. I ran away when I was twelve years old and joined a traveling circus on its way to Marseilles. I had always danced. Marguerite had taught me. I danced in the circus, and they made me an acrobat. I turned flips forward and backward and sideways. I swung from a high bar and I walked a high wire."

They listened, starved for interest and action and color. Feuille's practical mind went back to the core of the matter.

"If you are not a Protestant, how did you get here to work with the Huguenots in Silk Throsters Lane?"

"The circus troop came to London. We came on a slow boat that stopped in southern Spain and Portugal and western France. Whenever it put into port to load or unload cargo we would go ashore and give a performance. We were all happy, and they were all good to me. When we reached London we gave street shows every night. Then one night the wire broke and I fell. . . ."

Fleurette cried out, and Désirée jerked a thumb toward her.

"I've told her before, but she forgets. I broke several ribs, and they thought at first I'd broken my leg. It must have been only badly sprained, because it has healed perfectly straight, while I still feel little knobs on my ribs when I touch them."

They watched her explore her left side with her right hand while they waited.

"André was the head of the circus, and he was kind to me always. He explained that they had to leave me and go on, since they moved from place to place and I would have to be in bed for months. But he told me I would be cared for if I said I was a Huguenot. He said he wasn't sure just what Huguenots were, but that for some reason the English liked them and took care of them. There was a juggler in the troop who could read and write. André made him write a beautiful letter, saying that I was a Huguenot girl who had lost all her family and been injured while escaping from France. The juggler, whose name was Marcel-Robert, signed the letter 'Édouard le Piété, Pasteur of the Church of Morlaix.' They gave me the letter to keep.

Then, before he left London, André went to Threadneedle Street and told the committee he had discovered a Huguenot girl alone and injured and helpless. He gave them the address of the house where I was, and when they came I gave them the letter and moaned and refused to talk. That wasn't hard to do, for the pain was bad and I was silly from fever."

She paused to nod and smile with approval at the ruse.

"André was good," she repeated, "and he was clever."

One day Fleurette had a coughing spell and fainted at work.

She never went back to the weaving sheds. Her cough grew incessant, although Désirée and Feuille bought black nostrums by the quart. They discussed calling in a doctor, but they had no money to pay one. Together they paid Fleurette's board as well as their own, and Mrs. Riggs looked after her and fed her while they were at work. Alf knew how ill she was, and he no longer frightened or teased her.

He told Feuille, not unkindly: "She's going to die."

Feuille balled her fists at him, as if he were to blame.

"She isn't going to die! I won't let her."

"Bit of a spitfire, aren't you, Johnny Sevens? It isn't your fault. You and Daisy do all you can for her. What about a walk tonight, since it's Saturday? You're getting better looking all the time."

As she refused and turned away he caught her shoulder, and pulled her around and close against him.

"But I like you that way. I never did like 'em easy. No use to try to pull away. A kiss or two won't hurt you."

She felt his strength and knew there was no use to try to pull away. So she raised her foot and brought the sharp edge of its broad wooden heel down hard on his instep. He yelped with pain and let her go, and she ran into the room and bolted its door.

She had no desire to go with him. She wished to spend with Fleurette every waking hour that she was not at work. She had gone to the overseer and volunteered to work two additional hours a day, making her task sixteen instead of fourteen hours, in order to earn a few more pennies a week. She bought a warm nightdress for Fleurette, and every Saturday she squandered a halfpenny for sweetmeats. Fleurette smiled and ate them. She ate little else, and she smiled more and talked less as the time went by.

Except in her relations with the younger girls, Désirée was growing restless and quarrelsome. The son of the publican from whom Mrs. Riggs bought her beer was a friend of Alf, and he had looked upon the gypsy girl with desirous eyes from the first time he saw her. He was a young man of property, the best catch in the neighborhood; but Mrs. Riggs doubted the honor of his intentions and warned Désirée loudly and bawdily.

In Silk Throsters Lane there was restlessness too, and much talk of America. Alf boasted to Feuille that he was going there.

"A fellow like me could make a fortune. The land is rich as butter, and the towns are growing fast."

"It is so far away," she said, "and you would have no friends."

He winked at her. "Oh, wouldn't I? I know a chap would look after me. A proper toff he is too, with plenty of money and land."

She asked who the man was, but Alf shook his head.

"That's my secret. Here comes Daisy, and don't you be telling her. But you'll yet see me riding in a carriage of my own, and wearing a silk neckcloth."

Désirée overheard the last words as she approached. She stopped and surveyed him scornfully, with her fists set on her hips.

"Fortunes are made by work, my lad. You're a loafer from your heels to your ugly head."

His face darkened. "Why must you always give a fellow hard words? Go on and marry Hal Brown—if you can get him to jump the broom—and serve in The Brown Ale & Green Cheese for the rest of your life. I'm going to the New World, I am—no matter how I go. Last night I watched a ship clear with a load of covenant servants."

"I'm no man's servant," Désirée spat at him. "If I choose to marry Hal Brown, I'll see you pay for every pint you draw in The Brown Ale & Green Cheese."

"Hal can have you," Alf said. "God knows I don't want you."

He turned to Feuille, who listened with eyes round and blue.

"She's a proper piece, she is—little Johnny Sevens."

He winked at her. "What do you say to a trip to America with Alf?"

"I could not leave Fleurette," she said. "I will never leave Fleurette."

Alf was gross and brutal, the dregs of a London slum; but he was not brutal enough to tell her the answer to that. Besides, he found her attractive. He liked her small stocky body with its soft curves, and he found her square little face with its short nose and generous red mouth alluring. The blue eyes, instead of retreating into blackness as Fleurette's eyes did under stress, met the challenge by brightening until they sparkled like jewels between their thick short lashes.

His admiration was increased by the fact that whenever he persuaded her to go walking with him he saw other lads observing him enviously. In dealing with her he was careful to be more decent than he was with Désirée, and at last Feuille agreed to go to the neighborhood tavern with him.

She had never before been in such a place. The few wine-shops she had seen in France were open and bright, and men and women and children sat at sidewalk tables before them. The taproom of The Brown Ale & Green Cheese was paneled with dark wood and thick with smoke. It was not in the least sinister, and Feuille saw girls and women she knew drinking beer at tables; yet she balked on its threshold until Alf drew her across.

At the high counter he ordered two half pints, and when the mugs came he produced a fat bottle. She shook her head, for she knew it was rum. He laughed and took a long pull.

"Beer's only good for a chaser."

To Feuille the beer was sour and obnoxious. She sipped at the pewter tankard and the foam made her sneeze. Alf laughed loudly and Hal Brown came up to them.

"Where's Daisy Ray?" he asked.

"At home," said Alf. He hiccoughed. "I've got a girl I like better."

He tried to put an arm around Feuille's shoulders, but she wriggled away with eyes blazing at him.

"Give us another round," he told Hal. "I'm trying to thaw her out."

"I don't like it," said Feuille, "and I think it's a waste of money."

"Don't you bother your head about wasting my money," said Alf. He leaned close to her as he drank her beer as well as his own. "I've got enough money to waste a bit when I choose."

"How did you get it?" she asked him. "You don't do any work."

"Wouldn't you like to know that, Johnny? Maybe I'll tell you some day." He pulled her close, on the corner bench where they sat. "Stick by me, little Johnny, and I'll tell you all about it."

Disgusted, she rose to her feet. "I'm going back to Fleurette."

He caught her arm roughly. "Oh, no, you aren't! I brought you here and bought you a pint, and you aren't treating me that way!"

"Let me go!" cried Feuille.

Several men rose and started toward them, and the publican came up. "Here now," he expostulated. "What's the row? You let go of the little lady, Alf Riggs!"

"She's my girl," said Alf sullenly. But he released her arm. "She's my girl. If she's going home I'm walking with her."

"I'm *not* his girl," Feuille told the publican. "I'm sorry I came here with him, and I'm going back by myself—because he's half-drunk."

Alf raised his voice in protest as she turned away, but a man's voice said: "Let her be, Riggs, if you know what's good for you!"

As Feuille faced the door it swung open, and Désirée entered as if blown by the wind. Her face was pale and her dark hair rumpled, and she wore no cloak although the night was cold.

"Come, Feuille," she said in French. "Fleurette is calling for you. Alfie—"

She changed to English as she looked around the room. Then she saw his face flushed by drink.

"No, not Alfie! Hal, will you get a doctor quick?"

The two girls ran the short way back to the house. Fleurette lay still, with her eyes wide and the snuffbox held in both hands. She tried to smile as Feuille leaned over her.

"Shall I open the lid, Fleurette, and let it play for you?"

"Don't make her talk," said Désirée. "She's been coughing her heart out."

But Fleurette spoke clearly, although very faintly.

"No, I don't want it to play. I'm too tired even to listen. I asked Désirée to call you so I could give it to you—give it to you to keep—because I love you, Feuille."

Then she shut her eyes and seemed to fall asleep, while they bent over her and tried to rouse her.

Désirée ran for Mrs. Riggs. But Feuille sat with eyes burning blue and with Fleurette's little hand clasped tight in her own until the doctor came and loosened her grip and told her.

Life for Feuille now became less and less endurable. As the cold weather came, her skin chapped from exposure and the strain of the treadles caused the soles of her feet to crack and bleed. She missed Fleurette with the desperate sense of loss the doer has for the one who has been both beloved and done for.

Désirée grew even more restless and went out more with Alf and Hal. One night when Feuille awoke at her knock, unbolted the door and crawled back into bed, the gypsy girl came and leaned over her.

"Can you hear me?" she whispered. "I'm going now."

Feuille sat upright, suddenly awake.

"Where are you going? It's the middle of the night."

"It's between midnight and dawn. I'm going with the fair. Hal took me to see a traveling circus. I managed to slip off from him and talk with its manager. He needs a dancing acrobat, and he's hired me."

She was moving swiftly around the room, gathering her possessions. She came back to the bed where Feuille sat silent and staring, kissed Feuille quickly and spoke her brief farewell: "Bolt the door after me—and always keep it bolted."

Feuille sobbed for the rest of that night. While she dressed hurriedly in the bitter cold before dawn, she saw ahead of her only hard work and unhappiness. She would come home every night, after sixteen hours of hard labor, to a cold empty room and to loneliness. She had her choice between that and what most of the other girls chose: evenings in the tavern with a mug of flat lukewarm beer and a loutish fellow who tried to sit too close.

Alf waylaid her that evening on her way through the lane. He drew her into a doorway, out of the drizzling rain.

"Johnny, I've two tickets for America."

"I don't want to go. I have no friends there, and I might not even get work."

"All that's fixed," he told her eagerly. "These tickets are passages for people who want work. We don't pay anything; we just sign them aboard the boat. When we get to the New World, people who need labor are waiting at the dock. A man who's been there told me that a crowd meets every boat, every one of them anxious to pay a passage covenant and let the man or woman for whom he pays work it out."

Her practical mind told her that labor must be needed if such was the case. She lifted questioning eyes to his face.

"I'm afraid to go. Suppose nobody there needs the kind of work I can do?"

"They need every kind of work. You'd have your pick of jobs in towns or on farms. Wages are three times more than in London. You're a fool if you stay here, working your feet sore and letting Ma take what little you earn."

He added: "The sailorman told me the sun always shone over there, and the seed you put in the ground sprang up overnight."

She closed her eyes to squeeze back the tears, as she thought of her father's vineyard and the sun which shone in France. Perhaps, if she could get to this rich country of sunshine, she might earn enough to go back to France some day. But she did not let Alf's urging keep her from thinking it out.

"If some evil man or woman bought my covenant, I would not have anyone to help me."

"Oh, yes, you would! I told you I had a friend over there."

"You're just boasting! I don't believe you."

He brought from his jacket pocket a scrap of paper and unfolded it before her amazed eyes. Beneath a French coat of arms was written in a fine French hand: *Troyes Saint Lys, in Charles Town, in the English Lords Proprietors' Colony of the Carolinas.*

"I told you I couldn't pronounce frog names. But you can see—since you don't believe."

"Did he give it to you, Alf? Does he want you to work for him?"

"I got it from a—a friend of his—and I've got something to tell him. When he hears, I won't have to work any more."

She was impressed at the thought of Alf being a messenger to a Frenchman who had a crest. The address in French script seemed to her proof of the story.

"You mean the message is so important to him that he'll reward you for bringing it?"

"He'll pay pounds to hear it," said Alf. "The way I tell him, he'll be glad to keep on paying. But don't you go telling Ma anything about this, or she'll stop you from going with me."

"I haven't said I was going with you."

"Come on, Johnny. I don't mean you any harm. The sailorman showed me on the boat one place where the women stayed and another place for the men."

"When is the boat sailing for Charles Town?"

"It isn't sailing for Charles Town. It goes out at midnight tonight for a place called Virginia."

"Then there's no use to go, if Monsieur Saint Lys is in Charles Town."

"All those places are in the southern part of America. I've talked to the sailorman and I know all about them. When we get off the boat we'll just have a little way to go—say as far as from London to Gravesend. Ma took me there when I was a nipper, and we ate chips and fish and saw where that American Indian princess is buried."

Indian princesses . . . and sunshine . . . and land so rich that seed sprouted overnight. . . three times her pitiful wage, and no one to take it from her. . . .

She thought of beer-soaked Mrs. Riggs lurching heavily through the hall, of greasy food, of sixteen hours work at the sheds, of an empty room with a bolted door, and the mocking tinkle of the little snuffbox. . . .

She raised her eyes again to Alf's face. "Are you sure that on the boat the women will be to themselves?"

"Sure," he told her eagerly. "You can ask the sailorman before you go aboard."

So that night she let him lead her through wet streets where fog still lingered in patches. He had already gone ahead, taking his own luggage and the small bundle which she handed him through the window. Now he said: "Everything's fixed. I left our luggage in this house. Come on in with me."

She held back. "Where's the boat, Alfie?"

He walked her a block farther and pointed out a vessel moored at the end of a wooden pier. Figures laden with bundles such as her own or with small traveling boxes hurried toward it.

"We may get left," she urged him. "They are going aboard."

Alf assured her: "The boat won't sail before midnight. All these men and women have to sign their covenants in the presence of the captain and of Mr. Jonathan Horward."

She went with him then to the shabby house where he told

her he had left the luggage. They entered and climbed unlighted stairs. From one landing on the way, she saw a gleam
under a door and heard screams of laughter and hoarse cries
in men's voices. At the third level Alf pushed open a door.
While she waited he produced and lighted a candle and stuck
it by its own grease on the seat of a chair. She looked around
the room, and the first thing she saw was a fat bottle on the
window sill. But sure enough, her bundle was there, on the
floor by his. As she leaned to pick it up he caught her around
the waist and dropped his face to hers. She was sickened by
the rum on his breath, and she felt his other hand fumbling
at the neck of her dress. She ducked her head—her mouth
touched a thick finger—she closed her teeth on it.

He cursed and threw her from him so hard that she fell
against the window, steadying herself by her hands thrust
back against its sill. In the wavering candlelight she saw him
examine his finger. As he looked up, she shrank away from
him.

"You damned little fool, did you think I was taking you to
America for nothing?"

She tried to say, You're not taking me. I'm covenanting to
pay my way. You said I'd go with the women on board and
you'd go with the men. But she was so frightened that she
only heard herself gasping: "Don't you touch me, Alfie Riggs!"

Flattened against the closed window she slid away from
him, and as she moved, her hands behind her slipped along
the sill.

"Don't you touch me!" he mimicked. "So you're too good for
Alfie. You'll go to America with him, but you won't let him
touch you."

With his unbitten hand he drew from his pocket a batch of
papers, and waved them in her face.

"I'm playing fair with you. Here's your passage ready for
you to sign, and here's the letter from the French toff. You let
Alfie do the work, but you won't let him touch you.

"*The hell you won't,*" he screamed, as he reached for her.
"*I'm going to take you now!*"

Her right hand closed on the neck of the squat rum bottle on the window sill behind her. She ducked aside as she swung it high over her head and down. For just a second she saw his face—a fat comic mask of surprise—with blood and rum and broken glass running into its glazing eyes.

Then he went down—and, darting on papers and bundle, she seized them and dashed for the door and down the dark stairs.

Part Four

VOYAGE OF THE EAGLE

The *Eagle* slipped her moorings and moved with the Thames at turn of tide. She passed the lights of Gravesend north and of Chatham on the south. She swung from the bight with Margate and Ramsgate starboard, and the Channel caught her and shook her as a dog shakes a rat. She beat her way southwestward between Dover and Dunkirk, cleared the ragged West Country shores and turned the Lizard Point.

The hardships of the small vessel did not trouble Feuille. She had for more than two years now been accustomed to hardship. She counted every league between herself and London as one more league of safety, and to attain safety she was willing to bear much. Sleeping quarters were below water line, where the women were fenced off from the men like animals in a pen. Coarse flour and strong salt beef, hard peas and bread which grew moldy were their only rations as days and weeks went by. The covenant servants numbered a hundred and six, and they crowded a merchantman of less than a hundred and fifty tons. From the thirty-six women among them, Feuille found some who were kind of heart and some who were evil and vicious.

Life was toughening her, and she was able to hold her own. She was glad to have them about her and to feel herself one of their group. She felt no reproach or disgust for the worst of them. No one of them, she thought, can be worse than I. No one of them can be concealing a darker guilt. For I struck a man down and took his papers in order to make this voyage.

She reviewed that scene with horror, but she could feel no remorse. The only emotion it awoke was anxiety to escape it. She thought of it as she lay awake in the foul unventilated hold, or as she sat on deck by day watching the black-green swells recede. She figured coolly and carefully her chances of being caught. She was sure that she had not killed Alf, but she knew he was injured. If he lied and said she had attacked and robbed him, and if he exhibited a broken head as proof, she might be tracked down and arrested and put in jail. Alf would guess where she had gone when he missed the papers.

For she had taken the papers and run straight to the wharf. When she got there she had taken her place at the end of the line gang going aboard. The men and women around her saw only a small figure, as shabby and disheveled as they themselves. In the light of the first wharf lantern she passed she had examined the papers, for she saw that others were reading their own all around her. Folded in Alf's passage she found the scrap of paper with the Saint Lys name and crest. She refolded it and tucked it in the bosom of her dress. Then, with her own passage safely held, she tore Alf's repeatedly and dropped the pieces overside into the water. There had been no questions when, aboard, she passed in her turn between Captain Staples and Mr. Horward and signed her covenant *Johnny Sevens*.

Alf had called her by that name to tease and humiliate her. It was retribution upon him that she should use it now. He would never suspect her of using it, because he knew that she disliked it. When he went to make inquiries, as he would certainly do, he would ask if Feuille Joany had signed a covenant and the answer would be *no*. That would at least delay, if not put an end to the search. Feuille Joany, she told herself, had vanished, and the bond servant Johnny Sevens had started a new life when the *Eagle* cleared.

It had been late August when they cleared—late August of 1718. Now it was September in the North Atlantic. The wind from the ice fields chilled Feuille as she sat on deck wrapped in all the poor clothing she owned. But her heart had been even colder in Silk Throsters Lane. She was content and eager for this adventure. Time after time she got out the Saint Lys address and studied it, wondering what connection Alf had with the man. Possession of it gave her the feeling that she had a friend in the wide New World. Saint Lys was French, as she was. . . . Yet even if she found him, she could never dare make herself known to him. Not only was he a friend of Alf— whom she had injured—but Alf might sooner or later find Saint Lys.

A voice close behind her inquired: "What's that you're reading, Johnny?" —and a hand with long dirty fingernails reached over her shoulder for the paper.

Feuille jerked aside and stuffed the letter back in the bosom of her dress. It was where she kept the snuffbox—her only treasure. The girl called Spy smiled at her out of half-shut eyes.

"So you got a man you left behind?" Her voice was a sneer. "Of all I've had, there's not one I care enough for to carry his letters."

Feuille did not deny it. She knew that the girl would not have believed her, and she knew it was safer to let her think the paper no more than a letter from a man. The year in Silk Throsters Lane had taught her much, and the month upon this ship had taught her even more. She knew there were some bad characters among both men and women on the list of covenant servants. Some were convicts who had served their sentences, some were uncaught offenders or potential criminals. These quarreled with each other and disregarded the ship's laws. On several occasions she had seen trouble settled with fists or belaying pins. The majority, however, were decent humble people who were sincere in their desire to reach the New World and avail themselves of its opportunities.

Two of the younger women were known as Husk and Spy. Both were boldly attractive and a match for any man. Since they were nearer Feuille's age than were the other women,

they had sought her out. Two years before she would have
been afraid of and disgusted with them. Now she was grateful
for their rough kindness and cheerful companionship.

Spy doubled her long legs underneath her now, and shook
back her rough brown hair as she sank to sit on the deck.

"Keep your letter," she said, "and the more fool you! I'm
going to get me a rich man in the colonies."

Husk came up to them then. She remarked: "In a pig's eye,
you are! You don't yet know the name or address of one man
in America."

Seeing a quarrel brewing, Feuille rose hastily. She knew
that Husk and Spy often resorted to fisticuffs.

"I'm going to watch Mister Robinson shoot the sun," she
said, and she moved forward and away from their angry
voices.

She always enjoyed watching the work of officers and seamen, and she had experienced only kindness from them.
Captain Staples was a good master, and Chief Mate Edmund
Robinson was fair and efficient. She had noticed that a lookout
had been placed this day in the mainmast. As September gave
way to October, this watch was incessant and the whole ship
appeared more alert.

One morning three weeks later she stood by the port rail
while the two top officers conferred a few feet away. She
heard Captain Staples say: "It is October the twenty-fourth,
and if your observations are correct we can be no more than
thirty-five leagues from Cape Henry."

"They are correct," Mr. Robinson told him. "We are now in
the danger zone, and I double check them."

She saw Captain Staples nod as he charged: "Keep your
keenest lads in the crow's-nest."

She pulled her ragged shawl closer and moved nearer to the
bow. From the *Eagle's* forefoot forked a triangle of foam. Its
white arrowhead pointed west and to a new life for the girl
who called herself Johnny Sevens. She was done with hard
work in Silk Throsters Lane, with Mrs. Riggs' drunkenness
and Alf's beastliness. She had no idea what was before her,

but whatever it was she would try to meet it with courage. All she had was willingness to work, and Fleurette's little gold box, and a piece of paper with the name of a man she could not dare to know.

From amidship and high above, the wind brought a sudden cry to her ears. It was the voice of the young seaman in the crow's-nest, and it was shrill with excitement as he shouted: *"Sail ho! Sail ahead and to starboard!"*

Feuille gripped the rail and stared. She could as yet see no other ship. But a tumult of activity had broken out on the *Eagle.* Captain Staples and his two mates were shouting commands. The bosun's high whistle was calling those seamen off duty to their stations. Sailors were running to and fro on deck and some were climbing the rigging. She felt the vessel swing to port, keeling as it did so. For a moment she saw the great sail slack and flap uselessly; then it caught the breeze and filled with the sound of a cannon's roar. Now the foam on either side of the bow boiled and hissed with the pressure of speed. The boy in the crow's-nest shouted again: *"A three-master— under full sail—headed south!"*

Until now Feuille had been so occupied watching the crew that she had not noticed the reaction of the passengers. Now she saw them pushing and fighting to get to points of advantage along the rail. Several women were knocked down. There were shrieks and curses. Mr. Robinson picked up a belaying pin and went toward them. She saw him stop with legs spraddled wide, and she heard his shout above the noise.

"Be quiet, you dogs," he ordered them, "if you know what's good for you!"

They stared and muttered resentfully, but it calmed them for the moment. The deck was rising and falling as the *Eagle* plunged southward. Mr. Robinson ran to the mainmast and began to climb. As he went up he shouted to the seamen above him: "Break out the last inch of canvas! She looks like the *New York Revenge!*"

Neither Feuille nor her companions recognized that dreaded name. But they were able to see her now: a dark hull with three low slanting masts. She was gaining upon them swiftly and grew larger as they looked.

Husk joined them. "What's the bloody rumpus?"

"Maybe it's Ed Thatch," said Spy. Her eyes glittered more greenly. "They call him Blackbeard, and they say he takes a new wife every night."

"Maybe you'll be his next," said Husk. "You've crawled into plenty of beds before."

"Maybe I will, you dried-up bitch! What business of yours is it? I'd as lief sail with him on the business they call 'The Account' as to sail on this tub with cattle like you!"

They fell upon each other, pummeling and clawing. A ring of men formed around them, to jeer and bet on the victor. Feuille pushed her way through and went toward Captain Staples. He noticed neither her nor the fight. He stood with feet set wide apart and his tanned face grim, alternately raising the Naval glass to his left eye, then dropping it and calling quick orders to his mates.

Within an hour the strange ship was closing in on them. She flew no flag, but the black snouts of cannon stuck from her gunports. She swooped alongside as easily as a hawk swoops on a duck. She was longer than the merchantman but rode lower in the water, and Feuille got a good view of the wild mob on her deck. A man with loose trousers tucked into folded-down hip boots and with a black handkerchief tied around his head, hailed the *Eagle* through a speaking trumpet.

"Ship ahoy!" he roared. "Heave to, and parley us!"

"Let us parley only with our guns," Mr. Robinson advised.

But out of the *Eagle's* company came a whimper of fear. A voice spoke. "Do as he bids you! You'll get us all murdered."

Captain Staples paid them no attention.

"I carry only a load of covenant servants. Some of them are ill with a kind of pox, and I'm trying to reach Quarantine."

There came back another roar, this time of jeering disbelief. One of the *Eagle's* convicts yelled: "He lies! We've no pox aboard."

Again Captain Staples parleyed them. He was still too far from shore for help. He knew that his guns were too few and too small to shoot the matter out. But his resistance had infuriated the pirate captain Richard Worley. Threats and curses came now to the ears of all those upon the *Eagle*. The black ship was closer than ever before, and her crew were yelling abuse in addition to the demands of the man with the trumpet.

"Heave to," he howled, "or by God's knucklebones we'll blow you out of the water!"

Twenty or thirty of the men from among the covenant servants edged nearer the officers and spoke threateningly.

"Do as he says, or we'll put you overboard and do it!"

Mr. Robinson faced them, and his pistols clicked as he cocked them.

"Get back to your kennel, you curs!"

But as he spoke a volley of small arms from the other ship smashed into the *Eagle's* hull and scattered upon deck, wounding several who began to scream aloud. Up the highest mast of the *New York Revenge* ran a dark, shapeless, fluttering bundle of cloth. At the masthead it unfurled, flapped and tautened: a black flag centered with a human skull and crossbones.

Captain Staples felt a cold wind on the back of his neck as he watched the ensign of evil unfurl. Mr. Robinson stared grimly, and the second mate cursed aloud. But they had not yet given up. They were three brave and determined men. Not only were they going to do all possible to save the ship for her owner; they knew what to expect if captured.

"Helm about," cried the captain. "We cannot be far from the capes."

But his words were lost in a snarl from the mob on his own deck. They moved upon him, repeating threats.

"It's overboard with you unless you do as we say!"

"You bloody fool, you'll get the last one of us murdered!"

The officers drew their pistols, but it was already too late. Forty men were about them, crowding them to the rail. The helmsman had either not heard or been too terrified to obey. The *Eagle* was wallowing helplessly, and the black craft had put out a longboat. It was rowing toward them, seeming to leap from the crest of one wave to another. As it approached, several of the convicts, hoping to curry favor, ran and dropped a rope ladder overside. Up it swarmed a dozen dirty brutal ruffians. Striking aside the traitors who had helped them they advanced on Captain Staples.

"What's your ship and cargo?" the leader roared. He did not wait for a reply, but poured forth threats and curses.

Captain Staples kept his composure.

"My ship is the *Eagle Galley,* and her owner is Joseph Skyring of London. Since you are a sailor yourself, you must understand that my first duty is to him and that I had no reason to obey a stranger's order."

The pirate cursed more savagely. "You have reason to obey the order of Richard Worley! What are you carrying, and where are you bound?"

"My only cargo is a load of covenant servants. They are being shipped by Jonathan Horward to be assigned in Virginia and Maryland."

Spy's voice called from the crowd which was listening.

"And there's some of us, mister, would rather take sides with you than to be landed for work in the colonies!"

"Hold your tongue," he yelled at her. "I'll have time to attend to you when I've finished with the man who defied Richard Worley."

He raised his long pistol deliberately and struck Captain Staples on the head. The captain went down on deck, blood streaming from the deep wound, and several of the ruffians began kicking him where he lay. Mr. Robinson tried to interfere and was at once seized and beaten. Leaving Staples unconscious, half of the raiders dragged Robinson and four seamen overside and into their longboat to appear before

Worley on the *New York Revenge*. Upon the *Eagle* were left
Worley's lieutenant James Cole and four other pirates.

Feuille, little taller than a child, had been overlooked during
the boarding and the fighting that ensued. She was watching,
eyes bright blue with terror, as she wondered what would
happen next.

There was a certain savage and direct efficiency about that
conversion of a merchantman to the status of a pirate's consort.
With drawn pistols in their hands Cole and his crew searched
the ship from keel to mast, taking whatever pleased them and
whatever Worley needed. Six great guns, a number of small
arms and ammunition, were at once conveyed to the *New York
Revenge*. Feuille saw barrels of beef and flour being lowered
overside. She heard cries of protest from the more affluent
passengers who had brought boxes of clothing and who were
now being robbed. Her own small bundle was torn apart, then
scornfully tossed aside. She thought of the snuffbox which she
kept hidden in her dress. But nobody laid hands on her, so it
was not discovered. The traitorous covenant servants who tried
to fawn upon or fraternize with their captors were knocked
down and kicked aside. The seamen of the *Eagle* who were
still left aboard were forced at pistol point to continue to serve
their stations. Sail was hoisted, and the ship began to move
obediently in the wake of Worley's flagship.

Then Cole faced them, legs apart and hand on the knife in
his belt.

"I'm your skipper now," he told them. "If you know what's
good for you you'll remember that."

He glared around at the littered decks.

"Step lively, you swine, and begin to swab! Make her shipshape and keep her so. And whatever you do, remember that
the *Eagle Galley* is sunk. She's down in the locker of Davy
Jones. She's sunk as deep as hell. You're sailing on Worley's
consort commanded by Captain Cole, and her name from now
on is the *New York Revenge's Revenge*."

For nearly three weeks that nightmare cruise went on. Cole jammed the small ship with canvas until her trees creaked in protest. He was a magnificent seaman, able to judge her endurance to a fine point, and he was trying to keep up with his flagship for business farther south. Sometimes they lost each other; sometimes there reappeared the long, dark, wicked craft leading while they followed.

Gradually Feuille lost her fear of the pirates. Because she was young and small they were less rough with her. She never knew their real names. They called each other Little Tommy, Barefoot, Fox and Long Will. Little Tommy used to seek her out and talk with her. His stunted figure and wistful, ugly face made him appear pathetic rather than villainous.

In reply to his questioning she gave the outline of her short tragic life. He shook his head, and the brass ring in his left ear swayed to and fro. His pale little eyes gazed at her with real sympathy.

"On the *Revenge*," he told her, "you'll not find a man who would treat you as cruelly as you have been treated by men who call themselves honest ashore."

She told him frankly: "I always heard that you drowned all the people you caught."

He sucked his few remaining teeth with a sorrowful lisping sound.

" 'Tis hard they are upon us poor souls. They do us injustice, for 'tis *they* that have made us outcasts."

He fancied the last word and rolled it in his toothless mouth, as if it were a sweetmeat too hard to chew.

"Outcasts we are, and all due to *them*. If they take us they'll see that we dance on air."

His voice was dripping self-pity. Feuille asked: "Who are *they?*"

"They are the ones as has all the luck and will not share it with their poor, hungry, unlucky brothers. Houses they has, and servants and food, and soft beds and gold by the bagful.

But they keeps it for themselves while we unlucky ones starves. When we take them and their ships it is no more than justice. We are doing no wrong, dolly, but getting back our rights."

Her early training had been too honest and decent for her to be confused by such sophistry. And she remembered the beastly and uncalled-for beating of Captain Robert Staples. But she was afraid to argue. She did not yet know what was going to be her fate. She said: "I don't see how anybody can dance on air."

Even Désirée, she thought—Désirée who leapt and floated and whirled—could not dance on air.

He grinned sadly and moved dirty hands around his neck, in the gesture of knotting a noose.

"Only those can do it as is hanged by the neck from a rope. They don't like to do it, dolly. It gives them no comfort or pleasure. But the rich and greedy ones as has made outcasts of us likes to see us in torment and swings us as high as they can. They laughs and jeers while they tortures us—us that they has made outcasts."

Barefoot came up softly behind them at that moment. For some reason he would wear neither shoes nor seaboots. He grinned evilly at his brother buccaneer.

"Likes 'em young and soft, you does. Tender—like a spring chicken."

Little Tommy's mild face was suddenly contorted by such horrible fury that Feuille's heart went cold. He looked what he was—a vicious, conscienceless murderer—as he jerked the knife from his belt and advanced upon Barefoot. But as Feuille turned to run Cole's voice roared across the deck.

"Put up your knives, you black-hearted sons of a devil fish! I'd like to see you both dead, but I need all hands aboard. One move, and I'll read you the Articles and have you spread-eagled and flogged!"

Like the pieces of a kaleidoscope Little Tommy's face fell back into lines of sadness and injury. He slipped his knife into its sheath as Barefoot, still glaring, turned away. Tommy's voice was gentle and coaxing as he called after Feuille.

"Don't let us scare you, my dolly, with a gentleman's disagreement. We abides by the Articles, so long as we sails
under Worley."

Still terrified, she looked at him. "What are the Articles?"

Although frightened by the violence, she was recalling that
this little man had been kind to her. After all, the dreadful
change in him had been caused by Barefoot's remark about
her. Little Tommy had championed her, and when he smiled
his grieved and toothless smile it was not hard to think him a
victim of injustice.

"The Articles are the Laws of Account," he told her. "We
have laws like the king's laws, only ours are fairer. Under His
Majesty's laws a rich man can escape punishment for a crime
he has done; but under Worley's laws man and man shares
alike."

She had not known there were laws under the black flag.
She regarded him in surprised silence.

"Didn't know it, dolly, did you? Didn't know we seafarers
had laws? We has them and we abides by them. You've been
treated fairly under Cole, hasn't you?"

She thought about that. She still had her treasured snuffbox,
and she had suffered no injury as yet. But she had taken care
to keep out of Cole's way. She had seen him knock down
several men and slap Spy across the mouth.

Little Tommy boasted: "Our laws give a man death if he
cheats in sharing the spoil or if he touches a woman without
her consent."

It was all a surprise to her, but it gave her a little more
hope. She stayed in the hold as much as she could, and she
tried to keep to herself when on deck. The weather was getting
rougher as they neared Cape Hatteras. Fog was closing around
them, and they had lost sight of the flagship. She wondered
where they were and what would become of them all. Some
of the covenant servants were telling tales of West Indian
islands where pirates sold captives as slaves. . . .

Then one day in the autumn mists, thirty-five miles from the hook-backed cape, the lookout of the *New York Revenge's Revenge* again shouted: *"Sail ho! A brigantine east!"*

The prize was an English merchant ship captained by Timothy Low, and the pirates at once stripped her of money and provisions. They continued their course southward, passing Ocracoke Inlet, the rendezvous of Blackbeard and his captains. Little Tommy explained to Feuille.

"I'll tell you, dolly, how it got its name. One night this Captain Thatch who is known as Blackbeard was standing off its harbor waiting to attack at daybreak. He was so anxious for dawn, he was, that as he paced his flagship's deck he raised both arms above his head and shouted *'O, crow cock!'* "

The low yellow line of the Outer Bank at last dropped astern. After they had passed the mouth of the Cape Fear River, they dared sail so close to shore that Feuille could see islands with white sand beaches in place of the skeletal Great Barrier Reef.

She thought they had reached the Indies, and so did many others of that unhappy company aboard. She asked Little Tommy about it.

"No, my dolly," he told her. "We are still off the coast of His British Majesty's American Colonies. They are rich, and fat shiploads of plunder come sailing out of their ports."

"Are we on our way to the Indies?"

"In a manner of speaking, yes. But we have important business on the way. When we get to the Indies, dolly, I'll buy you something pretty. I'll buy you a yellow shawl and a silver finger ring."

They had already dropped anchor when Feuille came on deck next day. Close to starboard was a long narrow island, its beach alive with crying seabirds. Long Will, the only man who dared offer advice to Cole, was arguing that they should sail farther in.

"If we slip into Breach Inlet and hide between the two islands, we'll have outcoming ships pinned between us and Worley."

He gestured across the harbor mouth, where Worley's ship

was lying under bare masts alongside the southern sentinel island.

Cole frowned. "I say *no*. We'll lie where we are."

For several days they lay there, apparently unobserved. The pirate officers were observing through their glasses several ships anchored off a point in the inner harbor. Then, in a hazy November dawn, a thrill of excitement pervaded the raiders' decks. In ghostly single file the ships they watched were moving through the mists toward the bar and the open sea.

Reports came down from the crow's-nest, and Cole watched through his glass. The clearing vessels were four in number. They came on slowly but steadily, as if the fog hid their foe from them. No guns were visible upon their decks. They had every appearance of a small helpless merchant fleet putting to sea from its port.

Feuille could see them now, and pity was like a pain in her heart. They are unarmed and helpless, she thought, and sailing into the pirates' trap. They will be seized, as the *Eagle* and the *Expedition* were seized, stripped of what they are carrying and their men beaten or killed. She realized that both Worley and Cole had hoisted sail and were closing in, by gliding harborward with the beach, in order to get between their prey and the bar and cut off retreat.

As Cole drove down upon the nearest vessel Feuille could distinguish figures moving upon its deck. In triumph at the success of his plan, the pirate captain was roaring for surrender and demanding that pennants be struck. The small fleet slowed, as if confused by sudden attack. As it did both pirates swooped between it and the harbor mouth. In rage at not being obeyed Cole shouted to Long Will and Barefoot to open fire.

The cannon's explosion threw Feuille against the rail. But she gripped it and stared as she saw a flash of bright color ascending the mast of one of the ships. High and boldly there the British flag whipped out. Upon the apparently helpless merchantmen canvas was torn away from the cannon it masked. Cole saw his mistake and swung for open sea. As he did the Colonists' guns crashed in a ragged but thunderous broadside. An iron ball from one struck the *New York Revenge's Revenge* just above water line and pierced her hull. But Cole crowded sail and headed for the ocean.

He left Worley cornered and fighting the *Sea Nymph* and the sloop *Revenge,* with his back to the bar from which he had cut his enemy off.

Listing from the hole in her side, with her wounded men screaming on deck and her passengers fighting and howling with terror, the ship which had been the *Eagle* fled under all sail, with the *King William's Strike* and the governor's flagship *Mediterranean Galley* in pursuit.

Part Five

JOHNNY SEVENS

Feuille looked out on a harbor citron-green and smooth. Through her thin clothing she felt the late autumn sunlight, as pale but as warming as champagne. She had no idea where she was. The turmoil of that running fight had terrified her. In spite of what Little Tommy had said, she suspected that they had reached the Indies.

They were anchored near a long point of marsh, and the *Eagle* listed badly. Across a narrow stretch of the citron water, she saw a low infantry wall guarding a low white skyline. Rowing boats came and went from the city wharves. Mr. Richard Allein, the attorney general, came aboard every day. Feuille had been too frightened to ask any questions; but Spy and Husk questioned the men who rowed the boats and then gave lurid reports to their companions.

"Do you see that long white oystershell spit that runs south of the town? A pirate named Stede Bonnet was hanged there last month. The waterman who brought the attorney general told me just now that they were holding court, and that James Cole and Little Tommy and Fox and Barefoot and Long Will would be hanged there too."

Feuille shivered. "What is the name of the town?"

Husk said importantly: "It's likely Saint Augustine. We sailed a long way south, and that's in the South."

Spy turned upon her at once. "A lot you know about it! This is an English seaport, for everybody that comes aboard speaks English. The bloody Spaniards are down in the South. Long Will told me about them, and said they crucified Protestants."

"He was probably lying," screamed Husk. "I hope they hang you with him—or else sell you for a slave!"

At that point Spy grabbed Husk's hair with both hands and jerked. Feuille did her best to escape but was caught between them and knocked down. Struggling to regain her feet, she felt a hand grasp her shoulder and help her gently but firmly. As she rose she faced a young man with black hair and laughing black eyes. He spoke in English, but with a marked French accent.

"You are too small and too pretty, my child, to be banged about by these viragoes."

Feuille stammered: "I—I thank you—sir."

She realized that she had very nearly said "Monsieur," but had caught herself in time.

The man who had been pointed out to her as the attorney general was coming across the deck to them.

"What have you here, deRosset?" he demanded.

"A fight, Allein. Would you like to bet on the winner? I'm offering odds of a half crown to a florin on the skinny one who's biting the fat one's thumb."

Allein looked down his nose at Feuille, who was trying to shrink away. Her rescuer saw the glance.

"The little one is not to blame. I saw the battle's commencement, and saw that she was merely caught between the opposing forces."

Feuille gave him a look of gratitude. Allein looked more kindly at her, then spoke to the other man.

"We are not here to watch fights. Get her, and all the rest, down to the cabin."

Feuille straightened her rumpled hair and disordered clothing and went below with the crowd. She listened while the attorney general told them that Judge Nicholas Trott had ordered the ship and her gear sold to pay damages, and that they were all to be assigned to any masters willing to take up their covenants.

Thomas Milksop—in spite of his name—spoke up for them.

"What damage have we done, governor, and what damage has the *Eagle Galley* done?"

"The *Eagle Galley*, my good man, no longer exists," said Allein. "I have just proved in court, to his lordship's satisfaction, that this ship is a pirate's consort, and that with Worley's flagship she blockaded this port and engaged in battle with Colonel Rhett's fleet."

He added, not unkindly: "As for you people, you are no worse off than you would have been had you landed in Virginia. This province has large plantations of rice and indigo, and men are needed by the planters. Besides that, artisans are eager for apprentices, and householders need domestic servants right here in Charles Town."

He went on to tell them that he already had lists of prospective masters, lists which would allow them to see what kind of work was in demand, and allow them at least to indicate what they wished and for what they were fitted.

But Feuille had ceased to hear his voice after he spoke the name Charles Town. Panic gripped her as she realized that the pirates' capture of the galley had brought her to the place where Alf's friend lived. I must avoid him, she told herself, by any means I can. For Alf is determined to find him; and whatever I do, I must not let Alf find me.

Spy interrupted her thoughts with a push: "Get behind me! Didn't you hear the attorney tell us to line up and pass by the toff at the table there?"

Feuille looked then and saw the dark man who had befriended her on deck sitting at a table with papers spread out before him. Step by step she moved with the line, wondering what to do. She thought of the plantations. All that she knew about them was that they were big farms out in the country. I will try to get employment on a plantation, she thought. That will take me away from this man who is Alf's friend, because his address on the letter Alf had is Charles Town.

When she came to the table deRosset recognized and smiled at her.

"The small victim of the hostile engagement on deck! What kind of work are you trained for, child?"

"For work in the country," she told him. "I lived most of my life on a farm."

He reached for a list he had laid to one side. "Ah," he said, "the plantations! Few of the women wish to go there. It is a pity, because work on the plantations is accounted harder, and for that reason a covenant servant is bound for a shorter term."

She smiled back at him. All was going well. She would work out in the country and avoid Troyes Saint Lys.

DeRosset said: "Five planters of the French Santee have sent in their names as being in need of help. Three wish domestic service."

He paused and looked searchingly into her face. "Can you cook and clean a house?"

"I can, sir—and sew as well."

He laughed. "My wife, Madame deRosset, would sign you at once if she were here. She dislikes housework, and always she sighs for a French maid to care for her hair and her clothes."

Feuille felt a flash of fear. Could he have sensed that she was French? But he did not follow up the remark. He was studying his list.

"Besides these three, Monsieur Marion is anxious for a maid: 'a maid,' he writes, 'refined enough to companion my young daughters and to nurse them through the small illnesses habitual to *jeunes filles*.' Have you any experience in nursing?"

"I have," she told him truthfully, "although no medical skill. I nursed my father through pleurisy once, and my aunt was a victim of recurring migraines."

He was looking hard at her. "The last place is the best of all but its demands are greater. You would care for an elderly woman. But she wishes a nurse who can read to her and sing to her as well."

Feuille's cheeks went bright and her eyes shone bluer. The teaching of my Aunt Tonpain will serve me here, she thought. DeRosset, watching her, told himself: I am right. This girl is the pick of the crowd. She is decent and well mannered and will be pretty when neatly dressed.

"Could you fulfill the last two requirements?" he asked.

"I could, m—I mean sir. I can read and write, and I have always loved to sing."

"Good," he said. "It shall be so arranged, for you seem to suit the place and the place is the best one offered. You shall go to the plantation *Bois Bleu* just as soon as Monsieur Troyes Saint Lys gets here to sign your covenant."

The color left Feuille's cheeks and she felt her heart beating faster. This could not be possible. She would not allow it to be. . . .

She heard deRosset only faintly. "It is fortunate for Troyes and for Madame. Few young girls are willing to leave the town and go into the wilderness to work."

He broke off as he saw her face. "What is the matter, child?"

She would not lie and yet she could not tell him. She took refuge in half truth.

"It is—the wilderness. I—I am afraid, sir. I had better find work in the city."

"Nonsense," he said. "You could not find a better place than with the Saint Lys. Troyes appears stern, but you should see my wife tease him and break him down."

"If he is stern I am afraid—of him as well as the wilderness. You said that Madame deRosset. . . . Would she have me as her maid?"

"My dear child, to attend my wife is a difficult task. I have done it for five years, so I should know. Besides, the term set for domestic service in the town is three years to work out your passage. If you go to a plantation it will be only two."

"I would rather—rather work three years—in the town than in the wilderness."

A note of annoyance sounded in his pleasant voice.

"Well, you will have to stand aside while I deal with the rest of the line."

Miserably she moved to stand behind him. She watched her fellow voyagers as, one by one, they indicated preference for a type of employment. It was several hours later when deRosset finished his classification and turned to her.

"Now," he inquired sharply, "have you changed your mind?"

"No, sir, I have not. If Madame your wife does not wish to employ me, I beg you to assign my covenant to some other lady in this town who wishes maid service or housework."

His black brows drew together. "You have a will of your own. But I shall ask Mr. Allein to let me take you to my wife. If she decides not to keep you, I am quite sure that we can arrange to place you with one of our friends."

Thirty minutes later he told her to get her bundle and follow him. As she climbed down the ladder along the ship's side and into the rowing boat, Spy rushed to the rail above and screamed abuse.

"Sly little mouse, what lies have you told in order to be taken away first by a fine gentleman?"

DeRosset merely chuckled. "Thanks to the attorney general," he told Feuille, "the ship's late officers are too busy elsewhere just now to restrain such harpies."

He pointed toward the long white spit on their left as they approached the wharf.

"We are arriving just in time for proceedings."

Even from the boat Feuille could see a procession of people going south. But she was still too afraid of deRosset's annoyance to ask him what caused the excitement. At the wharf he told her: "Come along. My house is near enough for us to walk."

As they reached the long Bay Street parallel to the sea wall, they found themselves in the midst of the crowd. It was

going southward so fast that it jostled them. Coaches rolled
by with ladies in elegant gowns. Gentlemen trotted on horseback, while urchins ran alongside. There were groups of Negro
servants, and some of them led small white children. Hawkers
pushed barrows with souvenirs and sweets and cakes for sale.
A sad-faced ragged fellow approached and held up a dirty
paper.

"Will you buy a ballad, master? A ballad describing the
hanging of Cole and his fellow villains."

"No," said deRosset, "because Cole is just about to be
hanged. I saw you only a fortnight ago at the hanging of
Stede Bonnet. I'll wager it's the same ballad that you're trying
to sell me now."

"I've changed the names," said the poet. " 'Tis a lengthy and
erudite ballad, and it goes into all details. Upon the last
occasion it sold for ninepence a copy, but since it's not what
you might call fresh you may have a bargain for sixpence."

"Get along with you," ordered deRosset. "You should be
hanged along with Cole for selling a secondhand ballad."

Now that Feuille realized what was afoot, she looked with
horror at the people hurrying to their ghoulish amusement.
She knew that Worley and Cole and all of their men were
villains, but she could not help recalling that Little Tommy
had been kind to her.

The deRosset house was just off the bay, where a salt water
creek ran west on a side street. A neat Negro maid admitted
them and took deRosset's hat and cane and her tiny bundle.
Feuille had never before seen an African, although she had
heard that slavery was a practice in the colonies. The very
word *slavery* sounded barbaric; but this girl was not only neat
and attractive, she was fine-featured and looked intelligent.
As Feuille was staring after her, a slender pretty young woman
with hair as black as deRosset's ran down the stairs. Her husband seized and embraced her, but she pulled away and
went to Feuille and spoke in French with the eagerness of a
child.

"So you got an attendant for Madame Saint Lys."

She put a white hand bright with rings upon the coarse shawl pulled around the small shoulders.

"I had no idea that unfortunate ship carried such a nice-looking young girl among her passengers."

Feuille knew that she was far from nice-looking. Her clothes were by now both worn and torn. Her skin and hair, naturally fresh and fine, were roughened by exposure during months at sea. But she was hungry for kindness, and she realized that deRosset's wife was kind. She opened her lips to say "Thank you, Madame"—then caught herself and went cold with fear.

Johnny Sevens from London must not understand French. The deRossets did not know that she understood what they said.

For deRosset was telling his wife: "She is an English girl by name of Johnny Sevens."

"It is a hideous name. I must persuade her to change it before she goes to *Bois Bleu.*"

DeRosset's eyes twinkled as he looked at his wife.

"Then, Camille, you will have to persuade her to change her mind as well as her name. For she refuses to go to the plantations. She wishes work as a lady's maid in Charles Town."

"My good little Pierre," Madame deRosset cried. "Do you mean that you brought her for me?"

"Have you not been telling me for years that you needed a maid, a maid to mend your clothes and pick up all the things you drop or forget?"

"It is true," said Madame deRosset, "but I meant a French maid, my angel."

She was scrutinizing Feuille. "This girl looks French."

Feuille tried to keep from her face the fear that came into her heart.

Madame deRosset was saying: "I cannot make up my mind. . . ."

"You never can," her husband told her drily.

"Nonsense," cried Madame deRosset. "It is far more logical

and consistent to keep changing one's mind until one is really certain. May I keep the girl and try her, before I decide?"

"You may, my love—despite all laws of the province. Even Allein and Judge Trott make an exception for you."

She made a little face at him. "And why should they not do so?"

She turned to Feuille, then, and asked in English: "If I find that you can do the work to my satisfaction, would you be content for my husband to take up your bond?"

"I would, Madame," said Feuille hopefully. She added: "I will do my best to please you."

It was quiet in Feuille's attic room, in the street where the creek ran west. She liked the deRossets and made up her mind to please them, but the black girl Mirabel was the friend who helped her most. Mirabel had brought her a jug of hot water and a tray of food, and later had tapped softly on the door. When Feuille opened it she asked: "You need anything more?" But her soft brown eyes were saying: I want to help you.

Feuille stared timidly at her. "Will you come in and talk to me?"

It was what Mirabel wished to do. She was lonely too. She hesitated, and Feuille asked: "Would Madame object?"

"No," said Mirabel. "Madame skittish, but she got a good heart. She gone out with M'sieu to a ball. She love to dance."

For several hours the white girl and the black girl talked together. Feuille learned about the town and the ships that came into its harbor, about the plantations set on its tidal rivers. Mirabel had once been to French Santee with the deRossets.

"That kinda place too lonesome," she told Feuille. "All night long I hear the owls talk and the wildcats holler."

"Where in the French Santee did you stay, Mirabel?"

"Stay with M'sieu Troy and Madame."

"Isn't Madame his mother ill?"

"I hear tell she sick now, but last time I see her she was walking round all right, with her hair curl on top of her head. Last time M'sieu Troy come here, she come with him in the coach and stay a whole week."

Haunted by fear of Saint Lys, Feuille wondered why he should be a friend of the man who employed her. She did not realize that Charles Town was a small community and that the French Huguenots in the city and throughout the province were allied both by religion and intermarriage. She could not have found in the Carolinas a Frenchman unacquainted with Troyes Saint Lys and Pierre deRosset.

Starting her new duties next day, Feuille realized just what Mirabel meant by saying that her mistress was "skittish." Camille sat before her dressing mirror in a mauve and rose peignoir, with the long waves of her dark hair falling loose over her shoulders.

"For the love of God, get my primrose gown and mend the lace on the flounce!" she cried. "We have guests for dinner tonight, and I shall be disgraced!"

But before Feuille had finished the task she had changed her mind.

"Leave it, and come brush my hair, child! It must have two hundred strokes, or else it looks like the mane of a wild horse."

Feuille, called hither and thither, kept going back to the gown of yellow brocade, and finally mended the tear and hung it again in the wardrobe. The day was spent in the half-doing of a score of other small duties. Camille deRosset either forgot or revoked her orders. That evening there was a wild scurry when she decided to wear white because her husband brought her a half-wreath of dark red roses. Feuille and Mirabel raced from attic to cellar to heat smoothing irons for ribbons and petticoats, to clean white kid slippers and shake out long silk stockings.

They had finished dressing her and were standing off to admire their handiwork when deRosset came into the room. She pirouetted before her pier glass, slim and lovely in the pale dress with his crimson flowers in her dark hair. As they

gazed the two girls forgot the harried hours which had gone
in accomplishing that perfection.

"Ah, my Pierre, do you like me? I dressed to suit your
roses."

He crossed and kissed her hand, bowing low. "You are
exquisite, my darling."

"Why then do you frown?" She put a hand upon either side
of his face and put her lips against his forehead. "Let me kiss
away the ugly wrinkle that creases your brow, my angel."

"It is Troyes," he said, and dropped into a chair. "I have
been on the ship with him all day."

Feuille pricked up her ears but tried to control her face, for
the conversation was in French.

"And he is coming to dinner? He *must*, for my dinner is
planned."

"He has already come. He awaits you downstairs."

"Then all is well, and you need not wrinkle your brow."

"All is not well, Camille, and I feel I have failed Troyes.
You know that he wrote both me and Allein, begging us to get
from the covenant servants a decent woman to attend his
mother."

"Did you not do so?"

"You know Madame Saint Lys. And Troyes is himself exact-
ing. He wants a woman young and strong, yet quiet and well
mannered—in other words, a girl like the one I brought you."

As Madame deRosset turned and looked at Feuille, Feuille
tried to keep the fear from her face. Her temperamental mistress stamped a white kid slipper.

"He shall not have her! She mends lace—and see how well
she dressed my hair!"

"Troyes' mother needs her for more important tasks than
mending lace or dressing hair, Camille."

"There are other women upon the ship. What would you
have? You are cruel! Would you have your own wife go
unclothed with her hair unbrushed and flying?"

She was working herself into hysterics. DeRosset rose hastily
and put an arm around her.

"There, there! I shall not be cruel!" He glanced at the two girls. "You may go," he said. "I will take care of Madame."

He had spoken in English, and they obeyed him. As Feuille closed the door behind her, she was thanking her luck that the mistress into whose hands she had fallen was going to hold her by the powerful weapon of tears.

She spent that evening alone, for Mirabel was serving the dinner party downstairs. But when Mirabel brought her breakfast next morning, Feuille saw trouble on her face.

"M'sieu say you must come downstairs soon as you finish eating."

Feuille went downstairs with her heart in her throat. Camille deRosset had already furnished her with the neat black dress and frilled apron of the usual French maid. Excitement made her color high and her blue eyes bigger and brighter. A strange young man turned from where he stood by the chimney place, and his gray eyes narrowed with surprise and something like pleasure. For seconds she stood staring back at him: at his thin, almost-ugly face, with its high-bridged nose, dark gray eyes and strong mouth.

Then Madame deRosset cried with childish delight in her voice: "Eh, my Troyes, I can see that she pleases you! It is well. Tell Madame that I send her a treasure."

Feuille forgot that she was not supposed to understand French. She turned a stricken face to her betrayer.

"But, Madame, you said—"

She stopped. All three were staring at her, and she knew she must recover her blunder.

"What is it that you said, Madame?" she stammered.

"It is that I am unselfish toward my friends. I have agreed to let Monsieur Saint Lys sign your covenant."

"No," cried Feuille, forgetting herself. "No! I cannot—I will not go!"

She saw Saint Lys' face darken as he inquired in French: "Am I then an ogre, Pierre, that a bond servant refuses me service?"

"No," said deRosset. "She is from the slums of London, and she fears the country. That is all."

But his voice was stern as he addressed Feuille in English.

"It is not for you to say, wench. If I refuse to sign your covenant, you will be allotted to the next who offers to do so."

"Oh, the ingratitude!" cried Camille. "I tell you to do as my husband says!"

"But, Madame—sir—you said when you brought me here—"

"I said only that my wife would try you. She likes your work but is generous enough to yield you to an invalid."

"I—I would rather—go anywhere else!"

"Let her do so, then," said Saint Lys. "I will have no unwilling service."

DeRosset could be as grim as he could be gay.

"Let me deal with her. I am accustomed to women and their foibles."

"Now"—he turned on Feuille—"you may take your choice. You have already told me that you can do nursing. I think you are lazy and trying to avoid fulfilling your covenant."

"No," said his wife, "not lazy. She may be wicked—a criminal—but she is not lazy because she mended—"

"Leave the affair to me, Camille! The girl can either go to a good mistress like Madame Saint Lys and do high-class work like nursing, or else she can go back to the ship where a public auction is being held and be sold to anyone who chooses to buy her bond."

As he paused, Feuille shook her head. But the word *criminal* had struck her like a whip.

"Very well. Get your belongings. I will take you to Mr. Allein. As a lawyer who deals with all legal affairs of the province, he will examine into this. But I warn you that he will give you no choice. He will assign you to any master who pays your passage. And in spite of your stubbornness, I shall be sorry if you fall into the hands of some buyers I saw."

He saw the misery in Feuille's eyes and thought it caused by his warning of some rough master. But she was thinking of the attorney general. . . .

If he dealt with all affairs, he would know even sooner than Saint Lys did about Alf's inquiries or Alf's arrival. It would take Alf more time to reach a plantation in the wilderness than to reach the seaport of the province. She recalled that Désirée had said . . .

"I will go with Monsieur Saint Lys," she said sullenly, "and nurse his mother, if he signs my covenant."

Except for Mirabel's visits, Feuille was left alone until called to start at daybreak next morning. The volatile Camille had forgotten all disagreement. She patted Feuille upon a cheek and charged her: "You are to ride in the coach with Madame. See that you wait upon her well, if you wish to please Monsieur."

Feuille was surprised to hear that Madame could travel, but she asked no questions. She was rebellious in her heart, but practical enough to know that she had to make the best of a bad matter. DeRosset helped her into the vehicle, and handed in to her a large basket.

"My wife has packed it with dainties, so do it justice." He added: "Good luck, little Johnny! Serve your new mistress well."

As Feuille accepted the basket she looked anxiously at the woman she faced. She saw an oval face, tinted like peaches and cream, surrounded by ringlets and surmounted by a widow's bonnet. The handsome, full body lolled languidly, and one hand swayed a lace fan to and fro. But although attitude and gestures suggested languor, the woman appeared amazingly young and healthy to be the invalid mother of Troyes Saint Lys. She spoke now in an affected drawl.

"Put the basket on the seat by you, girl. I am made ill by the odor of food so early in the day."

"Certainly, Madame Saint Lys," Feuille answered respectfully as she obeyed.

Pierre deRosset's head was still in the carriage. He burst into delighted laughter.

"Is it the voice of prophecy which speaks, Rosalie?" he asked.

The woman sat upright, her dimples in full play. She folded the fan to a stick and tapped deRosset playfully.

"Naughty Pierre," she said coyly, "even to think such a thing!"

She turned her beaming glance of delight upon Feuille, who now realized her mistake.

"Madame," she stammered, "I ask your pardon. I thought—"

Madame was plainly pleased and wished to prolong the moment. "It was a natural mistake. Who did you think I was, girl?"

"Madame, I thought you Monsieur Saint Lys' mother, the lady I am going to serve."

DeRosset's laughter ended in a strangling noise. He said quickly: "Johnny, the lady is Madame Wentworth, a neighbor *and an especial friend*—of Monsieur Saint Lys."

The lady's big warm brown eyes, which had just cast soft glances on him, were flashing hatred now at Feuille.

"The wench is stupid and ignorant. Tell my coachman to drive on, Pierre."

Feuille huddled unhappily on the cushioned seat with her back to the coachman. She longed to sit on the box with him and the Negro maid Bindy. So far, she told herself, I have offended everyone except Mirabel. I do not like these colonists, and I shall run away from the plantation as soon as I get a chance. She glanced fearfully to the rear of the carriage where Troyes Saint Lys rode proudly on his tall thoroughbred.

But amid all her troubles and new experiences, her thoughts returned regretfully to her *faux pas* in regard to Madame Wentworth. Even had she not realized the situation at once, the stop for lunch on the roadside would have shown her that the lady had set her cap for Troyes. And she was undeniably beautiful as she lowered her lashes and dimpled at him and gave orders to her two servants.

"Bring my trunk from the luggage rack, Joseph, and place it here as a table for two. Bindy, get the cushions and the linen and service. Sit by me, Troyes, and tell me you don't think me silly because I must have dainty things about me, even on the road."

He did not appear to think her silly. There was admiration in his eyes as he waited upon her hand and foot. He seated himself beside her upon the cushions from the coach and leaned toward her as they ate, laughing gayly and talking. Feuille, eating her own lunch on the grass across the road, saw him holding his wine glass for her to touch it with her lips.

As they drove farther from the seaport the country became wilder. To Feuille the land journey seemed as unreal as her strange voyage with the pirates. The road was narrow and bordered by trees from which hung curtains of green-gray moss. When she remembered the small, orderly farms of France, she found the landscape dreary and depressing. The man who held her bond called himself a planter, and Feuille wondered what he planted. They rumbled along with the wooden wheels sinking into ruts and puddles and Saint Lys sometimes was forced to follow far behind when the road was narrow. Madame Wentworth never addressed her, except for an occasional order, and she grew more and more lonely and desolate. She not only disliked Saint Lys, she was afraid that he would be prejudiced against her because of her mistake in regard to the lady with whom he appeared to be infatuated. But Feuille's feminine instinct told her that however angry the lady might be, she would never repeat to a suitor the words of that mistake.

Just then the narrow trail widened, and the lady saw its advantage.

"Wench," she commanded sharply, "lean out of the coach and ask Mr. Saint Lys to ride alongside so that I may speak to him."

Feuille obeyed, and Saint Lys appeared almost immediately at the door. Madame leaned toward him.

"The crying of the frogs always terrifies me. Will we arrive at Wentworth Ways before nightfall?"

"If you are nervous I shall see that we do so—although I hate to speed our parting. As soon as we cross this causeway your coachman can drive faster."

After that they bumped swiftly along, with him trotting beside the coach to protect the timid beauty from the perils of twilight and of frogs. At the Wentworth plantation a man servant waited on horseback with a small brown pony side-saddled.

"This is the young lady, Ree," Troyes called. "Take charge of her and lead her home."

Then he turned back, assisting Madame Wentworth from the coach and carrying her fan and reticule and vinaigrette into the house, where he could take his leave of her in private.

The black man helped Feuille gently into the saddle. "Little Missy tired?" he crooned.

It was her first gentleness since she had left Mirabel. Darkness hid the tears in her eyes, but Ree heard them in her voice.

"Thank you. I'm not tired, but—but I'm afraid of this horse."

His low laughter had no derision. It was comforting.

"You got no right to be scared of this pony. He not only gentle, he bone-lazy too. But don't you worry. Ree'll lead him if you want."

He produced a piece of thin rope and tied it to the pony's bit ring, then mounted his own horse.

From there on it was too dark for her to see where they rode. She clung to the saddle with both hands and rocked precariously back and forth. Ree spoke frequently, in his rich gentle voice. Saint Lys rode up behind them and passed and took the lead.

Frightened and hopeless, she at last saw two torches blazing upon stands. Between them appeared the wide steps of a country house. Saint Lys sprang from his saddle as lightly as though he had not been riding all day, tossed his lines to Ree and spoke in French.

"Take her around to the back door, and send her to my mother's room by Jane or Juba. That will give me time to tell Madame about her."

A Negro girl in a white turban led her through the house. In the hall they paused before a cypress-paneled door. In response to the knock a sweet high voice said: *"Entrez!"*

As Feuille went in, Troyes Saint Lys was standing by his mother's bed and describing her in the French that he did not know she understood.

"Madame Wentworth finds her ignorant and uncouth. What else can one expect from a shipload of covenant servants? But she appeared the best of the lot—in fact the only one to be tolerated. Camille deRosset liked her and wished her for a maid, but resigned her in your favor. She is at least clean, and Mr. Allein assured me that she was not the criminal type."

Part Six

THE COVENANT SERVANT

Feuille stood just within the door, looking toward the big French bed. A woman sat upright within it, her head resting wearily against the headboard which was upholstered in blue silk. Her hair was white, and it was carefully arranged. She wore a pale blue bedgown with deep lace at wrists and throat. Her face seemed modeled of clay and only its eyes were alive. She fixed them on Feuille for seconds, then raised a hand and beckoned.

"Come nearer," she commanded. "You look only a child."

Feuille moved forward until she stood on the opposite side of the bed from the young man.

"I am sixteen years old, Madame, and I am strong and healthy."

"That is well," said Madame Saint Lys. "You appear polite and willing."

She turned to her son and spoke in quick French, gesturing as she did so. Feuille watched the jewels flash on the thin bloodless fingers. She could not help hearing and understanding every word that was said.

"I am pleasantly surprised, after what you told me, Troyes."

He frowned. "I have hardly had a chance to judge. Rosalie was unfavorably impressed."

His mother lifted her eyebrows. "Where did Rosalie see her?"

"Rosalie happened to drive to Charles Town the day after

I rode down. Naturally, she asked me to escort her back today."

"Naturally," said Madame Saint Lys. "Go now, my dear; for I know you are weary and hungry."

As he left the room she turned to Feuille.

"You will stay next to me, in the room on the other side of my dressing room. You may go now and wash your hands and make yourself ready to bring me my supper."

Madame Saint Lys was a hard mistress, but Feuille learned to please her. The girl had not forgotten her training by Madame Tonpain. After the squalor of those intervening years, it gave her joy to handle again silver and French china, delicate doilies and dainty food. She still disliked Troyes Saint Lys, and she did not love his mother; but she loved her work and she was a perfectionist. Trays which before had arrived in the sick room laden but uninviting, now came with immaculate linen and with food and drink temptingly arranged. There was always upon them a flower or a spray of fresh green leaves. Never was a wine glass too full, never a helping too large, never was a dish allowed to grow cold between oven and bed.

In spite of her first reaction of strangeness and fear, Feuille not only made friends with the house servants but soon grew to love them. Their racial patience and kindness of heart, their loyalty and humor, made a deep impression upon her. She saw they were trying to help her in every way they could. She taught the cook Tee Val to make *petits croissants* and a Bordeaux sauce of white wine for fowls and veal. She directed the maids in their housework, and she nursed the sick woman: bathed her and dabbed her aching temples and wrists with rose water, brushed her hair and dressed her in lacy gowns for her son's visits.

When he came she retired to her own room. It was a large room, with several windows which looked out on the piazza surrounding three sides of the house. Like all other rooms in the house it had a big brick chimney and a long wood box alongside the fireplace. One of the plantation boys kept this full of oak logs and pine splinters and came in every morning to kindle a blaze. That was a comfort she had not enjoyed since she left Bordeaux; and as soon as she dressed by its warmth she started on duties which kept her busy all day. In the hours between tasks she read aloud to Madame Saint Lys. One day while she read in English the patient fell asleep. Feuille laid down the volume of Shakespeare and reached for the French Bible on the table beside the bed.

It was the Protestant Bible, and except for services in Threadneedle Church she had not read or heard one read since her escape from France. For more than an hour she sat, turning the thin pages slowly while the winter twilight began to darken the room. Every few minutes she glanced at the sleeping woman, to assure herself that no ill change took place. But Madame Saint Lys breathed evenly and Feuille read on.

As she did so she was back again in the homes of her father and uncle. Although she had been young when she left the Cévennes, she remembered every detail of the farm. Its bright orderly vineyard was as different from this great tract of forest and swamp as day was different from night. She had loved the farm, but she hated and feared the plantation: hated its woods and dark water, its lonely nights and its crying frogs. When she went outside the house, which was not every day, she walked only in the garden laid out behind it or on the path from the garden down to the river.

As she read now the same verses which she had read aloud to her uncle and aunt she recalled those nights in Bordeaux. She recalled the Huguenot pastor's voice as he read them on that last afternoon before Captain Evan had saved her by getting her into his ship. Where was the *Lass of Lizard Point*? And where her kindly skipper? Had she been destroyed, or was she under a different name serving the pirates as the *Eagle* had been made to serve them? Were her uncle and aunt in prison or dead? The hopes she had held in London had drained to bitter dregs. She knew now that like her father they had suffered persecution for the Protestant faith. So had she, and been driven from one land to another. But this planter of rice and indigo lived in a house which was her idea of a château and owned land far more extensive than the farms of Joany and Gouttes and Lerac put together. His mother wore jewels; and when he rode in from his fields he changed to clean linen and a satin coat and his narrow face showed no emotion. What had he done to deserve all this? She could not see that he had suffered. Yet he laid claim to being, like her, a French Huguenot in exile.

Her eyes moved from the page and went again to the sleeper's face. As she raised them she saw him standing on the other side of his mother's bed. His gaze was fixed upon the book in her hands, and he stepped lightly around the footboard and took it from her.

"So," he said, "you fooled me, and Camille deRosset guessed right. She insisted, both to her husband and me, that you were a French girl."

She rose to her feet, cheeks blazing with sudden color. Her eyes were brilliantly blue and they flashed; but she remembered to keep her voice low.

"And I was right," she told him, "in my first impression of you. You bought me as you would a horse to make me work in harness. You even sink so low as to sneak into the room in order to reproach me if I read while Madame sleeps."

His face did not flush like hers, but his eyes darkened with anger. Her outburst surprised him; and even more he was surprised by the sudden beauty which angry sparkling eyes and crimson cheeks gave to her face.

"You have been in this room long enough," he told her, his low voice icy, "to know that I walk softly whenever I enter it. Also I think that you know in your heart I do not reproach you for reading."

Fear was cooling her anger. She was sullen again—sullen and hopeless like the bond servant he had bought.

"What do you mean then?" she asked defensively.

"I mean that like others upon the *Eagle* your name is an alias."

He made her a little bow as he held the Bible out to her, but she heard the note of mockery in his voice.

"I mean," he said, "that Johnny Sevens reads French."

Since Troyes rode off to his rice fields before daybreak and did not return until after sunset, Feuille managed for a few days to avoid him and further inquiry. But three nights later he found her in his mother's room, and he spoke to his mother.

"I hate to trouble you, but I must talk to you about Johnny Sevens. I made a discovery several days ago but waited to speak until she was present and could defend herself."

"Johnny defend herself?" asked Madame Saint Lys.

"Yes. She understands French but did not see fit to tell us. Consequently she has heard things she was not meant to hear."

Feuille's cheeks were scarlet and her blue eyes angry. "You never asked me if I understood French."

"That is the reason," said Saint Lys, "that I shall ask you questions now. I cannot allow a woman of whom I know nothing at all to be with my mother while I am absent."

Madame Saint Lys said: "Johnny, sit down."

She turned to her son. "I know that your action is prompted by consideration for me, but after all, we have said nothing that she should not hear. In fact I am happy that I can talk with her in her own tongue, rather than in this barbarous English."

"I do not object to her speaking French," he pointed out. "I object to her not telling us that fact. It makes me feel I was wrong to bring home to you a girl from a ship of covenant servants."

"Be practical," said Madame Saint Lys. "You knew when you signed her bond that every man and woman aboard had some reason to leave England. The girl may have left because of something for which she was not to blame. We—of all people—should understand that."

"I still think," he said stubbornly, "that she should tell us where she comes from."

"I came from London," said Feuille. "Before I sailed on the *Eagle,* I worked for a year with the French Huguenot weavers in the Silk Throsters Lane."

She did not intend to admit to Troyes that she was French. She knew now that the lawyer who hanged pirates was one of his friends. If Alf tried to find her, his inquiries might go through the channels of the law. She could be put in prison for a long time for breaking his head. It would take him longer to find an English girl than a French one, for he would inquire for Feuille Joany. So long as Mr. Allein did not know her by that name, she had a good chance of working out her bond and going on to another province.

"I shall ask her one question," said Madame Saint Lys. "Are your people Protestants, Johnny?"

"Yes, Madame," said Feuille. "They have been Protestants for many generations."

"Then," said Madame surprisingly, "you shall go next Sunday to the Huguenot Church at Jamestown."

Troyes opened his mouth to speak—and checked himself as he saw Feuille's face. He could not bear to dispel the joy that transfigured it. Her guard was down and she forgot all disguise.

"Madame," she whispered, "—a Huguenot Church? And you will let me go to it?"

"I approve of young people attending divine services. When you return, you must be prepared to tell me the pastor's sermon and—and can you sing?"

"Yes, Madame. I love nothing better."

"Then you shall take my hymnal and sing to me the hymns that are sung at the service."

She turned to Troyes. "I do not think that we need any further questioning."

He answered drily: "You are cleverer than I am, my mother. But—but Rosalie has already asked me to escort her coach to Jamestown on Sunday."

"I counted upon that," said Madame Saint Lys, "—although Rosalie prides herself upon being Church of England. You can arrange for Ree to lead the pony over to the Marions' place Sunday morning. Madame Marion is coming to visit me tomorrow, and I shall ask her to let Johnny ride on to church with her daughters."

The plan moved on schedule. Feuille started early with Ree, and she enjoyed the pony ride of two miles to the next plantation. He told her how to sit easily in the saddle, and he told her about the woods and fields they were passing.

"Mas Troy plants indigo on these thirty acres."

Feuille looked at the swampy ground from which dead stubble bristled.

"Does it die down every year?" she asked.

He told her about the crop, and she forgot herself and told him about the vineyard in the Cévennes.

"But please, Ree, don't let anyone know what I told you."

"Don't you worry," he reassured her. "Nobody ever going to hear it from Ree."

At the Marion place she was put in a coach with Monsieur Marion and the girls Pauline and Marie. They were friendly and talkative.

"This is the same river that runs by *Bois Bleu*. The Indians call it *Zantee*."

Feuille was alarmed. "Are there Indians in these forests?"

"Oh, yes," said Pauline. "They are not fierce. They trade with the French people and sell them game and hides."

Marie inquired: "Haven't you seen Troyes' huntsman, Santee Sam?"

Feuille shook her head. "I haven't been far from the house."

"Santee Sam has a cabin he built down by the rice fields. Troyes pays him an English pound a year to keep the table supplied with game. It is the custom with most of the planters in the French Santee."

Feuille listened eagerly, enjoying the friendliness as much as the information.

"Do you mean that there are other French families here?"

"The river is lined with plantations, most of them French Huguenot. We will point out to you the avenues as we pass.

Jamestown was one of the first Huguenot settlements in this colony. It is about twelve miles northwest, and the French Santee church is there."

Two hours later they drove into the village and drew up in front of the little house of worship. Feuille's heart rejoiced as she heard the French names uttered and the French language being used in conversation. She went with the Marion girls directly into the church, but the men remained talking outside.

Pauline whispered: "I heard Monsieur Vaillant say that he feared Monsieur Gendron was lost. He set out for Charles Town weeks ago, and nothing has since been heard of him."

Feuille thought of the lonely path from Charles Town to *Bois Bleu*. But the pastor was on his feet and reading aloud the first line of the Hussite hymn.

"Service will open," he announced, "with the singing of Ziska's hymn, and I charge everyone to join in singing. That is—"

His voice grew stern and his glance came to rest upon a mild-looking man in the pew across from Feuille.

"That is, I charge everyone to sing except *you*, Monsieur Gignilliat. You I charge *not to sing*, because you sing like a goat!"

The mild-faced man relapsed in the corner of his pew. Feuille felt sorry for him, but her voice soared like a lark. Oh, what joy to sing again the beloved words in the beloved tongue! At home and happy among her own people, she forgot all danger of revealing her identity. Heads were turned toward her as her voice rose sweet and strong and true.

Troyes Saint Lys was not singing, and he heard her with mixed emotions. He sat beside the lovely English widow, fanning her with a turkey-tail fan of iridescent feathers. His brow creased as he realized beyond all doubt that the girl was French and her name was not Johnny Sevens. But in spite of vexation, his ear rejoiced in the liquid loveliness of her high, flutelike voice.

When the hymn ended the pastor began the first prayer.

"Let us ask God for help," he said, "in a matter which troubles us all today. We have reason to fear that Monsieur Gendron, beloved of all our parish, has been lost or has met with some mishap in a journey through the wilderness."

With the informality of his priesthood, he discussed the virtues of Monsieur Gendron. He pictured the dark rushing waters which a traveler must cross. Feuille shivered as he told of long miles of lonely road and of occasional treachery by supposedly friendly Indians. She watched him raise his grave face, stamped by intensity of appeal.

"Oh, Lord, who led all present safe from dark forests of persecution," he prayed, "lead safe home again to us Thy servant and our friend!"

As he uttered the last words facing the open door, Feuille saw his face light suddenly with joy.

"God has granted our prayer!" he cried. "*Voilà Monsieur Gendron!*"

He abandoned the chancel and rushed down the aisle and out of the church, followed by his congregation, and with Feuille trotting among them.

Against the Santee's wide flood labored a small canoe, paddled by a vigorous-looking man of middle age. Cries of thanksgiving and joy went up, and hands were stretched toward him. Monsieur Gendron was returning to friends who loved and who prayed for him.

Feuille's happiness was complete. To her it was a miracle which made the French Huguenot service more beautiful and sacred. But just behind her she heard an amused and drawling voice which she recognized.

"Such a lack of dignity and formality," Madame Wentworth commented. "It could never have happened, Troyes, in any Church of England."

Spring came early on the Santee, and Madame Saint Lys appeared briefly to be better. Days were long, and sunlight poured like Bordeaux wine into the big room. Feuille went outdoors oftener. She had discovered that mushrooms grew wild all around the house and that the invalid would eat them when she refused other food. Feuille knew how to cook them in a dozen different ways: with wine or cream, in sauces, *pâtés, omelettes aux champignons*. Tee Val welcomed her in the kitchen, because she treated him with the respect he demanded.

"House servant different from field hand," he warned her. "Some of them people down on the Street still wild, and they talks African. When Mas Troy send me that fat gal for kitchen maid, she call my meal pot *sojo* and my pancake *flim*. When I tell her go bring water, she say, 'Where *juba haltuh?*' That why I call her Juba."

As Feuille walked down the avenue with her mushroom basket on her arm, she wondered what had been the kitchen maid's real name and whether she objected to being rechristened after a water bucket. Madame Gourdin had come this morning to sit with Madame Saint Lys, so there was no reason to hurry back. She walked on, gathering mushrooms around the damp roots of the oaks, and looking between their trunks she saw she had come to the indigo plots. Their appearance had changed greatly since she had seen them on her arrival, for young plants were sprouting in place of last season's dead bushes. She stood for a long time looking at them. My father would have loved them, she thought.

For the first time then interest stirred in her heart, interest about the plantation and its crops. She felt herself wondering just how the indigo grew, how it was harvested, and by what process made into dye. Later she asked Madame Saint Lys if there were books telling about it. The lady was pleased.

"My son has books describing every stage of indigo culture. They are in a glass-faced desk in his room, and you may get any you wish. I am glad to see you take an intelligent interest in his work."

Not in his work, thought Feuille. But she did not let resentment keep her from reading his books hungrily. Here was a subject far more appealing to her than the plots of Shakespeare which Madame Saint Lys enjoyed. These seeds of *Indigofera* of which she studied held for her more drama than the stories of Hamlet and Macbeth. In their small hard capsules, which were sown in the spring, was the promise of blue silk for queens and of blue cotton for servants. She longed to work with them, as she had worked with her father's grapes.

It was her only interest, and it became an obsession which reconciled her to life at *Bois Bleu*. In her first terror at having her bond assigned to Saint Lys, she had fully intended to run away from him. But as that first terror subsided, both her conscience and her brain advised her not to do so. Huguenot conscience warned her: You must not be dishonest and cheat your employer of what he paid for your ship passage. And her clear-thinking brain decided: Troyes Saint Lys is no friend of Alf Riggs. The two men are worlds apart. There is something mysterious, which I cannot understand, about Alf's possession of his name and address. Possibly Alf was lying, in order to boast to me, and he may never even come to America.

While the isolation of the place frightened her, it reassured her about this matter. Even if Alf reaches the seaport, she told herself, he will have both difficulty and delay in finding his way to the French Santee. If he sends a letter ahead, I shall know of it, because it is my duty to prepare for guests. If he arrives without writing, I shall still have warning from the children who play in the avenue and run to announce all arrivals.

So she calmed herself and made up her mind to work out her bond, and interest in the indigo was her greatest help at the time. Every day she walked down to the field, and upon return she described to Madame Saint Lys the growth of the plants and everything else about them. She questioned Ree, who was her friend and who told her things that the books did not tell.

"Mas Troy do better with rice crop. He plant rice on the big place. This here indigo just a 'speriment."

She had not known that there was another and larger plantation. *Bois Bleu*, which seemed so vast to her, was only the house
site with a few surrounding acres for gardens and indigo trials.
Ree explained it.

"Mas Troy build the house here close by the river to please
Old Miss. But rice is the main crop, and rice got to have fresh
water from the swamp. When you see Mas Troy ride 'way from
this house ev'ry mornin', he goin' to ride the rice banks from
day clean till dark."

She could not imagine the man whom she disliked working.
She saw him ride off every day, dressed in old clothes to be
sure, but always dressed carefully and cleanly. She could not
think of him soiling his hands or straining his back at any task
on the plantation. For his back was uncompromising, and his
hands were well-kept and straight—except for one finger that
stood stiffly off at an angle. She had noticed it at once and supposed it was some deformity.

One day while she looked at the indigo he rode suddenly up
through the oak screen. As he dismounted and threw his bridle
lines to Ree, she turned away quickly. But he called after her:
"Wait for me!"

Frightened, yet angry with herself for obeying, she stood. He
talked at length with the field hands who were cutting, then
turned and approached her on foot.

"I'm going back to the house," he said, "and I wish to talk
with you. You have been for a half year in my employ, and
you have not yet questioned me about your covenant."

"Why should I question?" she answered defiantly. "Was it
not decided by you and the attorney general, before you
brought me here, that I should work two years to pay back my
convenant?"

He inclined his head in affirmation. "When you were assigned
to me the attorney general and I agreed that it would probably
take two years for you to work out the money I paid."

She made no comment, for she had expected a term as long.

"But," he continued, "you have done better work than I had
any idea you could do. I am obliged in honesty to tell you that

your services to my mother are worth half again what I had figured they would be."

A year and a half, she counted, instead of two full years. But he is not telling me this because of kindness to me; he is thinking alone of himself and his honesty.

"This means I shall have to release you at the latest a year from now."

He paused and frowned unhappily.

"I do not know what my mother will do without you."

She did not help him; she only walked in silence by his side.

"I have two suggestions to make. One is, I will gladly pay you a certain amount every week and so prolong our bond. The other is that you work on as you are doing now; but that when your covenant expires you allow me to hire you at what salary you think fair."

This was her moment of triumph. He had been able to buy her, but he could not keep her beyond her covenant. She saw that he realized it, for he added quickly: "It is your right to decide as you wish. I can only suggest. Much as I need your services you can go or stay as you like."

They had reached the steps, and she mounted one so that her eyes were level with his. As she spoke she looked him directly in the face. She was glad that she had decided to stay and not cheat him by running away. Honesty had truly been the safer policy. Running away would have made both Saint Lys and the attorney general suspect that she was a fugitive, and she might have been caught. Now that her term had been shortened, she would probably work it out and be gone by the time that Alf came—if he came at all.

Besides all that, she now had a chance to inconvenience the man she disliked and to refuse him something that he wanted.

"I shall fufil my bond to the last day I owe you," she told him. "But the hour my debt is paid and I am free to leave this place, all your money will not be enough to keep me one moment longer."

All through that summer Feuille followed the dye-making, although her only official duties were indoors. During the months she had been with Madame Saint Lys, she had gradually taken on work outside the sick room. The house servants liked and trusted her now, and of their own accord consulted her. By degrees she found herself overseeing linen cupboards and pantry stores. She inspected the basement, with its kitchen and laundry, locked rooms for supplies, and its office where herbs and medicine were kept and dispensed to the slaves. When the roses were at their height of bloom she gathered those suitable for making potpourri and the year's supply of rose water.

It was the habit of Madame Wentworth to send baskets of fruit and flowers several times a week to Madame Saint Lys. She frequently accompanied these gifts, and never failed to leave messages or billets-doux for Troyes. Although he responded eagerly to these, Feuille had reason to suspect that his mother was not as enthusiastic as he in regard to their fair neighbor. More than once, upon being notified of the approach of the Wentworth coach, Madame Saint Lys had instructed Feuille to make her excuses to the visitor. Upon these occasions Feuille conducted the lady into the drawing room and served her cakes and wine.

Tee Val, assisting in the background, spoke his thoughts on one such occasion.

"She got no call to come 'round here courtin'. She too old for Mas Troy."

Feuille recalled her own mistake, and she had no reason to love the lady. But she felt obliged to reprove the old cook.

"Hush, Tee Val! She might overhear you. You must be polite to her, for she is a friend of Monsieur."

But he was not to be silenced. "She ain't no fit friend for him. She don't treat her own slaves right, and I ain't goin' to work for her."

Feuille thought with a pang that neither he nor she had any choice in that matter. If Troyes chose to marry the handsome Englishwoman, she, Feuille, would be a bond servant and the old cook a slave to Troyes' wife.

She tried to forget it as she went about her duties and to think of caring for Madame Saint Lys and giving her small pleasures. Like her son, Madame was not talkative and was sometimes stern, but she was scrupulously fair. She never failed to commend or thank Feuille or any other servant for a task well done.

In Bordeaux Madame Tonpain had taught her niece to crystallize fruit and certain flowers in the French fashion. Recalling it, Feuille one day selected from a basket the finest cherries and pears, coated them with the sugar and spread them to dry. They happened to be ready when Madame Wentworth paid her next visit, and Feuille placed them in a bonbon dish and carried them into the room.

"I crystallized for you, Madame," she said, "some of the fruit Madame Wentworth sent, and I thought you might wish to share it with her."

Madame Saint Lys exclaimed, with pleasure in her voice: "I used to make them long ago! I recall that Violette—"

She stopped as if the word choked her and her already pale face went ash gray. Feuille ran to her, but she gestured the girl away.

"Take them—at once—from my room! Never let me see them again!"

Torn between desire to help and fear of disobeying, Feuille left with the dish of sweets. And as she left she carried the picture of Madame Wentworth leaning over Madame Saint Lys and looking angrily over her shoulder.

After the guest's departure Madame Saint Lys refused supper and lay without speaking until she slept. Feuille did what she could to make the invalid comfortable, and she accepted the ministrations in silence. But Feuille was troubled, because she knew it was she who had made some *faux pas* and caused the setback. She had acted only in kindness, and she resented being kept in ignorance of how she had offended and for that reason risking another offense. But she could not ask the ill woman and she would not ask an outsider.

Troyes solved the problem on the next Sunday evening. She knew he had ridden to Wentworth Ways that afternoon. He summoned her to the office where he worked late into the night.

"Why," he demanded, "do you disturb and distress my mother? Why do you intrude upon family affairs which are sacred to her?"

Feuille's eyes seemed to him to grow twice as large. She did not narrow them as he did when angry. She opened them as wide as she could, and they flashed blue sparks at him.

"Monsieur," she said, "my interest in your family affairs is even less than any desire you may have to tell me. But my interest in my own affairs is great enough to make me demand that you explain your accusation."

She saw that he was taken aback.

"The crystallized fruit," he said. "Why should you so cruelly remind her of Violette?"

"I had never heard of Violette and do not yet know who she is."

"But," he persisted incredulously, "Madame Wentworth told me you said—that is, did you not say that you made the confection because Violette loved it?"

"I did not say it, Monsieur. Your mother mentioned Violette. She is an ill woman, and I do not ask you to annoy her about it. But Madame Wentworth is surely healthy enough to give you a correct account of all this."

Two dull red spots came into his tanned cheeks.

"Had my mother never before mentioned Violette to you?"

"Never before. If there are in your family secrets, Monsieur, it might be well to warn me so that I may avoid them."

"There are no secrets," he said harshly. "Nor, upon the other hand, do I feel obliged to confide in you."

Feuille was so angry that she flung caution aside.

"I wish no confidence from you, as I told you just now. It is only that, in Madame Wentworth's place, I would wish to have the truth told."

"You are not in Madame Wentworth's place," he reminded her. And she saw him look nervously over his shoulder toward the hall, as if afraid that Tee Val and the maids might overhear.

She laughed aloud then, too angry to be afraid.

"It would embarrass you—would it not—to have your black servants hear your white servant reproach you? But it does not embarrass you to be rude or unfair to me. I have lived in your house for nearly a year, and I know you for what you are: cold and hard and selfish and unjust. Someone has told a lie about me; but you will not try to find out, because you know in your heart you may find that the liar is one of your friends. I realize now what Little Tommy meant when he said there were men who made outcasts of other men. I pity him—but I despise you. For you have wealth and ease and power and you misuse those gifts. I believe that, in God's sight, men like you are guilty of the evil which they force humbler men to do."

Then, before he could answer, she turned her back and walked out.

After that she avoided him, a little fearful, and did not come face to face with him until more than a week later.

She had gone to watch the work at the indigo vats, the great cypress tubs where the bushes were steeping. At harvest the work went on night and day, and Saint Lys stayed at *Bois Bleu* to oversee it. Its exactitude appealed to Feuille's careful mind, and she longed to take part in it. When she saw Saint Lys testing the granulating mixture in a glass, she moved close to him and watched breathlessly.

He tossed the liquid back into the vat and shook his head. "Not yet," he told the beaters.

Then he turned, took Feuille gently by the arm, and without words led her toward the garden. At the first low terrace he released her and pointed to its brick step.

"Sit down there and listen to me!"

He looked down into a small flushed face, with big blue eyes half-frightened and half-angry. They were as deep a color as the long cotton dress which she had dyed from last year's indigo, and he could see the light-brown braids coiled thickly and neatly around her head. He noticed that wherever a soft lock could escape, it twined itself into a half-curl.

Then a reaction of anger and disgust swept over him and drowned his dawning interest. This woman, he told himself, is probably a convict. What else can she be, since she is afraid to tell her real name and goes under an alias? She has some reason to hide her past. She deceived me about her knowledge of French, and by so doing overheard what she was not supposed to hear. In spite of her attractive looks she is sullen and hard and in sympathy with malefactors. Only a member of the criminal class could give voice to the false and dangerous doctrine that a pirate is not to blame but is a victim of fate.

"In regard to our last conversation," he told her sternly, "you may hate me all you like, so long as you continue to fulfil your agreement by caring for my mother. In fairness I repeat now that your work more than satisfies her. But I tell you at the same time that a person who pities a pirate is deficient either in intellect or in morals."

"What do you know of pirates?" she flung at him. "You in your fine clothes and with your fine friends, were wining and dining in Charles Town while Little Tommy and the rest were being hanged."

"Why should I have deprived myself either of wining or dining because murderers were receiving their deserts? Your question is too stupid to merit a reply. Yet I will tell you that I know more of pirates than you can ever know. They are enemies of society, bullies who prey upon those weaker than themselves, yet cowards who howl as Stede Bonnet did when their own time comes to suffer."

His usually composed face was twisted with emotion. It made her hesitate to reply, and he continued speaking.

"I have watched your work and judged you by it. I did you the credit to think you honest and self-respecting. Only the man or woman who does his or her part can be that. We were set upon this earth to work, in whatever station we find ourselves. Yet there have always been and there will always be those who expect to share in gains for which they have not toiled. As individuals they have different excuses, such as weakness, injustice or ill luck. Together they try to dignify their greed and laziness with some name referring to communistic advantage. But singly or in groups their cry is the miserable whine of those who wish to take rather than to earn. They are dangerous with the danger of weakness and decadence; for their whole creed is a tearing down instead of building up."

Her eyes still blazed.

"Who are you to talk? You have always had all that you needed or wished. What do you know of people who suffer and grieve?"

"I know," he told her, "because I have both suffered and grieved. But instead of whining and demanding help, I have tried to build up a life in place of the one I lost."

Now his voice was sharper with scorn than hers had been.

"There was a time when I had all—all that I needed or wished. But I was driven from all that, driven from home and country. I was young—almost as young as you then—but I had to plan our escape. I had to take upon myself a responsibility too heavy for any man to bear. In part I succeeded, in part I failed; and that failure will haunt me until I die. I brought my mother to this New World which promised men of all beliefs freedom of their religion. You are too ignorant to know the travesty that has proved. But what do you think I did when I arrived in this wilderness? Do you think I found this house standing and trained servants waiting for me? Do you imagine I did not have to hew timber from this same site, to buy slaves and teach them to labor and carpenter, to make for myself a home and an industry by not only personal but manual work?"

She shook her head slowly, for she had imagined him only directing while others toiled. He raised the hand with the stiff finger marring it.

"Upon the day I broke it I was working with ax and saw. There was no surgeon nearer than Charles Town. Ree called one of the blacks who was a tribal doctor. He cut away the mangled flesh and cured the inflammation with herbs, but the bone healed crooked although healthy."

He caught himself there, and fear of showing emotion made his voice harsh and his face stern again.

"But of what use to tell you what my family has been through? You have sympathy for pirates and murderers, but not for a woman who is dying—dying because—"

"Monsieur, if you mean Madame your mother, I charge you with being unfair to me. In spite of the personal dislike you have shown me, you told me that my work was satisfactory."

"I have no personal dislike. Perhaps I was—was misled."

He paused, and she rejoiced as she saw how hard he was finding it to continue. But he had been bred in the clear uncompromising austerity of the Huguenot creed, and he was obliged to right the wrong he knew he had done.

"I apologize," he said. "It was no one's fault except my own. I misunderstood Madame Wentworth about the crystallized fruit. Both my mother and she say that—that you did not—did not mention the name I accused you of mentioning."

Feuille rose to her feet. "Is that all, Monsieur?"

But as she walked away from him she told herself: Although I hate him, I am glad he has found Madame Wentworth out. For, while he takes the blame, I saw in his eyes and heard in his voice that he knows in his heart she tried to lie about me.

Part Seven

THE PLANTATION

The long southern summer was drawing to its end, but the storms that came with September only made the heat more oppressive. Feuille wondered often if the scene could have been more tropical had the pirates taken her on to the West Indies. The deciduous trees appeared to be crowding their branches thicker and thicker with leaves, as if to shade themselves from a sun that made them droop limply at midday. When the breeze fell the gray moss hung straight from the live oaks, giving the impression of columns of smoke rising directly upward. The house seemed walled in a prison of woods which thickened every day. Ree told her not to walk in the wood paths because the snakes were coming up from the flooded swamps to high ground.

"Me and Mas Troy kill a big rattlesnake-pilot right by the indigo shed yesterday."

"What is a rattlesnake-pilot? Why did it go to the shed?"

"Some people call 'em 'moccasins.'" His voice held a faint contempt. "But everybody knows they goes ahead of the rattlesnake to scout for him. When they sends back word the way is clear, then old Mr. Rattlesnake comes right along behind them."

She stared at him with round eyes, hoping that this pilot had been destroyed before it had time to send its message back.

Ree went on. "Snakes comes up in sheds and barns to ketch rats. In a dry drought they comes up around houses to get water. In wet seasons they hunts high ground so's not to drown in the swamp."

It frightened her so that she dared not leave the cleared roads when she went out. The trees which hemmed them were tangled with tawny wild bignonia, and with the honeysuckle that is called "goat leaf" in France. Its scent, heavy and poignantly sweet, followed her wherever she walked. It drifted into the deep-piazzaed, wide-halled house at night.

Those summer nights were dark and thick, with a salt breeze from the tidal river. Sometimes she was awakened by a great swamp owl yelping, or a small owl that alternately mourned and burst into maniac laughter. The gulls that drifted in from the Santee Delta mewed overhead like cats. Madame Saint Lys and the servants had warned her to bolt her shutters tight against miasmas which would cause fever. Down in the Quarters, along the "plantation street," the slaves sought protection by building bonfires.

Since the violent interview with her employer, Feuille had avoided him whenever possible. It deprived her of the interest of seeing the indigo-making, but she felt she could not trust herself in another such altercation. She thought about him resentfully, but her resentment was mixed with unwilling respect. She had had no idea that this slim, supercilious young man had by his own work converted a wilderness of timber, jungles and lagoons into the arable land of a large plantation. Even her father, industrious and tireless, had not had to reclaim his soil before he farmed it. She wondered what long-dead ancestor had cleared that loved slope of the Cévennes. She pictured him as strong and bold and undaunted by hardship. He had left to his sons a legacy more precious than gold and jewels. Love of the earth and the good little leaves was ingrained in her. She looked back on that unknown forefather with an admiration which approached hero worship.

With just that admiration, she thought suddenly, might his great-grandsons look back on Troyes Saint Lys. The idea was not welcome, but she was too just to dismiss it without thought. It stayed with her, and she never lost an opportunity to inform herself about the origin of the plantation. Ree and Tee Val were always glad to talk. They had been in the first small lot of slaves bought in Charles Town by Saint Lys and taken with him to French Santee.

"When we first rode up that avenue," Ree said with a pioneer's pride, "there weren't no avenue. There weren't nothing but woods and creeks and snakes, and owls yelping all night and wildcats yowling."

She had neither seen nor heard of a wildcat, so her imagination pictured an infuriated tabby. Ree was enlarging upon the subject.

"Mas Troy and Injun Sam used to shoot wildcats most every night. Sam nails they skins on his cabin to cure, then he sells them over to the settlement."

Hard as her life had been, she had lived it in old countries and well-trodden ways. She had not realized just how wild this new land was—so wild that even its cats were wild.

She left the basement kitchen and, with her largest basket, went on to the garden. The low brick terraces fell away in a succession of shelves, broadening as they fanned out from the house. Box was planted in formal patterns, and the late summer flowers were in their last burst of bloom. Feuille had in the spring made the year's supply of rose water, and she had never again crystallized fruit or flowers. But she was making rose-petal jam and rose-petal honey of the warm, undersized, overscented autumn roses. She had learned that they had more flavor than the handsomer early blossoms. She moved carefully; for the grass was high on the lawns, and she suspected every syringa bush of sheltering a snake or a mad cat. Suddenly she heard voices, and she shrank behind a laburnum. Troyes Saint Lys, in working clothes and riding boots, stepped into view. He was followed by a field hand with a spade on his shoulder. Saint Lys was speaking.

"I want the lawns cut tomorrow, Saraka. The rice is in, so you may take as big a gang as you need. But finish the job tomorrow, because guests are arriving."

"Yes, *Mahaba*," the man answered, and went on toward the Quarters.

Saint Lys was coming toward her and would discover her, so she stepped from behind the laburnum. He stopped and frowned.

"Do you never cease work? Even the field hands have knocked off."

"I needed more rose petals to finish my jam. If it rains hard tonight the blossoms may be destroyed."

"I did not mean to criticize you." It was hard for Troyes to apologize, but he could not resist a rush of tenderness for the girl as she stood framed against the rich setting of the garden.

"I realize that I speak sharply at times, without intending to do so. If I am rude, I ask you to forgive me. Now give me the basket and let me help you gather. If you do not make haste you'll be cooking all night long."

She could not help laughing at his ignorance.

"Not cooking at this stage, Monsieur. The petals must stand overnight in the syrup."

He shrugged, but his voice was kind.

"I know nothing of the making of jam, but I enjoy eating what you make. It gives a flavor to those small rocks which Tee Val calls one day buns and the next day *petit pain*."

"Shall I try, without offending him, to teach him to make the bread lighter?"

"You'll save both my digestion and my temper if you do." He added warmly: "I'll thank you and try to do you some favor in return."

He was being kinder than he had ever been, and she responded.

"You will do that, Monsieur, if you tell me why the man who just left the garden called you *Mahaba*. Ree and Tee Val and the maids call you Master or Mas Troy."

"*Mahaba* is African for master, and many of the field hands were born in Africa. They live in the Quarters and talk their own language to each other. The house servants pride themselves on being different. They speak French or English—in this house a jumble of both."

She remembered Tee Val's remarks about his position. The rose basket was full, and they started toward the house. She would have liked to ask him who were the arriving guests; but she merely thanked him and took the basket at the basement entrance.

By the time she had stripped the roses and set the petals to soak, and got up to Madame Saint Lys' room, he was sitting there neatly dressed and talking with his mother. Feuille saw that her cheeks were faintly flushed with excitement.

"Johnny, my dear, I am glad you have come. I have something to tell you."

"Yes, Madame," said Feuille.

"My son's Indian huntsman is just back from an errand to Charles Town. He brings word that Mr. and Mrs. deRosset and the attorney general, Mr. Richard Allein, will arrive next Thursday by coach to spend some days with us."

So I know who the guests are, Feuille told herself. And the man who hangs criminals is one of them.

"It will give my son pleasure to see his friends. Besides which, the attorney general is our lawyer—"

Her voice broke. Her son leaned and took her hand gently.

"Mother, do not let yourself have too great hopes."

She was trying to regain her composure.

"I—I realize of course—that we would have had a letter if . . . But I can't help hoping—always—Troyes!"

He kissed her hand and laid it back on the coverlet. She turned her head and tried to smile at Feuille.

"I wish you, Johnny, to take my place and assist my son with these guests. I have just told him that I think you capable of sitting opposite him and presiding at table."

Troyes watched Feuille blush as red as the roses they had picked. Unlike his mother, he was not sure that she was capable. He knew now that she was a Huguenot. Only a French Protestant could have sung in church as she did. But that very fact convicted her of being under an alias. She might have done nothing really wicked, but there was some mystery about her. He did not like mysteries, and he had suggested that Madame Wentworth would be glad to come and stay and play hostess. But his mother, who had bequeathed him a strong will, had one even stronger. She had waved a frail white hand and murmured: "Most inappropriate!"

He heard Feuille protesting: "But, Madame, I have no dress suitable for the table. Besides—"

"It is arranged," said Madame Saint Lys. "You shall have a suitable dress. We will talk about that after supper. Now go and tidy yourself."

Madame deRosset and Mr. Allein arrived in the deRosset coach with Pierre deRosset riding alongside. Feuille was waiting on the front piazza to greet them, while Saint Lys stood at the foot of the steps. The Negro children had been on watch all day long in the avenue. At first glimpse of the visitors' approach they ran full speed for the big house, knowing that gifts of cakes or tarts always awaited the bringers of news.

Dressed in her first taffeta gown, Feuille stood and saw them arrive. In Silk Throsters Lane she had toiled at weaving the light, stiff, glossy material; but she had never aspired to wearing a dress made of it. Madame Saint Lys had sent her to a locked closet of stores to get the roll of deep-blue silk.

"Lucille shall help you make it. I know that you can sew, for you have mended my garments and made bedgowns for me."

Feuille could have made it alone, but with the plantation dressmaker's help it had been completed on the second day. She stood before the long mirror in Madame Saint Lys' room, and Madame smiled as she looked upon the result of her planning. . . .

The long straight skirt gave slenderness and height. The high-waisted, low-cut bodice was modestly filled with cream-colored net. Above it rose a smooth young face with flushed cheeks and with eyes as blue as the dress. The long blond-brown hair was wound in its womanly coronet, but its shorter locks still escaped and curled with childish softness.

Troyes Saint Lys had been in the room and had watched without comment. His mother exclaimed: "But, my son, she is charming; is she not?"

He had bowed gravely. "The color becomes her."

The color was from the plantation indigo. Feuille thought resentfully that the compliment was more for the product of his own work than for her. She knew enough about silk-making to realize that the stuff had been woven from undyed skeins and piece-dyed afterward. As she stood now on the piazza, she ran her hands down her sides, listening to the rustle which was distinctive of close weaving and equal count in the crossing of weft and warp. Hour by hour and yard by yard, she had toiled to create this beauty for other women to wear. In order to wear it herself, she had been obliged to strike down Alf Riggs, to cross an ocean, be captured by pirates and brought to a port for which she had not sailed, and, finally, to be bought like a slave by the man at the foot of the steps.

Madame deRosset, who was being helped from the coach by Troyes, wore a scoop bonnet of rose color and a rose-colored gown cut low and without modesty vest. My gown is as fine and as fashionable as hers, was Feuille's first thought. It made her smile sparkle and her cheeks grow deeper pink.

Pierre deRosset was running up the long steps.

"I would scarcely have known you!" he exclaimed.

She tried to speak and to welcome him, but his remark and the sight of the attorney general behind him had taken her back to the purchase of her bond in Charles Town. Her hands clenched in the folds of the blue taffeta. DeRosset reached out and, with an accustomed gesture, lifted the small hostile right hand and bowed and kissed its clenched knuckles.

The courtesy restored her poise. "A full year has gone by, Monsieur," she agreed.

"It has been kind to you. So, I am sure, have been Madame and Monsieur Saint Lys."

Feuille turned without answering to greet his wife.

"Blue for a blond," Madame deRosset cried. "A brunette must wear the warm colors."

"A warm heart, Madame," said Feuille, "is lovely in any color."

She did not see Saint Lys' glance of surprise and admiration. The British attorney general stood by, expressionless but watching. Madame deRosset embraced her.

"You are witty as well as pretty. No wonder Troyes out-pirated the pirates and stole you from me."

Only a Frenchwoman could so have eased awkwardness and completely changed a situation. Feuille, although conscious of her taffeta dress, had walked out on the piazza stiff with sullen misgivings. I am doing this, she had told herself, because my employer orders it. Although I sit at the head of his table, I sit there at his command: a servant obedient to him.

But now her employer's best friend had just kissed her hand. His wife had kissed her upon both cheeks and called her "pretty" and "witty."

The shyness of her manner was that evening as becoming to her as were the blue dress and the deep flush in her cheeks. Troyes Saint Lys, watching her from his seat at the foot of the table, wondered why he had ever thought her uncouth. DeRosset and Allein were seated on either side of her, but she deferred to Madame deRosset. The courtesy delighted Camille, who appeared to have forgotten all past friction and to give herself credit for what had come to be. She leaned and whispered to Troyes: "Did I not tell you the girl was French? Are you not grateful that I sent your mother such a jewel?"

He frowned. "You and Pierre knew her before I did. You know well enough that she is a London girl named Sevens."

"*Là, là!*" cried Camille softly and teasingly. She raised her wine glass and laughed at him across it. "A little actress may fool you with a stage name, *mon ami;* but you need not try to fool *me.*"

When he first suspected there was some mystery, his resentment had been directed at the girl. But now as he looked down

the table at her—fresh and sweet and innocent-appearing as
the blue forget-me-not which was his favorite flower—his
heart went suddenly cold with fear *for her.* Whatever she had
done, it could not have been criminal; yet the laws of the
province were harsh and Allein was a prosecutor. He tried to
hush the heedless Camille and to change the subject. The
church question was always good for a fight when French and
English met together. In a few moments it was Allein's turn to
wish to change the subject. He lifted his glass.

"Let us drink to Madame Saint Lys, whom we miss from
table. To her good health in your good Bordeaux!"

The kindness of the deRossets had given Feuille confidence;
the wine had warmed her heart and limbered her tongue. Here
was a subject on which she could speak as knowledgeably as
any of them. She leaned toward the Englishman, and her voice
was earnest.

"For many centuries, Monsieur, the Bordeaux merchants
have sued for laws to keep the name *Bordeaux* exclusively for
wines of the Gironde. The Bordeaux lawyers have pled in
court that no wines should bear that proud name save those
made from grapes grown in that department."

She was not looking at Saint Lys. Only Madame deRosset
saw the flicker of fear in his eyes and the hard set of his mouth.
Pierre deRosset and Mr. Allein were both watching the girl in
blue. It was a subject of interest to both, and for the lawyer
litigation held charm.

"Do you mean," he inquired, "that you can tell by the taste
whether a red or white wine is the product of grapes grown in
the Gironde or in another department?"

She smiled at him across her glass, and her lips parted to
reply. As they did her eyes met the warning in Troyes Saint
Lys' eyes. He and Camille deRosset saw the color drain from
her face. Allein and deRosset missed all significance.

Saint Lys spoke quickly. "As you know, I collect books on
wine-making. Johnny Sevens has, at my request, been studying
them with me and discussing with me the advisability of trying
a vineyard at *Bois Bleu.*"

"A vineyard here?" cried deRosset. "In the lowlands of the great Santee Swamps?"

"Why not?" demanded his quick-witted wife. "Troyes was one of the first planters in Craven County to experiment with indigo."

"But grapes," insisted deRosset, "need a very different soil. They need slopes for drainage, and sun and open country."

His wife longed to be near enough to kick him on the shins. Feuille and Allein sat silent. Troyes shrugged his shoulders.

"As Camille says, I am fond of making experiments. I have, of course, decided that grapes would not succeed. All the money and work I can spend must go on the rice. I am not even sure that I can continue with indigo."

Around the table was running a little electric current of uncertainty and suspense. Being English, Allein distrusted anything he did not understand. He stroked his small sandy moustache and frowned at the rice birds on his plate.

Troyes and Feuille sat, grave-faced and silent. She had already known that he guessed her secret, but she had not guessed that he would defend her from the knowledge of others. It made her feel resentful rather than grateful toward him. And he returned the feeling. Why, he asked himself, should I feel I must protect a woman who is not only a bond servant but who is also a suspect?

Pierre deRosset looked from their strained young faces to his wife, and she lifted her eyebrows at him. Camille is up to something, he thought, and he held his tongue and drank his wine. I don't know what she's up to, but I know that I'll catch the devil afterward if I try to find out now.

Camille lowered her penciled brows and laughed with delight and with mischief. It would be scandal, she thought, if a rich high-born Englishwoman were displaced by a little servant girl from France. It would be scandal—but what fun it would be! Rosalie Wentworth is my best friend, and she is considered the most beautiful woman in the province. But after all, she must be nearly ten years older than Troyes, and she takes it for granted that she must have everything she wants. Troyes does not even know it yet, but he has a *tendresse* for this blue-eyed child. Otherwise he would not have lied so quickly to protect her. She has some secret in her life, and I adore secrets! I know well enough that she is not a princess in disguise. On the contrary, Troyes is the prince and she is the pretty pauper. She is not only pretty, I'm sure that she is honest and kind and good. I shall take a hand in this, for it is going to be fun to watch. The only thing which could make it even more fun right now would be if the lovely widow Wentworth were dining with us!

The three visitors remained for a week, and for Feuille the time of their stay was a mixture of pleasure and fear. Realizing how she had betrayed herself and been saved only by Saint Lys' intervention, she dared not talk and only listened. She heard Madame deRosset regale Madame Saint Lys with all the latest gossip of Charles Town. The men talked politics and discussed the rebellion against the Lords Proprietors, which had resulted in the election of James Moore as governor. Saint Lys was bitter.

"We French have no reason to expect fairer treatment from a Royal government than from a Proprietary. Every inducement was offered us to settle in either southern or northern Carolina. But those promises have not been kept. Huguenots are caught between the malice of their fellow Dissenters and your iniquitous Church of England Act."

"I am outnumbered," protested Allein. He looked ruefully at Feuille. "You and I are two English against three French who outtalk us."

"You gave us no chance to talk at all," Camille deRosset told him, "when the Act of 1704 made the Church of England the established religion of the province."

"My dear love," her husband chided, "women do not discuss politics."

"My dear imbecile," she answered, "we discuss nothing else in the drawing rooms of Charles Town."

Politics and church acts meant nothing to Feuille. Her pretense of being English kept her from any discussion or criticism of the situation, and she dared neither observe nor resent difficulties set in the way of Huguenots. She carried on her housekeeping, taking pleasure in making delicacies for the guests. Madame deRosset accompanied her to the basement storerooms and exclaimed in admiration at their laden shelves. She complimented the tarts, made of small yellow wild plums which Feuille had gathered and bottled in early summer. Not since her aunt had petted and mothered her in Bordeaux had Feuille been treated so tenderly. Although Madame Saint Lys was both fair and kind, she had the same reserve which in her son became coldness.

But Camille deRosset had taken a sudden fancy to the girl with indigo eyes who had been for a day her maid. The pretty, dark-haired matron was spoiled and romantic-minded. She wove in imagination a background for Feuille which, although improbable, was no more improbable than the truth of the matter. She had questioned Madame Saint Lys tactfully, and had found that Madame was also fond of the girl.

"She is unquestionably a French Protestant and a refugee. She knows the Huguenot service, and she sings from memory the Huguenot hymns."

"I, too, am sure of it," said Camille. "But what reason can she have to call herself by an English name?"

"I have lived too long, my dear Camille, to have any curiosity left in regard to the reasons of other people. The girl is innately good, I am sure, and that is all I need to know."

But Camille had curiosity, and it was driving her almost mad.

She tried to draw Feuille out. "All Huguenots have secrets, and they should confide in each other. Although Madame and Troyes hide their feelings, Mr. Allein has upon this visit brought them news of disappointment and tragedy."

Feuille shook her head stubbornly. "They have not confided in me, and I know nothing of their affairs."

"It is a family matter in which Mr. Allein represents them."

"I owe Monsieur my ship passage and shall work until I pay it. That is my only link with this plantation."

Camille shook her pretty, inquisitive head. The girl is as stubborn as Troyes, she decided. And the very fact of her reserve makes me even surer that she is fine and sensitive, strong enough to endure without complaining for the religion which we all love. But unless I do something to hurry matters, Rosalie Wentworth will marry Troyes before he even finds out that he cares for Johnny.

She consulted her husband that night in their room, and he lifted his hands in horror.

"Camille, I warn you—I implore you—I order you not to meddle with Troyes' affairs!"

"But my darling, just suppose it were you and I? Imagine my agony if a designing woman many years older than you had caught you—right under my nose—"

There were tears in her voice and in her dark eyes. He took her into his arms.

"But it is not you and I. No designing woman ever tried to catch me, and we are married to each other and happy."

"Then it is even more cruel of you to disregard the happiness of your friend and of the girl he loves!"

"I see no sign that he loves her or that she loves him. She did all she could to prevent his taking up her bond, and I thought him unfavorably impressed."

"You are so unromantic! Conflict is necessary to a passionate love affair. Troyes must be stirred from his customary coldness. His love would awake if he were alarmed—if he thought that something dreadful threatened Johnny...."

"You are the cruel one, Camille, to plan to terrify Troyes. I shall have nothing to do with the matter."

"Then I shall have to do it alone," she warned him.

And she fell asleep, smiling as she made her plans.

Two days later, on the verge of departure in her carriage boots and gloves, she led Troyes into the basement.

"I must speak before I leave about a tragic matter. Where is little Johnny Sevens?"

Camille saw the muscles of his jaw tighten. "A moment ago she was in my mother's room, planning with my mother to pack a box of conserves for you."

In the preserve closet next door Feuille could hear them plainly. She had run down the stairs ahead of them and had the box already packed. Her only exit was cut off, for the closet door opened into the laundry room where they stood discussing her. Should she call out and warn them of her presence? No, she told herself; for I am the one who needs warning. This may be the news I dread: the news that Alf is following me. Self preservation gives me the right to listen in order to save myself.

She caught every word of Camille's low quick French.

"I tried to make her confide in me, two days ago in the garden. I realize of course that she is a French Huguenot who has met with misfortune."

"I realize it too," he said. "But it is none of my business."

Camille gave a little cry of exasperation. "That is the trouble! You are cold and reserved and stubborn, and she is enough like you to be your own sister. But it *is* your business if she is being pursued and needs protection."

Feuille's cheeks burned, but her heart was ice. Camille's prevarication was near enough the truth to terrify her, at whom it was not aimed. She could not see Troyes' face, which had gone pale enough to please his tormentor. She heard the harsh note in his voice, and she took it for anger against her rather than fear for her.

"What do you mean, Camille?"

"I mean that there are rumors." She spoke evasively. "One hears them in Charles Town, even if you do not."

"How do you know they refer to *her?*"

"I cannot, of course, be certain; but I felt I should warn you, Troyes. It may be some enemy who is tracking her down. I am sure she is good and innocent, and of our own faith. I implore you, *mon ami,* to be on your guard!"

Feuille, shaking so that she feared she would rattle the jelly glasses, heard him say between his teeth: "Thank you, Camille. I shall be on my guard."

Those words remained in Feuille's mind and tormented her: *I shall be on my guard.*

What terrible suspicions he must have of me, she thought, if he has to be on guard against me. I was wrong to imagine, as I did that night at table, that he was shielding me when he spoke of planting grapes. He was guarding himself and his mother and his property from any scandal or danger my presence might cause them. He is now watching me, guarding against me, and waiting for my arrest. The rumors of which Madame deRosset spoke must mean that Alf has reported me to the police and that they are tracking me in Charles Town and will find me here. If the constables come and take me and put me in prison, Troyes Saint Lys will say I am getting what I deserve and will sit sipping his wine as he did while Little Tommy was being hanged.

She dwelt upon the matter until her fears became certainties, and she determined to get away before the constables came. Terror so twisted her interpretation of the words she had heard through the pantry door that she came to believe Saint Lys might even inform against her. She had recognized the cold rage in his voice, and she thought it directed against her for daring to shelter in his home. At night she lay awake, wondering how to make her escape. As she did her work in the day, she started at every sudden noise outside the house, expecting to see the patrol riding up the avenue.

She had been badly frightened that night at the supper table when she saw she had betrayed herself by knowledge of Bordeaux wines. But afterward her cold fear had been thawed by a small warm spark of gratitude: gratitude that Troyes

Saint Lys had without hesitation come to her rescue and saved her from consequences.

How foolish I was, she now told herself, to believe it was kindness for me. He tried to deceive the others because he abhors any scandal; but he knows I am not Johnny Sevens and he has me now in his power. There is no way by which I can leave this plantation. Forests and water shut me in as if I were in a prison. He is cold and cautious; and knowing I cannot escape, he is only waiting to make sure. When he is satisfied that I am the girl in question, he will send his Indian huntsman who runs his errands to Charles Town to inform the attorney general.

Madame Saint Lys observed with anxiety the change that came over her looks and movements. The bright cheeks had lost their soft rose flush, but they flooded with painful red at a step in the hall or knock at the door. The big blue eyes which had sparkled like sapphires above the shining taffeta dress were clouded with unhappiness. There was no briskness in her step as she came and went in the sick room, doing the daily tasks that she had done so lightly before.

"Are you ill, my child—or troubled? You do not sing any more."

"I will sing for you, Madame, whenever you wish me to."

"It is not that. No song is sweet unless its singer wishes to sing. I used to enjoy hearing you, as you went about your work, singing the beloved lyrics of Clément Marot or humming the air of *Amaryllis*."

Feuille thought of the snuffbox hidden in her room. She dared not let it play in the house, but more than once she had taken it on her walks. When under an oak far down the avenue, or upon the farthest terrace where the garden met the river, she had sprung the lid and listened to its lilting music.

It was her only possession. While she thought of escape she thought, I will take it with me wherever I go. Fleurette loved me and gave it to me. No one in all the world cares for me now.

She was in the kitchen next morning planning meals with

the cook when Ree's little son rushed in with news that a cart was approaching. Her heart stood still as she wondered if the law would come in a cart. . . .

She heard Tee Val grumbling as he handed the child a waffle. "Ain't nobody but gypsies and hangmens goes round in a cart."

It was not the hangman but a traveling tinker. He sat upon one shaft of the two-wheel vehicle, which was piled with his merchandise, and urged his swaying ox with a wooden goad. Behind him, with the same splay-footed gait of the beast of burden, plodded his large, swarthy, dirty wife.

Feuille saw that the house servants were excited. They chattered of buying beads and bracelets with their few pennies. Although Tee Val still grumbled, he grumbled happily as he went around collecting steel from knife boxes and drawers. He charged the maids: "You good-for-nothin' gals better watch that gypsy while he sharpen these. I make you sorry if you let him steal one of my carvin' knifes."

Feuille's native thrift caused her to protest.

"But Tee Val, the plantation carpenter always sharpens the cutlery."

He only stuck out his mouth and grumbled more loudly.

"Zeke don't sharpen my knifes as sharp as gypsy can sharpen 'em. Gypsy-sharp is sharper than any other kind of sharp."

She left him and went upstairs to tell Madame Saint Lys of the impending arrival and consult her about the knives. The lady of the house appeared as excited as the servants.

"It is quite true that the carpenter Zeke can and does sharpen the steel. But on a lonely place like this we enjoy the tinker's visit. So we allow the cook to have his knives sharpened by the tinker who does it no better than Zeke. It is such a pleasure to Tee Val to stand over him and give him orders and find fault."

She continued: "I wish you would have the maids bring me samples of what the man has. I sometimes buy ornaments or dress lengths of calico to use for the house servants' gifts at the next New Year."

According to custom the tinker and his wife were issued a meal, while their tired ox was watered and fed. Madame Saint Lys bought lavishly of bright cotton and scarves and brass trinkets, as well as additional pots and pans which were demanded by Tee Val.

"The tinker's coming is an event," she repeated to Feuille. "Usually he comes once a year, but we have not seen him for the last eighteen months."

"Where does he go?" asked Feuille. "How can he travel any distance with that slow ox?"

"He goes from Santee to the Albemarle, stopping at plantations and camping on the roads. He will probably spend the night here and start before daybreak tomorrow. The first time he came my son told him that he and his woman could sleep in the basement. But both protested they could not sleep with a roof between them and the sky. So we merely give them food and allow them to make camp."

After the one word *Albemarle* Feuille had ceased to listen. She was thinking her own thoughts. Here was her chance of escape. She had heard the Albemarle discussed by Saint Lys and his friends. It was a vast country, fringing upon vast sounds. A fugitive could be lost in it . . . and from it could flee farther north. . . .

In the late afternoon before Saint Lys rode in from his rice fields, she walked out in the stable yard to the small untidy camp. Over a fire of fat lightwood knots the woman was cooking the provisions that had been given her. The man lay on the ground, but he leapt to his feet and came toward Feuille as she beckoned. His close-set eyes glittered with expectation of some commission which would bring him gain. His headkerchief had slipped to one side, and she saw that that ear was cropped. She knew what it meant, but the knowledge did not deter her.

"If you will do a service for me I will pay you fairly," she told him.

His teeth flashed. They were beautiful, but his face was repulsive.

"You can trust me, my lady. I carry many letters for ladies." His smile was evil. "They are letters to lovers on other plantations—letters which cannot be carried by slaves, for fear that husbands should know."

"My errand is not a letter. Can you carry a person hidden under the rolls of cloth in your cart?"

She saw the flash of fear in his eyes. If caught, this would mean more than ear-cropping. But she had to escape. She pictured prison and disgrace awaiting her. She opened her doubled fist and showed him the coins in her hand.

For a half moment uncertainty played like shadows on water over his greedy knife-sharp face. Then he smiled at her and touched his green headcloth.

"If the lady will be in the avenue before the morning star rises, I will do the thing she asks—provided she pays me before we start."

That night Feuille dared not let herself fall asleep, for fear that she might not awake in time. She had bathed Madame Saint Lys and done for her other services, with added tenderness in her heart and gentleness in her touch. Now she had finished and was in her own room; but the doors between stood open and the invalid might call. In that case her absence would be discovered before the oxcart had taken her away. Upon the other hand, she could not risk being late. The tinker might not return for another year and a half.

She had tied into a bundle only what remained of the possessions she had brought to *Bois Bleu*. She would not take away with her a dress or a petticoat or shoe which had been supplied her at the plantation. She set a candle in its French china rest on the floor, and she looked around the big room with its four shuttered windows. The ten months she had spent there passed in review before her. There she had had comfort and courtesy for the first time since leaving France. A pang of nostalgia gripped her heart at leaving the garden terraces, where she had watched the yellow tide of the Santee. The live oaks in the avenue had grown and spread since she had arrived. She thought of the Negroes' rhythmic song as they beat the fermented indigo. What would Madame Saint Lys do without the accustomed care? After all, Troyes Saint Lys, although brusque, had treated her fairly. . . .

But, she reminded herself, I cannot indulge in such thoughts. Even if I am foolish enough to have let myself grow fond of *Bois Bleu* and of its mistress, its master has turned against me and is going to cause my arrest.

She watched the dull stars from a window, and when midnight was three hours past she blew out her candle and let herself into the hall. It was dark as pitch, but she knew every step of it as she inched her way toward the front piazza. Here was the coat-and-hat rack made of antlers from stags Troyes had shot. She wiped each prong carefully every day to be sure that the maids left no dust. She had to pass both Madame Saint Lys' and Troyes' bedrooms as she went, but no sound came from either and she moved soundlessly. At the foot of the steps she paused, longing with all her heart to go back. West and toward the slave quarters the moon was a thin bright knife.

She had never been outdoors in the night by herself before. Except for the lean orange moon and the stars that it was dimming, she could see no light anywhere. She gripped the banister post where she stood, and tears ran down her face. But she forced her legs to take her on toward the avenue, which yawned like an ink-black tunnel between the trees.

The hour she waited seemed very long. She sat on a tree root and trembled. The cough of a squirrel made her jump, and the bullfrogs bellowed as loud as alligators. Only ten feet away from her a shadow slunk across the road: a gray fox returning to its lair before daylight. She was thankful when she heard the creak of wheels at last. The tinker was walking beside his ox, and his cat's eyes saw her through darkness. He told her to climb on top of the goods, using the wheel hub as a step. As she mounted he held out his hand, and she poured her coins into it.

"But I must hide," she told him. "I must hide under your goods."

"It does not matter," he said—and added, "for it is still night."

As he spoke she heard the woman behind the cart tail laugh deeply.

Feuille saw faint gray light ahead as they neared the end of the avenue. She thought of the night she had entered it, riding on the small brown horse alongside of Ree. Ree was her friend and protector. He had never failed to do anything he could to help her and guide her. Her bond had been bought in almost the same way that he the Negro was bought; the difference between them was only in term of servitude. In spite of being a slave he loved the plantation, with greater charity and faith than she a white woman showed. She began to weep afresh as it came over her that she too loved it and was leaving it forever. What would Madame Saint Lys do without all the accustomed care? The maids could not care for her properly, and Tee Val sometimes put the wrong wine in her mushroom sauce. When she awoke this morning she would not only be in distress, she would think of Johnny Sevens as ungrateful and faithless.

Through her tears she could now see that they were well without the gate and in the belt of longleaf pine. The oxcart swayed like a ship at sea, and she would have preferred to get down and walk. But she knew she could not risk it; she must hide in the bales of cloth.

She began to push them right and left in order to make a space between. The sun was not yet visible; but she knew that it was rising, because the pine trunks now stood like dark separate columns to the east. Just then the narrow rutted road made a turn toward the highway. The ox had scarcely drawn the cart around it when she heard hoofbeats behind them thundering to a crescendo.

Like an animal going to earth she burrowed down in the

merchandise. But Troyes Saint Lys was upon them before she could get into hiding. She had never seen him ride so fast. The bay horse was in full run and passed them before he could pull it up. As he wheeled it around on its hindlegs she saw his face and cowered.

He threw himself from its back and came toward her, with the bridle rein over an arm. As he did so the tinker checked the ox and went to meet him, flashing his white teeth in a grin and touching his green headcloth.

Saint Lys addressed Feuille briefly. "Get down, you little fool!"

She burst into tears and obeyed him. When she stood on the ground he dropped his bridle rein and stepped toward her, his gray eyes as dark and as dangerous as steel. She saw that he was drawing a paper from his breast pocket. He held it out.

"What have I done that you should do this thing to me?"

She tried to answer, but her voice came in sobs.

"I–I had to. You–know–why."

"I know nothing except that Ree found this stuck on the stable door when he went to get my horse just before daybreak this morning."

He extended the dirty fragment.

"Take it and read it. Have you lost your mind to trust yourself with thieves and rascals like these? If you wish to leave I will cancel your bond. I do not care to hold you by force."

Through her tears she tried to make out the crooked charcoal scrawl.

MASTr Yr WYFE BE RUNNING OFF. Yr HOSS
CAN OVERTAKE THEE OX BEFOR WEE CROS
THEE FERRIE.

Feuille looked up, and as she did blue anger burned the tears from her eyes. The wretch had betrayed her. She might have known by his evil face and his cropped left ear. He was daring to push between them, with his back to her. He touched his forehead with one hand and extended the other toward Saint Lys.

"You have her safely now, master. Give me what I deserve."

Feuille heard herself shrieking: "What you deserve is a flogging!"

"And you'll get it," added Saint Lys.

His whole face lit with a smile of joy as he reached and twisted one hand in the neck of the grimy shirt and with his other raised his leather riding whip.

At the first blow the tinker roared and tried to fight back, and the ox took off in a rocking gallop, scattering goods from the swaying cart. The woman, screaming curses, threw herself against Saint Lys. Without letting go of her husband he brought the whip down across her broad behind with all his strength. She squalled like a scalded cat, and clapping both hands to the injured place started to run down the wood road after the ox.

Then Troyes Saint Lys devoted himself to the tinker, while his horse cropped dead grass by the road and Feuille stood staring with parted lips.

When he threw the man from him his voice was even but menacing.

"Never put foot on my land again—unless you are anxious for double the twenty lashes I gave you."

He straightened his coat with both hands, stooped to pick up his trailing lines, and started off leading the tall horse back toward the plantation.

As he passed Feuille he gave her a glance and spoke shortly. "Now come home."

Just within the avenue gates Troyes Saint Lys stopped and looked back. She approached him slowly: a small, disconsolate figure with a torn dress and a tear-stained face.

"Are you tired?" he asked her. "Do you wish to ride on?"

She tried to answer and choked again.

"I was awake all night—and scared."

With no further words he put a hand on each side of her waist and swung her up to sit sideways in his flat saddle. She clutched the mane of the horse's crest, and he put his own hand over hers.

"Johnny," he asked her gravely, "why did you do this thing?"

"Because I was afraid that you—that you thought me a criminal—and were going to tell the attorney—and that I would be put in prison."

"I was afraid it was that," he said.

His face was set, and he stared beyond her. But she felt his hand tighten over hers.

"I was afraid of that before. I feared it ever since Camille said . . ."

He paused, and his eyes met hers and his voice became stern.

"But did you not realize that by running away you were calling attention to and convicting yourself? Had you really escaped and then been caught, I could not have protected you."

She shook her head in dumb misery, closing her eyes to hold back tears; but he saw them squeezing slowly through the thick lashes. He watched them, and the freckles on the bridge of her short straight nose. She did not look like a criminal, but evidence was against her. He had learned that among covenant servants there was always a percentage of men and women escaping from justice. He knew that she was French and was using an alias. For that reason he had believed what mischief-making Camille had said in order to stir him up. It was consistent with what he already knew that the girl should be sought by the authorities. Now to clinch the matter of her guilt, she had taken flight after giving herself away about the Bordeaux wine and had tried to get away in the cart of a crop-eared thief.

She opened her eyes, now turquoise-blue and washed of their sapphire sparkle.

"I did not know that you would—would try to protect me."

She felt his fingers close convulsively, then he took his hand away.

"You must come back to the house now. Only Ree knows what has happened, and he will not tell."

"Do you not wish me to tell you why the police want me?"

He frowned in silence as he thought, his Huguenot conscience at war with his every impulse and desire.

He was thinking, If bad becomes worst and the patrol is sent for her, I can truthfully swear that when I let her leave the place I did not know what offense she had committed. For he realized in that moment that he could not let her be taken, no matter what she had done. It must be serious, since she spoke of prison. Perhaps she had killed in self-defense to escape some cruel master. Even so, that master had probably been English, and she would be tried in an English province. He knew how provincial law discriminated against the French. What chance would she have in a Charles Town court? For a bond servant of alien race, fleeing under a false name from a crime committed in England, such a trial could well result in hanging.

"No," he said slowly. "It is better I do not know. I think I can help you best that way."

He had spoken the two magical words *protect* and *help*. Comfort flowed into her heart like warmth into a frozen limb. She still knew that in all the world nobody loved her; but she had learned there was someone who might protect and help her. He was going on.

"If I do not know of what they are accusing you, I can—in the event that they send to arrest you—warn you and get you away before they arrive."

She was thinking, as he was, of the Negro children who played all day in the avenue and raced each other to herald arrivals. She was thinking, as he was, of trackless swamps and lagoons that stretched around his plantation. His protection meant hiding, if hiding became necessary, in that hinterland which patrols could not penetrate.

A terror as great as fear for herself came over her as she thought: What will they do to him if he aids a criminal? Will they crop his ears like the gypsy man's, or will they hang him in my stead?

He was looking up at her, although he had moved his hand away.

"We must go on," he said again. "My mother wakes early."

She leaned impulsively and put a hand on his shoulder.

"I would rather be taken than—than that they should punish you."

He felt his heart give a little jump of relief and reassurance. No habitual criminal would feel or speak that way. Whatever she had done—and by her own admission she had offended the law—must have been of necessity and in self-defense. For a few seconds they looked into each other's eyes, closer in spirit than the eighteen inches between their faces.

He was the first to look away, as he reminded himself that his duty was to his mother and not to an indentured girl.

He led the tall horse, and it stepped quietly in the road between the live oaks. When the avenue ended and they crossed toward the stables, she summoned courage to speak.

"I do not know why you are so kind as to help me. I am your covenant servant, and you owe me nothing."

The moment had gone. In the full daybreak his young face was austere.

"We owe each other nothing, and it is better this way. If only you care for my mother as you have been doing, any protection I give you will be but fair return."

Madame Saint Lys never learned of the escapade. When Feuille went in to her she was lying awake.

"Have you needed anything, Madame? Have you been calling me?"

"I called. When you did not come I knew you had gone outside to gather mushrooms, or to instruct the servants."

"I was out of doors," Feuille told her truthfully. "I am sorry that you had to wait."

"It does not matter." The low voice was very tired. "For two years now I have been only waiting."

Feuille knew that it was true. Whatever the cause of her illness, Troyes Saint Lys' mother was steadily losing ground. Feuille had hoped at one time that care might restore her health. But she had come to realize that it could not even hold her, and that all to be done was to make her comfortable. Sympathy for the invalid and her bargain with Saint Lys had at first prompted her to do all she could. To these motives was added now her gratitude for the protection that he had promised.

The autumn came and went peacefully, and winter started with Christmas. At *Bois Bleu* its observance was only religious. Gift-giving and merrymaking were postponed for New Year's Day. The Huguenot plantation was still a small part of France.

Troyes Saint Lys came early to greet his mother, and the three exchanged *"Joyeux Noël."* He returned after breakfast and read to her from the well-worn Protestant Bible. Feuille had not kept Christmas so since she had left Bordeaux. She had neither been invited nor wished to stay in the room with the Saint Lys a year before. Now she sat and listened to the Christmas story with no attempt to hide her understanding of French. Even if Alf comes, she thought—no matter what comes —I have in the world one friend who will try to protect me.

As Troyes closed the Book he lifted and kissed his mother's hand. "I wish that I could sing for you, but that was always your part."

She glanced from him to Feuille and smiled. "He has no ear for music. The only tunes he can recognize are the hymns he has heard from childhood and the minuet *Amaryllis* to which he used to dance."

Feuille had never sung for him. She sang for Madame in the afternoons, before he came home from work. The only time he had heard her had been in the Jamestown church. She looked from his mother's face to his, and she blushed as she saw the eagerness in his eyes.

"Although I have no ear, I love music. Will you sing, Johnny?"

"I will be glad to. What do you wish, Monsieur?"

His voice as well as his eyes were eager. "Ziska's hymn," he said. "Your voice carries it like a silver trumpet."

> *"Faith of our fathers, living still*
> *In spite of dungeon, fire and sword...."*

She did not know its history, or vision as he did the Hussite soldiers chanting it as they went into battle, but her young voice, clear and true and triumphant, carried the noble words with passionate conviction.

> *"Faith of our fathers, holy faith,*
> *We will be true to thee till death."*

My own father died being true to it, she thought. Madame and Monsieur left France in order to be true.

Troyes and his mother asked for other hymns, and they thanked her when she had sung them. As she rose to go to the pantry and her duties concerning dinner, Troyes rose too.

"Your voice is lovely," he said. "May we meet like this again on New Year's Day and hear you sing the carols?"

She looked forward to it all week, and the thought bound her to *Blois Bleu*. She was just beginning to realize that there was beauty on the plantation. Before, she had only shivered at the hoot of night owls and at Ree's stories of snakes. Now she walked in the winter woods and saw the dull-leaved mistletoe clustering its waxen-white berries in the trees. The hollies were crimson with fruit, and smilax and other vines trailed strung beads of black or red like bright chains from branch to branch. There was beauty in the woods and kindness in the house, and she was going to sing for friends—as she used to sing for her loved ones in France—and share the celebration of the *Jour de l'Étrennes*.

She looked forward less eagerly now to the fulfilment of her bond. Troyes never referred to it again, or again asked if she would stay beyond its expiration to nurse his mother. Nor had he ever again said a word about her running away and his thrashing the tinker. What will he do, she wondered, for someone to take my place? And what will I do to get other employment? I dare not stay in Charles Town, for fear that Alf may come; so I must again move on to a strange place and strangers. Perhaps I would be as safe here as anywhere, since Monsieur said that he would help and protect me.

She recalled the carols she had sung in childhood on the Day of Gifts, and she practiced the ones she liked best in order to be ready. Sitting by the river or walking on a wood path, she caroled with the liquid ease and the bell notes of the wood thrushes. After breakfast on New Year's Day, she changed her dress and brushed her hair and went into Madame's room, her cheeks bright and her heart warm with pleasure.

Troyes stood by his mother's bed; but he held his riding crop in one hand and his riding cape over the other arm. There was annoyance in his voice.

"Had I known that you objected, I would have refused. But Ree has already carried my acceptance to Rosalie."

"I do not object. I am merely surprised. You asked Johnny to sing for us, as she did on Christmas Day."

"I did not then know . . . I mean that Rosalie . . ." He stopped again and his face darkened. "I ask you both to excuse me, for I have been invited by Madame Wentworth to a dinner at Wentworth Ways."

Feuille had still no love for Troyes, only gratitude; but the disappointment of that day stayed with her like a physical hurt. She was truly fond of Madame Saint Lys, but she was accustomed to daily reading and singing for her. Troyes' presence would have made the occasion a party, as it had made Christmas Day. But he, after asking her to sing, had excused himself at the beck of Madame Wentworth's white languid finger.

Madame Saint Lys was even graver than usual, and Feuille saw that she was taking no pleasure in the carols. After singing two she stopped and sat silently by the bed, wondering whether Troyes' mother disapproved of the wealthy and beautiful woman or was merely disappointed by her son's absence.

Disappointment and other small vexations were forgotten that night when Madame became suddenly ill and lapsed into an unconscious state. Feuille, at her wits' end, roused the house servants and sent Ree to Wentworth Ways for his master and Saraka riding to Winyah Bay for a doctor.

For those hours she worked alone with the apparently dying woman, stimulating her with brandy and *eau sucre* and ordering Jane and Juba to keep the bed warm with hot bricks and jugs of boiling water. When Troyes arrived she had no time for his white-faced misery, and only told him to get out of her way as she rushed to and fro on her ministrations. But when the physician finally left next midday, Troyes came to her.

"Dr. Hyrne says that without your care my mother would have died last night. I can only thank you. I have nothing valuable enough to offer you in payment for such service."

"Monsieur," she told him, "I owe your mother service by the terms of my covenant. Even if I did not, I care enough for her to do gladly what I have done."

No more was said of that matter. Dr. Hyrne had told them both that the illness had been a heart attack and would probably recur. Feuille, afraid to leave her patient, no longer dared go beyond the house. She was tired in mind and body, and yet her resentment flared when Troyes brought the Indian woman to her.

"This is Wancheesa, a medicine woman of the Waccamaws. She is skilled in nursing, and has been employed by many families of the Santee."

Feuille looked into the dark immobile face, and received no answer to her question. But, she reminded herself, the master of the house had brought Wancheesa. He had brought

her to supplant his supposedly English bond servant. No matter
why he had done so, she, Feuille, was obliged to give way to
the Waccamaw nurse in the sick room.

Suddenly then it dawned upon her. She had refused to
renew her bond or to promise to remain with Madame even if
Troyes paid her. He was not a man who would either argue or
beg. He had taken her at her word when she told him that
he could not pay her to remain one day longer.

She was obliged to admit to herself that he was right. Not
only was Wancheesa competent, she lightened the burden
Feuille had been carrying. For Wancheesa was not only a
natural nurse but had medical knowledge to meet an emergency. Wancheesa knew the herbs whose brew gave sleep or
strengthened a tired heart. Although she seldom spoke except
to answer a question, she watched her patient unceasingly and
seemed by intuition to foresee her wants.

That burden was lifted from Feuille's mind; but with its
lifting a weight settled on her heart, destroying all the pleasure
of relief. For she realized that she was no longer indispensable
to the household of *Bois Bleu*. Before I came, she reminded
herself, Tee Val and Ree were in charge of the house and
stables. Now Wancheesa is doing for Madame Saint Lys all
that I could do for her. June is approaching, and Monsieur
Troyes has already told me that my bond will then be repaid.

The Albemarle seemed too far away, and dread of loneliness
seized her. She realized that ever since Troyes had thrashed
the tinker and brought her home she had rested secure in the
promise of his protection. Home . . . She even called the plantation *home* in her thoughts. She had lost her babyhood home in
the vineyards of the Cévennes. She had learned to love her
uncle's home in Bordeaux, and then been driven away. *Bois
Bleu* was the third place that she had ever called *home* in her
heart. She would be leaving it, too, behind when she left the
plantation and tried to make her way into the unknown
country north.

But it is too late, she grieved. I told him nearly a year ago
that I would not remain one day after my bond expired. He is

scrupulously honest, and he has acted in accordance. To his mind my debt will be paid in June, so he will then send me away. That is why he has replaced me with Wancheesa.

Everything about the place began to seem dear and familiar. The avenue oaks were getting their new pale-green leaves. From a distance they looked like sprays of flower buds in the dark hue of the old leaves. After the April rains the Spanish moss came to life and curled delicate tendrils of citron color. She stood in the roadway and watched it hang, translucent against the western sun. The indigo beds are near, she recalled, and the seed will be sprouting now. I will walk on and look at it, for I shall be gone before harvest.

There was a sharp little ache in her heart as she went on toward the south fields. To her surprise the drained swampland stretched unplowed and unplanted. For the half mile where the indigo plots had run parallel to the avenue she saw only abandoned fields, growing up with tufts of coarse grass and weeds.

Her duty of nursing had kept her from walking this way for many weeks. But she had pictured the indigo growing toward its first cutting. A feeling of indignation was mixed with her disappointment. She knew nothing about the rice, but she loved the indigo. It had taken for her the place of the grapes in the Cévennes. Why had Troyes Saint Lys neglected to plant it this season?

When he left his mother's room that night she followed him into the hall. He stopped as he saw her come out of her door and turned to face her, but he did not speak.

"Monsieur, I realize that it is not my affair, and I ask you— I ask you to pardon me."

He raised one dark level eyebrow.

"For what do you ask pardon?"

"For—for speaking of something which is not my affair. This afternoon I walked out to the indigo plots."

He waited for her to continue. She had not asked a question.

"It is your affair entirely, but I love the indigo. All last summer I watched it and longed to work with it. I ask your pardon for asking, but—are you not going to plant it?"

He shook his head.

"Not this year—and perhaps never again. I too love the indigo, as I love all growing things."

He stopped and looked hard at her.

"What is it to you? Even if I plant it you will be gone before it matures."

"I know," she said.

She was twisting her hands, and looking down at them. He wondered what it was that she was trying to say.

"I have not yet told my mother, and I ask you not to tell her. It will distress her when she hears that I have made a failure of it."

"I will not tell her. But, Monsieur, how can it have been a failure? I saw your wagonloads of bricks of the dye drive off to market."

He smiled without any amusement.

"I did not mean by failure that I had lost money on its planting and sale. I meant rather that the giving up of any crop he tries is for a planter acknowledgment of failure."

She persisted. "But, Monsieur, why then should you give it up?"

"Because I myself cannot be in two places at once. My rice fields are far larger and they support *Bois Bleu*. I have no white overseer, and I do not intend to have one; because those I have seen are brutes. Ree and Tee Val must be at the house, to guard it in my absence as well as to do their work. My other slaves are all field hands, none of them fitted to superintend."

"If you had someone to superintend, you could furnish the labor, Monsieur?"

He answered impatiently: "Yes, *if*. But I have not. None of the hands know the full process; each one knows merely some part of it. What use to discuss it? I have tried and have failed. Why do you even ask? Are you not leaving in June?"

"Not unless you wish me to," she told him, trying to steady

her voice. "If you have the indigo seed and you can let me have twenty hands, I will start tomorrow to plow and plant. All last summer I read your books, and watched every step of the making. I will harvest three crops this summer for you, if—if you let me stay."

Part Eight

INDIGO

Five days later the plowing was finished, for Saint Lys had taken his best men from the rice to do it. Thirty acres of rich lowland lying south of the avenue had been broken into soft soil free of weeds or grass. Feuille had walked the banks of the drainage ditches which divided it into plots. She had paced the windbreaks of cassena east and west, and made sure that the mule-dragged shares cut every available foot of earth. Although the earth was lavish in this wild new world, she still measured it in terms of the small precious farms of France and her intention was to make use of every inch of it. When she returned to the house at nightfall of that fifth day her stout shoes were stiff with dried mud, but her heart was singing.

"This is all I need from your plowmen," she told Saint Lys. "From here I can go on with the gang of women field hands you have assigned me."

As she stopped and frowned thoughtfully he saw that the freckles across her nose and beneath her eyes had increased in number. Although he knew they were blemishes and no lady should have one, they did not appear unattractive to him. They were dark gold in color and small, and they twinkled when she smiled or frowned.

But they sat in his mother's room, and his mother had other ideas. She looked upon this venture with mingled amusement and horror.

"Lucille is making Johnny a set of sunbonnets," she said. "Without them her complexion would be completely ruined. They are blue to match your working dresses, Johnny. I wish you would try this first one on. And mind you never again go out in the sun without wearing one!"

Wancheesa brought it, and she stood watching while Feuille tried it before the glass where she had tried the taffeta dress. Troyes Saint Lys could see her small reflected face. He was recalling the wave of relief—and of something more than relief—which had surged over him when she said *"if you let me stay."*

He assured himself that relief was natural and sprang from two good reasons. His mother had grown to love the girl. Although the Indian nurse was now in charge of the sick room, the girl still came to sit with his mother in the evenings, still sang to her and chatted with her and made sure that all went right. In addition to that valuable service, she was going to try to make the indigo—to save a crop which he had been obliged to abandon.

With the blue bonnet still framing her face, she turned to the bed where Madame Saint Lys was propped on a pile of silk pillows to receive her evening visits.

"Thank you, Madame. I will wear it to shade my eyes and my face. I regret that the work will keep me away from you. But I shall still see you at midday and in the evenings, and I know that Wancheesa is a better nurse than I."

The Waccamaw woman's face gave no sign of appreciation or displeasure. She seldom spoke, except to her patient.

"Leaving you," said Feuille, "is my only regret, Madame. For work with the soil and its growing things gives me more joy than any work between walls."

She took off the bonnet and faced Troyes, unsmiling and businesslike.

"Whether the sun shines or it rains, I must begin sowing tomorrow. The seed should have been in three weeks ago."

"Fortunately for us the spring is late this year," he told her. "The rains this week are the first real rains we have had since the vernal equinox. Although we are three weeks late, the weather conditions are just right. What worries me most is that your gang is almost half Corymantyns. I would have liked to give you only Mandingo women."

She had lived long enough upon a rice plantation to know that rice planters preferred Mandingoes to other Africans. They were intelligent as well as strong, co-operative and willing to learn, able to adapt themselves more easily than others to the awful change made by slavery in their lives. Ree was a Mandingo. He praised his own tribe, and at the same time never failed to warn her of the shortcomings of "Coramantees." According to Ree they were savages, ignorant, stubborn, unruly. But she knew that Saint Lys had selected for her the best he could find in the Quarters.

"I have always got on well with your people," she reminded him. "I have seen the women and think them an exceptionally fine lot. While with them I made a list of their names, and then I went over that list with Ree. I have them numbered now according to their trustworthiness and ability, so that I know exactly which to appoint as my taskmistresses."

He laughed at her earnestness. "Is there anything you have forgotten?"

"I hope not, but there probably is. If I do what I can ahead of time, work will go more smoothly and faster."

His gray eyes lit with the hope of catching her in some small detail.

"Each of your twenty hands will drink at least a gallon of water a day. Had you thought of water carriers?"

"Yes," she told him tranquilly. "I have ten bucket boys. Ree's son Jolly picked them for me. I told him to keep the buckets under the avenue oaks and upon the other side in the shade of the south windbreak."

She added: "Ree said the women liked a dipperful of molasses in each bucketful of water."

"All the hands do. It is their *eau sucre,* and is more stimulating than wine."

"There is one thing I would like to ask. I expect to work

from sunrise until sundown. The indigo fields are exactly a quarter mile from the Street. That is near enough for my hands to go home and cook their own dinners. They are all women, and most of them have little children. I saw their cabins and asked about their families when I was listing them."

He looked at her intently. "Yes?"

"I would like to stop work at high noon and start again two hours later. I think they need that time to get back and forth, to cook and eat and feed their children."

"It is reasonable enough. If you start work at sunrise and leave the fields at sundown, you will still have a ten-hour work day outside of your two-hour rest."

"I calculated upon that, but I do not wish to break rules. I know that in the rice fields your gangs work different hours."

"They do, for the reason that they are too far away to get home for the midday meal and rest. With the indigo the situation is different. Besides, you are there in complete charge. I shall not interfere—unless you call upon me."

"I shall try not to call upon you, for I know how busy you are. I hope and expect to do this work without taking you once from your rice planting."

But in spite of her brave words and although she was tired, she did not fall asleep as usual that night. Can I really accomplish this thing I have promised to do? she wondered. Ree says that the women are more difficult to oversee than the men. Will they like me and obey me, or will they lose time and make trouble?

She seldom dreamed, but she dreamed that night of foaming indigo vats and of molded bars of dye rising higher and higher.

And she was still thinking of this when she left the house before day and started down for the south fields to meet her indigo gang.

She reached the field ahead of the gang, as she had planned to do; and as she turned and looked west and toward the Quarters she saw them.

Ree was walking at their head to guide them this first day. They strung out behind him in single file, silhouetted against the dawn, tall figures made taller by the turbans they wore. Each carried upon a shoulder the hoe or rake she would use. They were stately in their long full skirts; they held themselves straight and proudly; they seemed not to hurry but strode swiftly with a steady, reaching glide.

Ree halted them at the first field and spoke to them in a mixture of English and French and African dialect. Feuille had heard it used now for more than a year, and she understood most of it. While he talked the women laid down their tools and began to gird their skirts around their hips with pieces of rope. Most appeared to be listening, but others looked away; a few faces were contemptuous or sullen. Ree knew the reason as Feuille did not. They had always worked supervised by a man, overseen by Saint Lys himself and directed by Negro taskmasters. Here was a woman as young as the youngest of them. Her head reached only the shoulder of the least tall of them. Her white face and small stature made her seem by their standards frail and helpless. A brown giantess suddenly laughed aloud.

Ree wheeled and started for her, and she cowered from him.

"One more laugh outa your big mouth and I puts you to the plowing. This gang got no room for troublemakers. It's the best work on the plantation, so near the Quarters that you gets home to cook your dinner and to see 'bout your children. But the only way you stays in it is to do what *Maduba* tell you."

His eyes singled out two tall Mandingoes.

"Losa and Hanny," he told Feuille.

They were the two at the top of her list and she recognized them now. Losa was tall and thin with her head bound in bright yellow cotton. Hanny was a young girl with features like an Indian, with flashing teeth and eyes and a violent temper. Feuille had to tilt her chin and look up to both of them.

"You are my head taskmistresses. Split the gang in two and start the hoeing at once. You know the distance between trenches. Monsieur tells me the indigo hoes are all notched for a foot and a half."

Ree stood watching, with uncertainty on his face.

"Mas Troy told me to stay with you today if you needed me."

If she needed him. . . .

She needed him desperately, for she knew that next to Troyes he ruled the plantation. But she must not let either him or Troyes see her need. She had volunteered to do this work, and had known when she did so that she must direct a gang of field hands. While she read about it in books, or merely watched it as she had done the past year, it had seemed simple and she had had no doubts. According to the printed page, one laborer plus one acre of plowed land and the indigo seed must equal so many cakes of dye. Now she was faced with all the imponderables. She was three weeks late with planting, and the sun was hot for seed. Losa and Hanny were with her, but there was at least one rebel in her gang. She had heard enough about field work to know that a man or woman bent on making trouble could not only pretend to work and accomplish nothing, but could actually do damage. She needed Ree. . . .

But she turned to him and managed to smile with confidence.

"Thank you for bringing them. Please tell them to be at this place at this time every day. Then you may go. I do not need anything more."

She did not dare look after him as he went toward the house. She picked up her skirts with both hands and followed her gang, using the ditch bank as a path. Losa and Hanny had already deployed them. They stooped to measure distance between rows by the notches on their hoe handles. Then thirty hoe blades rose and flashed as they caught the rising sun, and the small trenches began to creep west to east in parallel lines. Feuille followed steadily, inspecting depth and direction. Her feet sank ankle-deep in the soft damp black earth.

As soon as the first acre was trenched Losa brought three girls back to her.

"You better start droppin' seed, *Maduba*. Bully knows how to drop seed, and Ludie and Fan can cover for you."

Feuille and Bully tied seed aprons around their waists. Bully had sowed indigo before and she knew the spacing. They followed the first two trenches, moving west to east. Behind them came Fan and Ludie filling the trenches with their rakes, covering the seed to the exact depth required, breaking or removing any hard piece of earth which might retard a plant or make it grow crookedly.

Before they reached the end of the row Bully was well in the lead. Her heavy body swayed easily while Feuille's jerked as it dipped and rose. She reached the east end of her row and turned to go west on the next one. Ludie followed her closely, in perfect time, apparently losing no second and no stroke of rake. But Feuille was aware that she was holding back Fan, who could have covered for a faster dropper.

"Shall I ask Losa for another dropper, Bully?"

"*Maduba*, you go right on. You doin' fine for beginner."

The praise was to Feuille a stronger stimulant than the molasses water, to which the women were now beginning to resort. She sent Fan to bring her a gourdful, and in the five minutes she got a start ahead of the rake. I'll keep the lead if it breaks my back, she told herself determinedly.

Row after row was filling in. The hoe gang had reached the third plot. Feuille's strong young back was aching. She straightened for a moment to look east. Bright blades on long wooden handles rose and fell to the rhythm of the high-pitched song. The many-colored turbans made the plot a field of flowers.

Row after row and hour after hour, in a rhythm of toil broken only by the cry of "*Juba haltuh!*" Then one of the

children on duty under the trees would come between
the trenches in a staggering trot, splashing the water from the
bucket as he stumbled, and the sweet gourd dippers would
soon empty it.

The sun was almost directly above, and its rays beat like
blows on the blue sunbonnet. The Negro women, Feuille
realized, had enough experience to keep several folds of cloth
between such heat and the tops of their heads. She made up
her mind to pad the crowns of her bonnets. Sweat was running
down her face, and she longed for the midday rest and for
sustaining food. Each step was now an effort. She looked up
and was thankful to see that the sun stood at the zenith. She
untied her apron band.

"Put the seed bags in the shade, Bully. I'll speak to Losa and
Hanny, and then we'll stop work for dinner."

Losa's gang was the nearer, and all went well with it. The
women dropped their hoes where they stood and turned
gratefully toward their cabins. Feuille turned toward Hanny's
gang—and as she did so trouble broke out. Yells of rage arose,
hoes were lifted in combat.

She scrambled through the drainage ditch toward them,
tearing her stockings on briars and getting her skirts bemired.
As she approached the fight she screamed: "Drop those hoes!"

To her surprise they broke apart, leaving Hanny and another
woman facing and glaring at each other. Hanny let go of the
weapon, but the other still grasped the handle of hers although
its blade rested on the ground.

Feuille went toward her, knees shaking and heart beating
fast.

"Obey me. Drop that hoe."

The woman relinquished it slowly, but her look was murderous.

Feuille spoke to her taskmistress. "Now, Hanny, what is
this?"

"It that Coramantee Cat, and I goin' to split her head open.
She done ruin my task, and she done it on purpose."

Hanny was pointing at the trench. It was crooked, too

shallow and too wide. It would not only have to be dug again, but the repairing would take longer than digging a new trench.

As she looked more closely at the other combatant, Feuille saw she was the woman who had laughed aloud that morning.

"You are Coramantee Cat?"

"No. My name Coramantee Cate. Them that hates me calls me Cat."

"Why did you do this, Cate? I have done nothing wrong to you. Ree told me you all had hoed trenches before. Did you do it on purpose?"

"I done it on purpose. Ree put the Mandingoes ahead of me. I make just as good taskmistress as Hanny or Losa."

"Lemme bust her head," shouted Hanny. "She cause us to work overtime."

The others had gathered all around. Feuille and Hanny and Cate stood in the center of a ring, and Hanny had picked up her hoe.

"I goin' to chop her head open. She cause us to work the noon time."

"No, she won't," said Feuille. "You will not chop her head open, but neither will any one of you do extra work because of her fault. Go to the Quarters—all of you except Coramantee Cate. She will stay here with me and mend every row that she has done wrong. And what she does not finish at noon she will do after sundown."

That evening Feuille did all she could to avoid a talk with Saint Lys. Not only was she achingly weary, she did not wish to own up to having had trouble on her first day. Just after he came to his mother's room she rose to go to hers. She tried to smile, and the sunburned skin on her lower face prickled like needles at the movement of the muscles. Her mirror had told her that chin and jaws, where the rays struck below her bonnet's shade, were a fiery and painful red.

Saint Lys saw it too but did not comment. He asked: "Will

you come to my office and give me an account of the day's work? I know that you are tired, and I will not keep you long."

"Do not," said his mother. "Johnny must be worn out. She did not even get back to the house for dinner. I wish, Troyes, that you would tell her she must always come home. Unless she has rest and food the work will break her down."

Feuille sat in the high-backed plantation-made chair, facing him across the desk where he did his book work. He looked at her with one eyebrow drawn higher than the other.

"Why did you stay at the field during the midday hours?" She told him the story.

"Did I do wrong, Monsieur? It seemed to me the only fair thing to do."

"It was fair—a fairer thing than I would have done."

"What would you have done, Monsieur?"

"Turned the woman over to Ree for punishment. He would have replaced her in my gang and put her on harder work."

"I know that you chose prime hands for me, and I shall be ashamed if I cannot handle them. Besides, in spite of what she did, I am sorry for Coramantee Cate. The other women already dislike her. They will hate her and may do her harm if I make them do extra time on account of her bad work."

"That is just and ethical. But can you afford to lose time by stopping to consider any individual to that extent?"

"I lost no time today. We trenched and sowed exactly what I had planned."

"I did not mean that. I meant that you could not yourself afford to lose your noonday meal and rest. If this Corymantyn does anything wrong tomorrow, call Ree at once and turn her over to him."

"I will," she told him unwillingly. "But I hope that I shall not have to. The others are unkind to her and call her Cat."

"From what you've told me, the name suits her."

"She may be only suiting herself to the name because she is unhappy and is goaded by them. She did every foot of her bad work over today, and while she was sullen she obeyed me."

He raised the eyebrow higher.

"Very well. I told you you were to handle this your own way. I think I know you now, Johnny, although I did not at first. Camille deRosset said that you were just like me—which means you are proud and stubborn and fond of your own way. But do not let pride and stubbornness keep you from coming to me if you need help."

As the workdays went on into weeks her sunburn settled into freckles, and her nervousness into alertness and understanding. Losa and Hanny never failed her. Coramantee Cate obeyed, although she still looked resentful. Most important of all, the other women no longer abused and taunted Cate. Feuille realized that their antipathy had been rooted in a natural cause and was dying as naturally since that cause was removed. Each one of them worked ten hours a day at manual labor. A task well done in that time meant leisure for the other fourteen hours and certain privileges accorded the trustworthy. Leisure and these small perquisites were precious to them. They were earned by hard work and not to be endangered by troublemakers who spoiled the common task. So long as the Cat did them no harm they would leave her in peace.

That realization helped Feuille to understand her women. She could not blame them for striking back when what they cherished was threatened, for she knew how little they had to cherish in their lives. She admired and applauded the sense and charity which enabled them to forget the injury as soon as it ceased.

Now that the indigo seed was in the ground she was tranquil. All to be done until it sprouted and bore its first leaf was to keep the earth soft with rakes and free of every alien growth. For this short interval her gang worked only from dawn until midday. They were a large gang for thirty acres of indigo. Saint Lys had given her a generous number because they were all women and because he knew the planting had to be rushed.

Instead of enjoying her half day rest, Feuille could not stay away from the field. When she started her full day work she had formed the habit of arranging all household matters in the evenings. At that time she planned with Tee Val the meals for the next day, inspected the maids' housecleaning, questioned Wancheesa about her patient, sat with Madame Saint Lys and told her all the day's news. Now she found herself with a long afternoon on her hands. She was too strong and young to need any rest except the night's sleep. As soon as the sun was behind the pine tops she started down the avenue.

She loved the very look of the plots: smooth and as soft as loam, clean of the greedy weeds and grass that tried to push their way in. Every night she described it in detail to Madame Saint Lys.

"Soon there will come the good little leaves. I wish you could see them yourself, Madame. I will dye a piece of wool with the first cake of dye we mold, and make you a winter bed jacket from this seed that is now in the ground."

This afternoon the sun was low and she was walking a lateral ditch, her head bare and the blue bonnet swinging over an arm. Saint Lys saw her through the oaks before he reached the edge of the field: a bright splash of indigo blue against the green of the windbreak. He had left the rice fields early in order to see her work, and he came toward her now, walking between the seed rows.

She waved the bonnet and cried aloud: "Monsieur, I am glad you have come! Tell me what you think of the sowing."

His eyes went up and down the rows where the young plants were beginning to sprout. They were in line and evenly spaced, and except for their tiny blades no other growth was aboveground in the field.

"I could not have done it better with a gang of my best men."

She knew that he was not quick to praise, and she flushed with pleasure.

"Losa says that just as soon as the first leaf uncurls we must begin to work the plants. I looked up that stage of the work last night in one of your books, in order to refresh my memory."

"Losa is right. Also you must keep the soil loose and pulverized, as it is now. Next to hoeing and sowing you will find that your hardest work."

"I can hardly wait," she told him, "to get from one stage to another. It is like a beautiful story: seed, earth, plants, flowers, leaves—and from all this a color like the noonday sky, which can be transferred to cloth and used and enjoyed by men and women."

Her face was glowing. The wind that always sprang up in the pines at dusk was blowing her hair into loose curls across her forehead. The sun had burned it a shade lighter, and it was more blond than brown. He smiled, both with amusement at her enthusiasm and with pleasure at the sight of her.

"You make it sound romantic, while it comes from hard toil. On the debit side, my mother still grieves over your freckles. Too—" he looked at her harder and a little anxiously—"it seems to me that you are growing thinner."

She laughed, and the freckles twinkled.

"The freckles cannot be helped, and growing thinner is for me an improvement. Even if it were not, I would count it a fair exchange for the happiness of being close to the earth again and to the good little leaves."

"The good little leaves," he said slowly.

He repeated the words in French, and he wondered why her eyes grew bigger and startled as he dwelt on the last one.

"Most of us overlook the leaves in greed for the flower and fruit. I have always loved them, Johnny, and I am glad that you do. In fact I have often thought that the most beautiful word in all the French language is our word for *leaf*."

June found the indigo plants ten to twelve inches high. The workers had long since gone back to a sunup to sundown task.

Worms and insects of all kinds were attracted to the succulent leaves. Every leaf and twig of every plant had to be examined daily, and the pests picked from it and killed. In addition to this the raking continued all during growth.

The women worked well, and Feuille kept up with them. Her task was no longer strange to her. She had systematized it, as she did all her duties, and avoided loss of time or motion. She had broken each gang of ten into two small gangs of five, and assigned to each of these its portion of the fields. Cora-mantee Cate was the taskmistress of four other Corymantyns, and they were doing as good a job as any other group. Arriving in the daybreak the women girded their skirts, broke at once into units and went to their starting points. Feuille, moving steadily, went from one to the other, inspecting work already done, directing, checking time, examining hopefully each plant for the first hint of a flower bud.

"Losa, the plants on this side of the field are at least an inch higher than all the others."

"Yes, *Maduba*. They gets the morning sun. Climbing sun give strength, falling sun give nothing but hot."

"Will they bloom first?"

"Yes; you can count on that. We always begins cutting from that side the field."

"Good. It will be easier for us if all are not ready at once. Oh! I've found a worm under this leaf! The row has already been worked, so somebody has been careless."

Long hot days in the blazing sun, while the succulent plants grew taller. Rainbow turbans swaying, rakes rising and falling, always in rhythm to the weird unintelligible songs. Showers, or short spells of drought when the fine loosened soil blew in dust clouds over the sweating laborers. Feuille's shoes were gray with it; it sifted down her neck and gritted between her teeth. When she returned to the house she tried to reach her room unobserved, in order to wash her body and brush her hair before anyone saw her. Saint Lys laughed at her one evening as he saw her dodge through her door, and he referred to it that night when they talked across his desk.

"Do you still think that Huguenot planters spend their time wining and dining and making outcasts of humble men like pirates?"

She flushed scarlet.

"I did not know. Is it fair to blame me for ignorance?"

"Not for ignorance, but for doing what so many others do: passing judgment on a thing of which you are ignorant. The average Huguenot planter rides and walks his rice fields and inspects and directs his work as I do. Like me, he lends a hand with the labor when he is needed. When—and if—he gets to the place where he can afford leisure, he has earned it and has a right to it."

"I know," she said. "The work I am doing makes me understand what you do. Your rice crop covers hundreds of acres, while thirty acres of indigo keep me busy from dawn until dark."

"It is thirty acres more than any other woman I know would undertake or could accomplish. I walked in the west plots this afternoon, and I think the plants will bud soon. By extra work and care you have overcome your handicap of being three weeks late with the planting."

"They are budding now in the south plots," she told him proudly. "Unless the weather changes we will cut in early July."

Long and hot and monotonous, the June days wore on. In the south fields the buds were opening, changing from brownish-red to reddish-yellow as they uncurled. Feuille had watched the flowers come the summer before, but she still felt they should be blue to forecast the dye from a common sap. Ahead of her in the savage sun the rakes rose and fell, and the brilliant turbans bobbed in a primitive ballet.

Sunrise, with the dew still cool on the drinking indigo leaves —mockingbirds in the windbreak—dust from the bruised black-purple earth as the tines tore it into loam—brassy heat of noonday and sweat and thirst—gourd of molasses water cool from its place in the shade—descending sun, which as Losa said gave only fiercer heat—first dark fingers of shadow pointed by the oak trees on the west—little breeze from the pineland that always came at sunset—time to knock off, Losa—call your women, Hanny—dusk and rest and food and sleep, and a world gone twilight-colored.

Then the first week of July and the south plots ready for cutting.

Feuille knew it by heart from the books and had watched it done the past year, but she was now responsible for it and its result. The plants were healthy and well-grown, the leaves full and juicy and rich with the fine powder that gave luster and brilliance of hue to the dye. At this critical stage any rough handling could undo the labor of their planting and cultivation, and cause the whole crop to be of second-rate quality and thus bring a lower price. As the cutting knives sliced the stalks to the ground and the carriers bundled and shouldered them, she tried to be in three places at once. . . .

"Hanny, some of your women are slashing at the stalks. They will jar the farina from the leaves. You must show them how to cut. . . ."

"Oh, Cate, you have bound that bundle too tightly! Do not try to carry such a big load at once. Squeezing or bruising will injure the indigo. . . ."

"Losa, go along with your carriers to the shed, and stay there until I come. See that the plants are not crushed on the way, and that they are not laid too deep in the vats."

Saint Lys rode in early that afternoon and went at once to the shed. He recognized Feuille: a small figure darting here and there, sleeves rolled above her elbows and skirts girded like the slaves, displaying stained white cotton stockings halfway up to her knees. As she turned and saw him behind her, she gave a scream and quickly untied her skirts and dropped them to cover her ankles.

"It is so hot, Monsieur; and the pumpers splash water in puddles on the ground."

"I know," he said. "The hands are far more sensible than we are. They go barefoot for this task."

He went from steeper to steeper, inspecting the contents.

The great cypress tubs varied in length from twelve to fifteen feet, but they were all four feet in depth. In six of them now the cut plants were piled more than a foot deep. Six women were pumping water over them, and Feuille was going from vat to vat and leaning over to check measurements with a long stick.

"Where are the indigo measures?" he asked. "Why are you using a notched stick?"

She straightened and faced him, pushing her hair away from her flushed damp face.

"I am not quite five feet tall, Monsieur. I cannot reach with the short ruler. Cate cut this smooth pole for me, and I have notched it accurately."

He tried not to smile.

"You do everything accurately. And you appear to have tamed the Coramantee Cat."

"She is one of my best laborers now, and is taskmistress of a small gang. She offered of her own accord to come back here at midnight with me, so I sent her home several hours ago."

He shook his head.

"Ree and I will have turns with the short shift from midnight until daybreak. I know that it is important and that someone of experience must be here then. But I cannot allow you to come out at night with a Corymantyn slave."

She shook her own head back at him, until the loose curls flew out again. Her full red mouth was as stubborn as his thin lips could be.

"You cannot refuse to let me, Monsieur, unless you go back on your word. You said I should plant and cut and harvest and make this indigo, being in full charge of the crop and receiving for my work ten per cent of whatever you got for the crop."

She paused, with her face tilted up to his and her eyes defiantly blue.

"More than once you have said you would not interfere unless I asked you for help. I need no help, and I intend to do it alone with these same women. I am your overseer, with whom you have made a contract. I am no longer your covenant servant."

Surprise and indignation had made Saint Lys drop the subject without argument. He felt that she had told him in no uncertain terms that she could and would do as she pleased since her bond had been canceled. She had warned him not to interfere.

He forgot that Camille deRosset had pointed out to him that this girl had the same traits of character he had. She is what my friends in Holland called *stiff-headed*, he thought. She is determined to carry this through in her own way, and is jealous of letting even me have a part.

But he could find nothing wrong in the work at the steepers, so he left without comment after looking around.

Immediately after supper his mother told him: "Johnny has gone to bed. Do you think this work is breaking her down, Troyes?"

He realized that the girl was trying to get some sleep before midnight, but was keeping from Madame Saint Lys the fact that she was going out then. Even that fact did not soothe his ruffled feelings.

"No," he said. "I think she is strong—and quite able to take care of herself."

Yet, tired as he was from his own long day at the rice fields, he could not fall asleep as he always did. He kept waking with sudden starts, and listening for a step in the hall. At last he sat up, lighted his bedside candle and looked at his watch. It was a quarter past midnight, so she must have already gone. He got up and began to dress.

Feuille had been sleeping soundly when Cate tapped on her window. She ran barefooted across the floor and whispered: "Wait for me!"

Memories of her other trip into the night were with her as she struggled into her clothes without making a light. Terror

had been her spur then—terror which made her risk everything. In the time since, she had day by day become more
confident of security. She was going out into the darkness now
of her own choice. Darkness had for her its especial horrors:
horror of that night by the cave when she had been taken
away from her father—horror of waiting in a windowless
closet in Toulouse—vertigo of a spinning cask in which were
only blackness and herself—jar and thunder of cannon above
the *Eagle's* dark hold....

She was grateful to find Coramantee Cate with a lightwood
torch at the foot of the steps. She forgot her fears and began
to think of the indigo. Not for anything in her small world
would she have missed the sight of her first crop beginning
to macerate. She had hardly realized that she spoke shortly to
Saint Lys. The night watch seemed to her both her privilege
and her duty. She hurried along by the tall Negress without
a thought of him.

The shed lay close by the wood's edge and about six hundred yards from the house. Four lanterns hung by chains from
its center roofbeam. Cate began lighting the nearer two at the
end where the filled vats stood. Feuille ran to lean over them.
Their fermentation had begun, and the mass was rising steadily. Reaching to dip a finger, she felt the water warm.

"There is no use to light the other lanterns," she told Cate.
"This first steeper has risen almost to the top peg hole. We
must hurry to lay the bars across it."

The bars were solid pieces of wood just less than four feet
in length and heavy enough to hold down the indigo plants.
Starting with the highest vat, the two women placed them
crosswise. Around and over them the disturbed water rose,
now a soiled yellow hue and erupting in sluggish bubbles.

Feuille sat on a log bench and took off her shoes and stockings. Then she went back to work with Cate, for the vats were
fermenting faster and faster. The first two, she knew, had been
filled before noon, and twelve hours was the minimum time
for soaking to result in fermentation. As soon as the water
reached its high mark and began to fall, the vat cocks would

be opened and it would be carried through short pipes to the beating tubs nearby.

The July night was close in the shed and the earth floor cool to her bare feet. They and her arms were now splashed with yellowish froth. She looked around for her long measuring stick, and recalled that she had left it leaning with the other measures at the farther side of the shed. She walked between the double rows of the great cypress tubs, going more slowly as she left the lantern light behind her. She had turned back with the stick in hand when she heard the low snarl. . . .

She stopped in her tracks and looked up—into two eyes of green flame.

It was crouching on the center beam between her and the lanterns, and she saw its long cat body in silhouette. She saw the broad whiskered face, the little tufted ears, the tiger teeth in the snarling mouth, and the green fire of its eyes.

In the first second of horror, before she found voice to scream, she realized that she must have walked underneath it in the darkness. Now it was between her and help and did not intend to let her pass.

The Coramantee felt her wave of terror like a touch. This woman had been fair to her and had given her dignity by allowing her to work up to a position of importance and command. For other whites who enslaved her, and for her own blacks who tormented her, she had only hatred. This was her only friend, and some primitive instinct told her this friend was in trouble before she even cried out. She wheeled from her work at the vat, and her jungle-trained eyes saw both the frozen figure below and the wildcat at which it was staring. With a yell more savage than that of the beast itself she snatched up the live torch she had stuck in the ground and leapt toward the place with the blazing weapon.

At the same moment Feuille's shriek and Saint Lys' shout added to the uproar and confused the enemy.

Saint Lys had just a few moments before arrived and paused outside in the darkness, undecided whether to make his presence known or merely to assure himself all was well and then go back to bed. The Coramantee knew he was there but gave no sign of that knowledge. The behavior of white people was just as peculiar to her as the customs of her tribe were to them. Since she had not been at the shed when he offered to take the night work, and since she herself had no fear of the night and felt herself able to protect Feuille, she did not guess his motive in coming. In fact she suspected him of designs upon her young mistress, and had he made any move in that direction she would have attacked him with the torch as she attacked the wildcat. As it leapt for escape from fire and noise, she bounded upward and struck out with the flaming brand.

Saint Lys, also running at full speed but making a poor second to Cate, collided with and was almost knocked down by Feuille as he reached the shed. In her unreasoning terror she fought him, but he caught her with both arms and lifted her from her feet. She was shaking with fear and still struggling in his grasp, and he heard her breath coming in quick gasps. His own knees gave way as he thought of the savage bay lynx crouched to spring only a few feet from her. He dropped to a sitting position on the edge of the nearest vat and hugged her even tighter against him.

Instead of yielding she pulled away, and he released her. Her voice shook, but she stood upright before him.

"Monsieur—was it—a mountain lion?"

"Of course not. There are no mountains and no lions around here. It was a wildcat, and a very large one. It is a dangerous beast, and it would have sprung upon you if Cate had not done what she did."

"Was it there all along—watching us from the dark?"

"Yes, because it would never have come in the shed when you were in here. It must have come out of the woods and been prowling the place for poultry when it heard you and Cate crossing the yard. If it were near the indigo shed it would have jumped up to hide on the beam, for it could not know you were on your way to that place."

He saw her shiver.

"I walked under it. Why did it not jump on me then?"

"Probably it thought you did not see it. But when you turned to come back you had a weapon in your hand. It can see in the dark, and it saw you pick up that pole and thought you meant to attack it."

Cate was coming back from the farther side of the shed, where she had pursued her quarry.

"You're a brave woman," he told her. "I can see why your missy made you a taskmistress. From now on I shall see that you have every chance."

She looked at him expressionlessly, then turned to Feuille and grinned broadly.

"Don't you be scare no more, *Maduba*. Old Yowler won't come back no more. He git way, but I swinge he tail good before he go."

D ay and night now, the indigo-making went on. Saint Lys gave orders, and Feuille agreed, that Santee Sam the plantation huntsman should be at the shed from dark until dawn. Being an Indian by birth and a hunter by occupation, he refused to do any part of the work and merely patrolled the place or sat chewing tobacco while the women worked.

At sunrise the field gang began to cut the bushes in blossom, and before midday these were bundled and soaking in the steepers. Liquor from the first day's cutting had by now been drained into other vats. The bottomless pails on their long handles rose and fell in the hands of the beaters, whipping this liquor into a froth that heated and rose in foam and would have overrun the tubs. At this critical moment oil was added by the taskmistress. Feuille had taught only Losa, Hanny and Cate how and when and in what proportion to do this. So one of the three was always in charge at the shed and ready to hasten at the beater's warning cry.

After the oil was added and the liquor subsided, it was beaten steadily until granulation commenced. Since this might take place anywhere from fifteen minutes to a half hour, according to consistency, temperature, violence of paddling and other factors, a skilled worker had to watch the vat for the first sign of the granules. As they separated themselves from the muddy liquid Feuille dipped samples with the glass containers kept from year to year for the testing. She knew that upon her judgment depended the decision as to when this process had gone far enough to demand addition of the lime water.

This decision troubled her more than any other. It must not be too soon, yet unnecessary delay was just as dangerous. She tried to make her voice confident as she halted the paddlers.

"Stop beating now, Fan, and stir the lime gently as I put it in."

To her it was each time a new miracle when at this juncture the yellowish hue began to assume a purple tinge, and the slowly moving paddles turned up more thickly the flakes of forming dye.

"Leave it now to settle, and go and help Ludie scrape the vats which have just been drained. Do not spill a handful of the stuff left in them. We need every bit to fertilize the plants and make them put out again."

And while the emptied vats were scraped for fertilizer, the tubs to which lime had been added were drained into other tubs which were again drained. When all waste matter had been left behind the process was reversed. The mud at the bottom of this last vat was the desired indigo dye. The clearing water above it was carefully dipped away.

"Do not let them dip too deep and disturb the settlement, Hanny. Cate, we are ready for the first drying bags."

The bags were broad-mouthed and of strong, coarsely woven cloth. They were filled with the purplish mud remaining in the vat's bottom, and then hung in rows from hooks attached to the beams of the shed.

By mid-July cutting was finished. The long field stretched dark and flat, and ugly with the stubble of cut plants. But these roots were alive and were banked richly with waste from their own production. This feeding and working of the earth would cause them shortly to bear stalks and leaves for a second crop.

At the shed the gang worked in three shifts on the different stages of the process, for the latest vats were ten days behind the earliest steeping.

From midday until nightfall Feuille took her rest and left Losa in charge. Feuille herself took the night shift, with Cate as lieutenant and the Corymantyns as crew. They did not resent taking orders from her and Cate as they did from the Mandingoes, and at this season of heat night work was no disadvantage. Before dawn Hanny brought her workers to relieve them. But Feuille spent the morning between field and shed.

Night and day the fermented plants were processed steadily: paddlers beating harder on sluggish, delayed vats; mixers stirring slowly to cause precipitation with the lime; drainers moving from tub to tub and opening cocks or dipping as the contents settled; fillers putting the last thick residue into bags; dryers taking this drained mud and spreading it with small wooden trowels on boards to dry; molders packing it into frames which shaped it into cakes.

The season's first cakes of indigo dye, the harvest of almost four months' toil!

Feuille remembered that first morning when she had gone out for the sowing. There had been a broken field, a gang of strange women with hoes and rakes, the baglike aprons of dormant indigo seed, and herself to effect the synthesis. By human labor and sweat, through one of nature's seasonal miracles, brick after brick of deep blue dye was coming into being. They were being packed in the square boxes, each made to hold three dozen bricks, from which they would be transferred to the shipping containers. She examined them lovingly: firm and healthy-colored, they had passed the water test; they were not sweating, nor yet were they dry enough for brittle edges to chip.

All morning she moved between shed and field, sunburned and thin but happy. The bushes were already sprouting new stalks, and the greater part of the gang worked and wormed them daily. The last vats had been run off and scraped, and the last bags were hanging to drain. Her fingers loved the feel of the greasy mud as she spread and patted it on the long drying board. Free at last from constant supervision of the whole task, she could take an active part in this last stage of it.

When Saint Lys came in at twilight he found her still there. She straightened up from the molding frames and showed him the boxed bricks.

"We have only enough cakes here in the frames to fill that half-filled one. Are they as many as you expected, Monsieur?"

He had already guessed how many dozens of cakes would be made, for he had seen the vats every night. Now he glanced at the boxes, multiplying by three.

"It is above average, even for July cutting." He hesitated before he asked: "Are you molding the last of the bricks tonight?"

"These are the last. That is why I am working late."

"The reason I ask is that I wish you to see the nearer rice fields in growth. It will take only half a day. I'll send you back by Sam."

She looked up into his face, her own face alight with surprise and pleasure. And next morning she was still aglow with the unexpected joy as he helped her up into the big sidesaddle strapped on the back of the small brown pony.

"Put your left foot in my hands and your left hand on the pony's crest. Now give a little jump as I lift you."

She had gone up lightly and then sprawled, clutching the saddle bow with both hands. He steadied her.

"Get your right knee over the pommel and your left toe in the stirrup. No; do not try to jam your whole foot through it. Now you can smooth your skirts down. Do not hold onto the saddle or mane. Keep your hands for your bridle lines."

The last order seemed unreasonable to Feuille. The pony's long mane and the saddle bow seemed to her to have been provided both by nature and by artifice as holds for a timid rider. But except for a nervous grab now and then she did as instructed.

The next five hours went on wings, swifter than the bobo-links between the green paddies and the blue sky. Saint Lys shaded his eyes with a hand as he glanced up at the sun.

"The time has gone too quickly. Some day we will come again. Sam is instructed to meet us at his cabin before noon, and you'll have to make that lazy pony trot."

Obediently she urged the pony to keep behind his horse. They left the long embankment upon which they had been riding for a tongue of high land with a grove of huge sym-metrical live oaks. Sam had there a cabin built of logs, but steep-roofed like a tepee. He sat on its step with his long gun beside him, and as they rode up he spat tobacco and squinted at the sky.

"You ride plenty slow. I look for you hour ago."

"Missy was interested in the rice," Saint Lys explained.

The Indian approved of that. He had seen her work with the indigo. This squaw, he thought to himself, will make the white man a good wife—if he does not spoil her by pampering, as white men do.

He rose, shouldered his French flintlock, and took a grip on the pony's bridle. He knew the pony would make its way home if turned and given a slap on the rump, and he thought Saint Lys foolish to make him lead it back. But the foolishness of white men could in such a case be used to advantage. For he, Sam, would reach the Big House at dinner time and conse-quently be given a real meal instead of having to cook scantier fare for himself. As he led the pony and chewed, he reflected with pleasure that it would probably be fresh beef or hogmeat instead of the venison and wild duck and birds of which he was weary.

And behind them Troyes Saint Lys sat his horse and watched the small blue figure on the brown pony out of sight, astonished and almost incredulous at the pang of loss in his heart and the sudden tumult of thoughts in his mind.

Part Nine

THE STORM

By the end of August the indigo was ready for the second cutting. There had been the same long hot days of work, the hoeing and worming, the same anxious watching for the first flower buds. But all had been easier because Feuille now knew her women, and both she and they knew procedure.

"No, Losa. Never put Diffy and Mary on the same shift. You know they fight, and you told me yourself that Diffy's name meant *fire*."

Once again the steepers beginning to rise and froth—the long line of women bringing green bundles on their heads—the fields left naked under a ragged stubble—the hectic haste at the shed where the great vats fermented.

To Feuille's disappointment she saw that the harvest of dye would be smaller; but Saint Lys explained that it was always so with a later crop.

"The quality of the first growth is better. The leaves are both juicier and higher in farina. You'll be fortunate if you make a third as much in October as in June."

"Is it because of the heat? The cut plants put out again so well that I hoped for just as large a yield of dye."

"Indigo does not mind the heat if its roots are moist. Our spring rains are as a rule gentle but adequate. Drought is more apt to come in midsummer."

"I have noticed that. In spite of the fact that we hoe it daily, it has been difficult to keep the soil as soft as we kept it for the earlier crop."

"And for the third crop it will probably be too wet. I do not mean to discourage you, but these are the hazards of planting. Even if September does not bring storm, it will probably bring excessive rain."

In the less busy interval of those few weeks after the dye-making, before the third crop's leaves had put out and when only hoeing was needed, he suggested that she ride again to the rice fields with him.

"They are the color of dull gold now, and cutting is about to begin."

Her eyes grew bright and wistful, but she shook her head.

"I wish to be with your mother, Monsieur, every hour I can. I leave Losa and Hanny in charge in midmorning while I go back to the house for a visit with her."

His face was troubled. He knew what she meant.

"I see it too. Shall I send for Dr. Hyrne?"

"On his last visit Dr. Hyrne told me he could do nothing more. She takes the medicine that he left, and we try to tempt her appetite. But she eats less and less and grows weaker and weaker."

"Do you find Wancheesa competent?"

"Entirely competent and very kind. She is so silent that she appears unsympathetic; but she talks to Madame when they are alone. From my room as I dressed last evening I heard her telling the story of two little lost Indians who were taken up in the sky and placed as guardians for the Pole Star."

"I am glad to hear that. Madame Marion appears to trust her. Once when her daughters were young she had to leave the plantation, and she left Wancheesa both to care for them and to chaperone them."

"She is trustworthy," said Feuille. "Your mother is safe with her. It is only that I have grown to care for Madame, and I do not like to be much away from her because—"

She checked herself, but he knew what she meant. He too had the feeling that he wished to be with his mother more because the time for that opportunity was running fast. But his work was in the rice fields all day. The rice was their living— both their living and means to continue a quest which he felt was hopeless but which his mother refused to relinquish.

His rice-cutting was well under way in that early and sultry September. He felt he must hurry it all he could, for he knew that the heat would bring rain. He had shaken his head when old Deloe warned him.

"*Mahaba* best put all hand in field. *Mahaba* best take 'em from indigo. Storm on he way now, and storm travel fast. All last night I dream bout *deloe* running, and I hear *maulin a bumba*."

Both because she was the oldest African on the place and because her name meant water, she was said by her people to be a weather prophetess. He had turned away impatiently, but he could not forget it. Twenty strong women were in the indigo field. If he took them, as Deloe advised, he would harvest his rice at least two days earlier. But they were Johnny Sevens' gang. He had assigned them to her. If he took them the indigo soil would bake hard in the late summer sun, and the worms play havoc with the tender new leaves.

So he went about the rice harvest with his regular crew, starting on the advanced fields and leaving the slower. Every day brought wagonloads up to the threshing floor by the barn, where a dozen women were wielding the leather-hinged flails.

Feuille went there to look at the work. She had seen the rice growing green. Now the heaps of blond grain were piling, ready to be hauled to the plantation landing and shipped to the *Bois Bleu* factor in Charles Town.

Although she refused to spend a half day away from Madame Saint Lys, she would have given much to see the harvesting. She rejoiced at the promise of these first wagonloads just as sincerely as she had rejoiced in the indigo yield.

"Madame, the threshers told me just now that the grains were fatter and sounder this year than any grain they had ever threshed before."

Even less than Saint Lys did she look for danger from the south.

It came after two days of cloudless brilliance and brassy heat, came with the suddenness of the West Indian cyclones. A belt so black that it looked dark blue appeared on the southern horizon, creeping every hour higher into the sky. The women in the indigo field stopped work to lean on their rakes, dashing sweat from their faces and shading their eyes to look. In the utter stillness of the early afternoon no leaf stirred in the windbreak, no bird sang in the trees. Through that heavy, breathless stillness they heard the galloping horse.

Saint Lys did not stop to dismount. He jumped his thoroughbred over the boundary ditch and rode the cross drainage bank in a canter toward Feuille.

"Let me have your gang at once! We'll lose what rice we don't get in before darkness."

They left the indigo field in a trot, dropping hoes and rakes at the barn, and running to catch the wagons which were going out. Feuille climbed into one and saw that it was driven by the little old dried-up cook.

"I ain't no field hand," he reminded her sharply; "but I ain't gonna sit in kitchen and let storm ketch *Bois Bleu* rice crop."

He lashed the mule to a gallop along the causeway. As they neared the first field they met returning wagons piled high with dull gold sheaves. One was driven by Santee Sam. He held the cooter back of the road and forced Tee Val's empty one to take to the slanting side. Tee Val scowled at him as he passed without a look.

"Big trouble must be comin' if Mas Troy kin get that lazy Injun to work."

As they reached the main bank Feuille saw that practically everyone on the plantation had been called out. Children from eight years up were there, carrying sheaves to the wagons. She followed her women, who seemed to know what to do, to the second field where Deloe was in charge.

"*Mahaba* gone to the far field and tek most all the men with him. I taskmistress here. Losa, take your gals cross the next ditch and start cuttin'. *Maduba,* if you kin mek those chillun carry proper, all my gang and Losa's kin cut and bind."

Feuille took the children in hand with good results. They were not only willing but pleased at the excitement. She sent the half dozen biggest, who had done such work before, farther along the face ditch to carry the longer way for Losa's gang. She herself followed Deloe's workers, loading the small bearers as they came empty-handed.

"That's enough for you. If you take more you'll drop it. Don't run. Walk fast or trot. Keep your place in the line and don't shove. When you get to the wagons drop the sheaves and come back. Don't stop a second. The drivers will do the loading."

As far as she could see, the curved knives flashed and swooped: sickles which had changed little since they had harvested Boaz's grain. The women were working faster than she had ever seen them work. But these were only a few acres of the two hundred in rice, and every acre which was not cut and got under shelter would be lost. How was it going with Troyes a mile away in the east fields? Was the boat at the landing? If so, he might load the grain on the straw. Would work not go faster if, when they passed the high land with the live oaks, they used the Indian's house as a barn for bundles from that field? At the rate the women were cutting they would reach it well before twilight.

Meanwhile the false twilight of the cyclone rolled up the sky, and the hot stillness was broken by gusty sighs of wind.

The children were obeying orders, and the tied bundles were going in a steady stream to the wagons. Feuille, still keeping an eye on them, began to help with the binding. By five o'clock they had reached the oak grove and the children were carrying the sheaves to the cabin.

More than an hour passed, while the clouds boiled up like black smoke from a cooking pot. In the south a citron streak opened and widened in the sky, casting a weird yellow light over the rice fields and the moving figures. They cut faster and faster, but they did not sing. The only sound in the close hot silence was the swish of the sickles and the children's voices.

Then a noise like a giant's sigh rose and came from the east fields. Acre by acre the rice bent west, flattening before the wind. A lash of lightning whipped the sky from horizon to zenith. Upon its heels the thunder cracked and roared.

Old Deloe straightened and gestured to her gang with her sickle.

"*Maulin a bumba* talkin' now, and he say storm got here. You gals grab cut rice and run for Injun's cabin!"

Night and day, without respite, the cyclone tore at the rice banks. Upon one side of the long riverward dyke lay the planted fields, flooded by rain water now. Upon the other the storm-swollen tide backed from the Santee into the creek, overflowing and rising high in the marsh. Never before had the floodgates had to endure such pressure. Day and night the lashing rain melted the earth from its log supports, while tides which refused to recede gnawed steadily from below.

Saint Lys and a crew of his best men fought the losing battle. They worked all day and far into the night, repairing the breaks with timber and bags of earth. Feuille could do nothing except try to comfort Madame Saint Lys, and see that Troyes got hot food when he came in drenched and dejected. She appealed to Tee Val.

"How long can the storm last? It has been raining and blowing for five days now."

"First storm gone on," said Tee Val, "but another come right behind him. Deloe say this weather gonna last three days more."

That night she told Troyes, and he nodded.

"Ree and Saraka say the same thing. They have ways of knowing that we have not. But if wind and rain last three days more the bank along the river will go."

She raised eyes full of sympathy to his tired face.

"I wish, above all else in the world, that I could help you, Monsieur."

His eyes lit for a second. Then he shook his head tiredly.

"It is the worst storm since I came to the colony. I selected my rice land carefully and was sure that it was protected. Now I have failed—and I can blame no one except myself."

She reached out and touched his wet sleeve.

"You have worked all day long in the rain, and you can do nothing more until morning. Will you not go now and get into dry clothes? Madame has had a bad day. She must not see you as you are, or know how troubled we are."

That small word "we" went with him as he went to his room to change. He was shaking with cold, for he had worked in wet clothes since early morning and the wind was still blowing a gale. But he knew now that the girl was as troubled as he was. Her sympathy showed in her voice and her eyes and warmed him like a blue flame.

That night his mother no longer had strength to sit against her pillows. She lay flat in the bed, as white as clay, while the wind rattled the board shutters and the rain hammered the shingle roof.

"You were obliged to go out in this weather, my son?" she asked him.

He stood close beside her, washed and brushed, with face and voice under control.

"Yes, my mother. I think it well to watch the banks in time of storm."

Feuille applauded him silently, for she knew how distressed he was. As she watched him smile reassuringly at the sick woman, she thought: I was mistaken to believe him hard and cold. He is disciplined and self-controlled and brave. He keeps his troubles to himself, no matter how unhappy he is.

"The banks are in God's hands," Madame Saint Lys said. Her voice was low and slow, but the words were clear. "Do not let them or anything else disturb your peace of mind, my

son. The greatest Huguenot of all said that God lent him
courage. Remember to borrow it from God. He will lend it if
you are worthy."

Those days and nights merged for Feuille and Troyes into
a strange crepuscular time of anxiety upon her part and of
stress and labor on his. He knew that his mother was dying.
He could not let her know that the very home which sheltered
her was threatened by other disaster. At the day's end, when
he saw that no more work could be done—and when he knew
in his heart that other weak spots would cave before morning—
he would go back to his house with no expectation of comfort,
but rather with a forced smile on his lips and a prayer in his
heart for the courage to comfort Madame Saint Lys. But as he
worked in the rain and wind he recalled the expression in the
eyes of the girl who never failed to meet him at the door. Her
voice would be cheerful as she said: "Your mother is no worse.
But you are shivering, Monsieur! You must have some hot soup
at once, in your room. I ran out of doors between squalls today
and found some mushrooms."

The soup would arrive, borne by Juba, who warned him
that mushrooms were "frog bread"; and Troyes would swallow
it, scarcely tasting its flavor, but savoring with gratitude the
sweet flavor of sympathy.

Her voice will be cheerful, he told himself each night as he
called a halt to the work, but I will see in her eyes that she
understands. I do not know what she has lived through or
what sent her to this colony. Some day I will make her tell me.
I can wait without fear, for I feel sure she has suffered as my
people suffered. I am sure in my heart that she has done nothing unworthy.

And Feuille, although she smiled whenever she went in to
Madame Saint Lys, wondered and worried about him all day
long. She had terrible visions of the yellow river rolling in on
the rice fields—green, rich, happy fields which he had shown
her in their prime. She wondered how much of the crop he had
lost. She knew now that he was not rich, and that the annual
sale of the rice crop must pay the expenses of *Bois Bleu* every

year. Her duties had taught her something about those expenses. She knew what was used in the house, and she had kept account of supplies issued the Quarters for two hundred slaves.

Even more she worried now about Troyes himself. It was hard to associate illness or even weariness with him. He was one of those men who are slenderly built but apparently built of steel. Now she could see the strain in his face and the load on the shoulders he tried to hold erect. Her practical mind reminded her of illness caused by exposure. She knew how high the plantation death rate was from chills and fever and diseases which started with simple colds.

On that fifth and last night she watched the clock while its hour hand went steadily on toward midnight. At last she heard him come, and she picked up her candlestick and crossed to the room which he used as an office. It was unlighted; and as she paused on the threshold she thought it was empty too. Then she saw him and went swiftly to him.

He sat in his chair that faced the door, where he had sat to talk with her about the indigo planting. But his arms were crossed on the writing table before him, and his face was hidden upon them. She could see only the top of his head, dark and wet and disheveled, and the desperate weariness in his bent shoulders.

She heard herself whispering: "Troyes! Oh, Troyes, what is it?"

He raised his head slowly.

"The riverward bank is gone. Salt water is on the rice."

He heard her catch her breath, stifling a cry of dismay.

"I knew how great the danger was. But I hoped to the last. How much of the crop is destroyed?"

"Seventy per cent," he said—and again dropped his head wearily on his arms.

"You worked so hard to save it. Is there nothing more to be done?"

He moved his head tiredly, in a gesture of negation.

She put out a hand and smoothed the wet hair from his forehead. She knew that she must give him even sadder news, for a definite change for the worse was occurring in Madame Saint Lys. She was obliged to tell him, grieved as he already was, and to advise him to send Saraka for Dr. Hyrne. But at the touch of his bent dark head something warmer than pity flooded her heart and her body.

"I wish"—he heard her voice catch and break—"with all my heart I could help you."

He straightened suddenly, and caught the small strong hand in both his hands. "Do you mean that, Johnny? Do you mean it with all your heart?"

His face was close to hers, and she could not mistake the look in his eyes. Shy and unsure of herself, she tried to release her hand. But he only held it tighter and pulled her closer against him as he rose.

"I beg you to mean it, Johnny," he said; "because I love you!"

His mouth was still against hers in that first kiss when Wancheesa spoke harshly from the door. "You come quick," she urged. "Old Missy plenty sick!"

For the next week Feuille and Troyes put aside their own love as they worked together to save his mother. When Dr. Hyrne arrived he remained for two days and nights, for the heart attacks were now frequent and violent. Feuille and Wancheesa took turns at the bedside, and Troyes stayed within call. On the third day the patient rallied, and the old doctor rode away on his big rough-gaited buggy horse. As he mounted and Troyes handed up his medical bag, he shook his gray head resignedly.

"I am too old for equestrianism, and my Bucephalus is too broad in the back and too clumsy of foot. But no wheels can go the roads that I must travel, for trees have fallen across them and the tide is still up in low places. I shall return on Sunday—if you do not call me before."

They did not have to call him, for Madame held her own during the short interval. She lay, as fragile as a Dresden figurine, but making no complaint of the pain that wracked her. Whenever she gathered strength enough, she smiled at her son and Feuille. For the past two years Madame had realized that she was growing to love the girl who nursed her. At this time her inherent formality was brought into focus by what she knew to be final and fatal illness. Beside the fact that she was going and leaving her son to a hard task in a new land, certain rules to which she had been born and bred appeared petty or meaningless. They were laws laid down by family and society. Her family had been torn apart by religious persecution, and the ramparts of society had crashed about her head. Survivors were those who fought their way through because they had courage, and because they loved the Huguenot faith enough to suffer for it. Although accustomed to formality and artificiality, she was intelligent enough to realize that a new civilization was being founded in this new land and that its founders were worthy to father and mother it.

Her son was her sole thought, and she tried to think clearly about him. She had told him that she had no curiosity about the true name and the origin of the girl called Johnny Sevens. But she was now seized with a terrible longing to know the truth. It was motivated by love rather than by curiosity. While she lay too weak for speech, her eyes followed Feuille and her heart said: This is the wife I would choose for my son. He would not be fortunate with the lovely English widow. He needs someone of his own faith, someone young and earnest as he, someone sympathetic. I would like to know her story, although I know she is honest and good—this blue-eyed little one that he brought me as a bond servant. I will rally my strength and question her, and I know she will tell me truly. And I shall then confide in her the grief that Troyes and I share. . . .

But she could not rally enough to talk. The cyclone had brought misfortune greater than loss of the rice crop and destruction of the banks. Looking back now, Feuille could see that trouble had ridden its wings. Not only had Madame's illness been aggravated, there had been also an outbreak of chills and fever in the Quarters. When Dr. Hyrne came back he visited there as well as at the Big House, and he left a supply of drugs. In the medical storeroom in the basement he showed Feuille how to weigh doses on the tiny scale, and he instructed Deloe and Losa, the nurses. Deloe's husband Balonga was one of the sick, but he was a tribal doctor and he refused the white man's medicine.

"I know the root to cure me," he told Dr. Hyrne; "but it has to be digged from the earth under a setting moon."

Feuille listened in horror. "What shall I do?"

"Leave him alone," said Dr. Hyrne. "I don't doubt that his root is just as good as my physic, and he probably knows as much medicine as I do."

That had been two weeks past, and Balonga was now recovering. Feuille had seen him that morning, sitting on his cabin step to get the early sunlight. She had asked him about the root, and he had showed her the jar in which it was crushed and steeped: a dark muddy liquid with a sharp odor. But she found that the patients whom she and Deloe and Losa had dosed were recovering too. So honors seemed even between Balonga and Dr. Hyrne.

But neither root nor herb could save Madame Saint Lys. In spite of precautions she had taken cold in that time of wild wet weather that followed the tropical storm. As soon as Dr. Hyrne saw her this day and heard her labored breathing, he leaned his ear against her chest. When he rose Troyes and Feuille saw the verdict in his eyes.

The patient's lips were moving. "Let me—talk to—my son and—"

Troyes caught her hand and begged: "Do not try! Save your strength, my mother."

Dr. Hyrne's voice was kind and reassuring, but he told the truth. "Talk if you wish, my friend. Nothing can now hurt you any more. Talk if you choose, but stop as soon as you feel weary."

He left the room, and Feuille moved close and took her other hand. The dark blue eyes looked black as they moved from her to Troyes.

"Johnny—is now one of us. I wish—before I go—to hear—all about her—and—and to tell her—"

The voice grew fainter. Feuille whispered: "Madame, I will tell you gladly. But are you not weary now?"

"Very—weary," said Madame Saint Lys.

She closed her eyes and they had to bend over her to hear her words.

"I will sleep—and then—I will—listen. Go now—but—but come back—to me—when I have—awakened—my son and—and my daughter."

Madame did not awaken again, and the story went untold.

There was now too much to do even to think of stories. Ree and Saraka were despatched on horseback to summon a few neighbors, in the tragic haste of a plantation burial. When the two men returned Troyes took them to the garden, to measure and lay out the plot and to set at its corners four cypress posts.

Down the rain-washed terraces and between the wet sweet syringas, the pine coffin was carried by Troyes, Monsieur Marion, and Ree and Saraka. There by the yellow river slept under the new-turned earth a woman who had danced to the minuet *Amaryllis* at the glittering court of the *Grand Monarque*.

But Feuille and Troyes felt that she slept peacefully in a clean new country which had given her sanctuary and allowed her to live and die in the faith she loved. Although they mourned her, they were young and the same thought was comforting them: they knew they had her approval because before she died she had smiled at Feuille and called her "daughter."

For days they found it impossible to be alone together. According to plantation custom, the neighbors who came to help had remained to visit. Dr. Hyrne was old, and when belated he was accustomed to spending the night. Madame Marion had arrived within a few hours of her friend's death and had stayed to act as chaperone and to help in every other way. The deRossets did not reach *Bois Bleu* until after the funeral, but they were now house guests and showed no inclination to leave.

Camille told Troyes: "I am free to remain, even after Pierre must go back. We have to be careful, you and I, of what gossip may do to Johnny. In her position she is even more vulnerable than is the average *jeune fille.*"

"What do you mean," he demanded, "by gossip about Johnny? Why should anyone gossip? There is no girl in the world more modest or careful, and besides this is her home; is it not?"

"It is if you make it so, *mon ami.*"

She fluttered her dark lashes to hide the laughter beneath them as she watched dull red creep into his thin cheeks.

"But let us be practical. You and I know that Johnny is fine and sweet and good, and worthy of all the respect to be shown a *demoiselle* of the *haut monde*. But there are some who consider her still a covenant servant who came to America in a shipload of convicts."

"They can go to the devil," he said succinctly.

"Would you consign Rosalie—the beautiful Rosalie Wentworth—to the devil, *mon ami?*"

He seized upon the question. "Is she talking, Camille?"

"How do I know?" Camille countered lightly. "But she is coming this afternoon, in her coach, for a visit of state."

Meanwhile Feuille had gone all alone down to the terraces. She recalled the one word "Violette," and it haunted her thoughts. She was dressed in her simple house dress of blue, and she carried a trowel and a basket of flower roots. At the long mound of clay she kneeled and began to remove the faded cut flowers and to plant the violets. Both the name and the color seemed significant; they had both played a part in her two years at *Bois Bleu*. She knew the plantation was named

Blue Wood because of the indigo. Why had Madame Saint Lys loved and yet dreaded the word "Violette"?

As she worked she was reviewing her stay at the plantation. She wondered that she had ever thought it wild and alien. For she knew now that it was to be her home. She loved it and she loved Troyes, and she knew that Troyes loved her.

She heard wheels and horses' feet and the bustle of Madame Wentworth's arrival. Camille is acting as hostess, she told herself. So I am not needed, and I would rather be here. It hurts me to see his mother's grave bare. I recall that she once told me she enjoyed her food more because I arranged flowers on the tray. Soon the ivy will make a green mat and the violets will bloom. . . .

At the house Troyes was assisting the visitor up the steps. She was radiantly lovely, and she allowed her generous charms to lean heavily on him. She did not realize that instead of being stirred by that proximity, he was contrasting her weight with Feuille's lightness. Johnny is light and graceful and agile, he thought. Although she doesn't know how to ride, she mounted the pony easily. I hardly knew when she put her foot in my hand to go up. It will be fun to teach her equestrianism . . . to have her ride with me along the rice field banks . . . to plan with me cheerfully and bravely for a recovery after this disaster. . . .

Rosalie Wentworth settled herself in the most comfortable chair and tapped him sharply with the fan she carried summer and winter. She had heard of his financial loss, in addition to the loss of his mother. She was complacently certain he would wish to marry her now. Not only would he be lonely for a woman in the house, but a rice planter who had lost seventy per cent of his crop was in desperate plight and could not afford to scorn a rich alliance. From Wentworth Ways, where they would live and entertain in the lavish scale of her present life, he could ride occasionally to *Bois Bleu* and keep up the pretense of being a planter. But she would see that he no longer acted as his own overseer. The English planters considered it best to employ a white overseer; a man who knew how to exact every inch of labor of which a slave was capable, and a man not too squeamish to use the lash to exact it. The French, she reflected, had always been too sympathetic with their Territorials and too indulgent and friendly with their slaves.

She tapped him again when he did not respond, and her charming English voice was sweet with sympathy in spite of her reflections.

"You are preoccupied, Troyes, and I do not wonder. But"— she included Camille in her glance—"you must permit your friends to comfort you."

"You are kind," he said—then moved out of reach of the fan and stood by the mantel. "Camille," he asked, "do you know where Johnny is?"

Camille nodded, her eyes sparkling with anticipation of whatever was to come. "Johnny has gone to the burial plot to plant ivy and violets."

"Presumption!" cried Madame Wentworth. "How can you allow it, Troyes?"

He took a step toward her. "What do you mean, Rosalie?"

"I mean it is unsuitable for a person like her—a girl who is a bond servant and comes from the criminal class—to intrude in affairs which are sacred to you."

Camille saw a muscle in his cheek begin to jump.

"Johnny is a French Protestant—a Huguenot refugee who fled as my family did—from persecution in France."

"How do you know? Why, then, does she use an alias?"

"My mother discovered as soon as she came to *Bois Bleu* that she knew the French Protestant service by heart. Do you not recall how she sang our hymns in the French Santee church?"

"I only recall that she sang so loud she caused everyone to stare at her."

Rosalie Wentworth caught herself there. She was far too clever to act the virago, no matter how angry. But Troyes Saint Lys hardly noticed. He was going on.

"I know she is sweet and good and true and lovable; so as to the name she calls herself, I neither know nor care."

The fan dropped from Rosalie's hand, and he did not stoop to pick it up. Even in great agitation, her voice was exquisite.

"I do not understand you. What do you mean, Troyes?"

"I mean that I love Johnny and am going to marry her. I asked Camille where she was in order to find her and bring her here and present to you, my friend, my future wife."

He recollected himself enough to stoop and recover the fan and bow as he handed it to her.

"Camille will entertain you," he said, "while I go and get her."

Camille watched him, her black eyes dancing with delight, as he turned and went out of the door.

Rosalie lay back in her chair and felt in her reticule for her vinaigrette.

Feuille, on her knees as she worked, saw him running eagerly down the terraces toward her, and she rose and brushed the earth from her skirt and held out both arms toward him.

Part Ten

SOMETHING THAT GOD LENDS

In the storm-beaten garden Troyes had taken her close in his arms.

"Johnny, why should we wait? My mother approved, for she called you daughter. Why should we not drive tomorrow to the French Santee church, and be married there?"

Head against his shoulder, she pressed close but did not reply. Dropping his chin, he could see dark lashes raised as she looked up into his face.

"There is no reason to wait, and I do not wish to wait. I get no chance to see you alone, and I am hungry for you."

Her arms tightened around his neck, but she turned her head away to look at the newly planted ivy and violets.

"It is just—just that haste might seem disrespectful to *her*."

"If I thought *she* would think it so, I would not urge you, darling. But I know she would wish whatever was best for you and me. Until we are married we are going to be kept apart by the good intentions of our friends. In order to chaperone you, Madame Marion and Camille deRosset have already informed me that one or the other will be glad to remain at *Bois Bleu*. I know, of course, that it is necessary. But the easiest way—and the way I want—would be an immediate wedding."

It was what she wanted too. The happiness of it made her blood run faster, as she stood held close against him and heard his heart beat under her cheek. To be loved and guarded again, as she had been with her father and with her Uncle

Tonpain! To have that blessed safety—and to have with it the love of Troyes whom she adored. . . .

She released herself and looked gravely at him.

"It is what I wish too, *mon cher*. But there is so much to do. I must open the storeroom and sun the linen before it molds. And the indigo is beginning to sprout again—"

He interrupted by catching her back to him.

"There will be time enough for all that when I bring my wife back from Jamestown. Losa already has her gang in the indigo field. Say you will marry me, Johnny? Let us be married tomorrow!"

She gave him his answer without needing words. Love was warming them both like wine, and its kisses were sweeter than grapes. I hold in my arms, he was thinking, all that I ask of life. Hard work lies ahead for me, but I can do it with her at my side. And she was reviewing all that she had suffered and contrasting it with this perfect joy. If anything should destroy it, she thought, I could not bear it this time. Trouble hardened me so that I could live through Silk Throsters Lane and the terrible voyage of the *Eagle*. But happiness has softened me now and unarmed me. I could not lose Troyes and live. . . .

She clutched him almost desperately and pressed herself closer against him. The sound of Camille's light laughter at last broke them apart. Troyes again caught her around the waist as he made a formal bow.

"Madame deRosset, I present the lady who is to be my wife."

She felt his arm tighten as he added: "Tomorrow."

Camille hugged her in real delight.

"I shall be your dame of honor. But what will you wear, Johnny? If Troyes insists upon such haste, you must come with me at once and arrange a suitable costume."

"Do not take her away from me," he cried impatiently. "It does not matter what she wears. I'd like to marry her in the blue dress and bonnet that she wore to oversee the harvest of the indigo."

"But you cannot, you impossible man," Camille told him

severely. "She must be married in silk, with satin slippers and bonnet to match. Would you take the future Madame Saint Lys to church as your Indian hunter would take his squaw?"

"He wouldn't take his squaw to church. He'd just take her home with him—which is where I want to take Johnny."

Camille's voice went high in a shriek of mingled amusement and outrage.

"You are as uncivilized as your wild Indian! But I shall protect Johnny from you. I shall find her a suitable wedding gown. You will not be showing her the proper respect unless you allow me to dress her suitably."

He released Feuille reluctantly.

"Then let your suitable dress be blue. Will you wear blue, my *bonne amie?*"

"Whatever you wish, Troyes. Blue is the color that I love the best."

"It is her color," Camille agreed; "and I shall dress her becomingly."

"It must be blue. And I want her to wear the turquoise bracelets and brooch and ring—"

His voice faltered as he glanced again toward the new mound which Feuille had just planted with young green.

"They were among the few things that we dared try to bring from France. My mother's mother had worn them at court. They were to be Violette's."

Feuille could not yet understand, but the sadness in his voice made her turn to him and lift her hands to frame his face. And as his mouth went down upon hers and he kissed her boldly before Camille, her heart quickened with a sudden and double joy. For she recalled in that second that she had a gift for him, a gift as lovely as any he could give her. She had come to him with empty hands, and he had loved her in spite of that. But she had for him a betrothal gift as exquisite and appropriate as any piece of jewelry that he could give to her. She would give him the only thing that she owned in all the world: the turquoise-studded snuffbox that played *Amaryllis.*

Alone in her bedroom that night, Feuille took out the musical snuffbox and examined it carefully for any speck of dust or tarnish. She rubbed it with a small piece of chamois skin until its gold glittered and its stones shone softly blue. It had been strongly as well as exquisitely fashioned, and at her touch the lid sprang up and the gay notes tinkled out. It was safe, she knew, to let it play; for the only room adjoining hers was now closed and empty.

She was taking pleasure in anticipation of Troyes' surprise and pleasure in her gift. She knew that he carried no snuffbox and had often wondered why; for Pierre deRosset and Mr. Allein carried and used them frequently. She smiled to herself at the happy thought that the one she was giving Troyes was far more beautiful than those of his friends. Besides that, the air it played was an air his mother had loved and an air to which he had danced. Together, she planned, they would listen to it, and it would be a link between them all their lives.

At this time she was thinking more of Fleurette. She had tried to avoid the thought before. It had seemed desecration even to think of Fleurette in the presence of Alf or Husk or Spy. During those first months at *Bois Bleu* while her heart was hurt and resentful, she had hidden the thought of Fleurette as she had hidden the snuffbox. But she had now a feeling that Fleurette would have wished her to give this dear gift to Troyes. She saw again, as she thought of Fleurette, the lovely fragile child with the lost expression which turned her blue eyes black. Except for the trinket, Fleurette had had nothing— not even identity. Yet it did not make her resentful and hard as it made me, thought Feuille. It did not make her tough, as it made Désirée. Her body was not strong enough to stand hardship, but her spirit was. I have a feeling that she not only wants me to give this gift to Troyes, but that she approves our love and even loves him too.

But in spite of Troyes' urgency they did not go to Jamestown that next day or the next. For they learned that the pastor was absent on a visit to the French Quarter upon Cooper River. They were obliged to wait two days longer at *Bois Bleu* while he baptized and married and buried French Huguenots.

Feuille did not fret about the delay as her bridegroom did. She went about the house, a sedate little figure with cheeks and eyes bright above her home-dyed blue homespun dress. And she tried to persuade Troyes that postponement was for the best, when he caught her and hugged her in a corner of the hall.

"So much has to be done, dear, indoors and at the indigo field. I can use every hour of these two days while we wait."

"On the contrary," he grumbled, "I cannot do anything. I feel as if a hurricane was blowing inside my head and heart. I shall not be able to work, or even to act normally, until I am sure that we are safely married."

She took his face between her hands.

"Safely is such a beautiful word. For the first time in years I feel safe—with your arms around me, Troyes."

He gave her a little impatient shake, then caught her up in his arms and carried her through the door of his office and closed it behind them.

"Safely is not a word which comes to my mind at this time. I can think of other words which better suit my feelings. Sometimes, Johnny, you act and speak more like my sister than like my sweetheart."

She lay still in his arms, submitting to but not returning his embrace. The blue eyes looking up at him were troubled because he was vexed.

"I love you just as much as you love me, Troyes. It is only that there is so much to do. I feel as if I belonged to you, but belonged to *Bois Bleu* as well. This morning Jane and Juba and I opened the linen closet and—"

This time he really shook her, then hugged her closer than ever.

"Don't talk about house cleaning when I want to make love to you! You can't love me the way I love you while you are so matter-of-fact. I've lost my head, my darling—for the first time in my life. I want more than affection. Love me the way I love you!"

She gave him the abandon he craved, and when his arms at last slackened she lay in them quiet and contented.

"Now will you let me tell you, Troyes, my real name—and why I ran away?"

"You need not tell me anything, unless you wish to, darling."

"I wish to, because you will like my name. In fact you have already said that it was beautiful."

There was real surprise in his voice. "How can I have told you that when I do not even know it?"

"In spite of that you told me," she teased him. "We were down at the indigo field, talking of flowers and fruit and leaves. But I shall keep my name for the last."

He saw her eyes widen suddenly and recognized the fear in them, and he pulled her so close that her voice was muffled against his chest.

"No! Let me tell you *now!*" she cried as he tried to stop her. "Let me tell you while your arms around me make me brave enough!"

He held her tight while she told him the story of Alf Riggs and the sordid house by the London docks. His face was grave, but his voice reassured her.

"I cannot believe that you killed the man, or even injured him badly. In the first place, you are very small and you tell me he was large. Although you are strong, you could not have reached high enough to bring a bottle down on his head with any great force."

"When I heard Camille deRosset tell you there were rumors about a girl whom the police were tracking, I was so afraid, Troyes. That is why I ran away."

"I know, my darling," he said, and his arms closed around her again. "And it was when I thought you had gone that I first knew I loved you and wanted to take care of you—no matter what you had done."

"Can you take care of me if they ever find me? Or will you only be taking my danger upon yourself?"

"I can take care of you, and I will. I think you have heard the last of Riggs. But if the matter ever comes to an inquiry, I can now tell Allein that I know all about it and that you fought in self-defense against a brute who should be hanged."

She clung to him, warm with happiness for his protection and love. Never again, she was thinking, shall I be alone. Never again shall I have to defend myself; for peace and protection, as well as love, are now mine. All to be done now is to tell Troyes that my name is not the ugly Johnny Sevens but the word he thinks most beautiful in our language.

Before she could speak someone tapped sharply upon the door. It opened, and Camille's dark curls appeared in the aperture.

"Pierre has arrived and brought word," she cried—then stopped short as she caught sight of them.

Feuille was trying to get out of Troyes' lap, but he only held her tighter. DeRosset was laughing, but his wife's face was horrified.

"Troyes, you should know better than to do a thing like this! To take your fiancée upon your knees—in a closed room—without chaperonage!"

"We may forget chaperonage in the message I bring," said Pierre. "The pastor rode part of the way north with me today. He has received your letter and messages, and he will be waiting for you tomorrow in Jamestown."

Camille insisted that there be a celebration that night. She dressed Feuille in the blue taffeta gown that Madame Saint Lys had given her, and she left enough hair free of the blond-brown braid to shape in a bunch of curls. Dinner was a banquet, with Feuille seated opposite Troyes and with their two friends sympathetic and interested. But it was not strange that the talk turned back to France. Pierre deRosset's family and the family of his wife had, it was revealed, made their escape together.

"We were able to buy a fishing boat and sail directly from la Rochelle. Our home was farther north, but in those terrible days one fled by any route left open to one."

Camille, who was speaking, turned to Feuille.

"Did you come from Bordeaux, *petite?* I recall another night at this same table when you gave yourself away by speaking of Bordeaux wines."

Feuille nodded, feeling her cheeks grow hot. Kind as Camille and Pierre were to her, she was not willing to tell them the tale of Silk Throsters Lane that she had told Troyes.

"You must have been very young, almost too young to remember. Pierre's little sister who was on that voyage with us says that she can recall nothing of it. But when we speak of it there is fear in her eyes, as if she remembered subconsciously and yet tried to forget."

Feuille nodded sadly, thinking of Fleurette.

"I know a case of a young girl who could not even recall her real name. She tried so hard, and it distressed her to speak of it; but she could do no more than to accept the little pet name by which she had last been called in England."

Troyes Saint Lys said to himself, I have never seen her eyes so sad. She must have loved this young girl. Or can she be speaking of herself? He rose to his feet and raised his glass.

"To my bride-to-be! I promise to banish all sadness and to make her happy."

It made her happy at once, and made her blue eyes and red mouth smile. After the toast he and she sat silent and looked at each other. They needed no words, and Camille was nothing loath to do all the talking.

"Because we had a boat we could take our smaller possessions. Troyes and his mother were not so fortunate. Have you anything brought from France, Johnny?"

Feuille laughed happily down the table at Troyes.

"One thing only—and it is to be my wedding present to *him.*"

His eyes met hers, with all the pleased surprise she had hoped for. Camille exclaimed in delighted interest.

"Will you tell us about it? No! Let it remain a secret—a secret until after dinner. For he plans to give you his gift tonight, so that you may wear it when you are married tomorrow."

Feuille had already been informed that his gifts were family heirlooms. She did not wish to let him think that Fleurette's snuffbox had been a possession of the Joanys. In honesty she tried to explain.

"My gift has not—not the same history. In fact I cannot be sure of its history at all. It was given its owner by someone whose real name she had forgotten because of loss of memory."

Camille, just as kind as she was rattle-brained, saw the trouble on her face and interrupted.

"Troyes will adore it, whether or not you recall its history."

Feuille was glad not to be urged to continue. The memory of Fleurette was still a sacred thing. When Troyes was her husband she would tell him all about it. If she tried now to do so, she might break down and weep before the gay and sophisticated deRossets. For the rest of the meal time she merely listened to them, and Troyes with his eyes on her talked no more than she did.

When they rose and went into the long plantation drawing room, he crossed to a table and lifted a small jewel casket. While Pierre and Camille stood and watched, he carried it to Feuille, placed it in her hands and opened its lid.

There were other trinkets of which he had not told her. But while she held it he singled out the turquoise set in heavy gold. He caught the pin of the brooch in the blue silk of her bodice, fastened the bracelets around her wrists and clasped the necklace about her throat. Then he made her a low bow. Camille clapped her hands.

"Exquisitely done, my dear Troyes! All you have done is *comme il faut*. Now you may kiss her—upon the cheek."

"I fully intend to do so," he said, "—but not upon the cheek." And when he had kissed her hard on the mouth he whispered: "Madame Saint Lys—and my own dear love—happiness is ahead for us both."

She was lovely as she drew herself gently out of his arms. It was her moment. Now she could give her gift to him. His eyes clung to her as she left the room. Pierre deRosset saw it and said: "I'm happy for you, my friend."

They heard Feuille's quick step in the hall, and she re-entered the room with something held tight between her hands. She went straight to Troyes Saint Lys, looking up into his face and placing both her hands between his. As she withdrew them he looked down and saw what he held.

She watched his face go gray as ash while he stared at it for seconds. The muscles of his mouth and jaw strained and tightened. Across the room Camille and Pierre looked on in consternation. Then Troyes spoke loudly and harshly.

"Where did you get it? *Tell me.*"

She was so afraid that her throat ached. He could barely hear her words.

"I told you—that I was not sure. All I know is it came from Boum-Boum—"

At the word he jerked his hands apart as if they were holding a snake. The snuffbox fell upon the floor, the lid sprang and it began to play.

"God in heaven," he asked, "what have I done to deserve this?"

"Troyes," she cried, and clutched him with both hands. "Why do you look so, Troyes? Is it something I have done?"

He pushed her from him so roughly that she fell against the table.

"Do not touch me," he told her. "Never touch me again!"

After that she had run out on the piazza, with Camille catching and trying to hold her back. But she had clung to the banister, calling his name repeatedly into the darkness where he had gone. She had stood there until she heard the hoofbeats of a galloping horse and realized that he had ridden away. Pierre deRosset had come back up the steps and had spoken gravely to his wife.

"Take her to her room. I could do nothing with Troyes."

"But what is it?" Camille had cried. "Could you not even make him explain? Is it that he has gone mad?"

"He has not gone mad," said Pierre, "and I could not make him explain. Whatever it is, it is something in which we cannot interfere. Take her to her room and give her something to make her sleep."

Feuille's next memory was of Wancheesa beside her bed: Wancheesa, a tall dark ghost with a cup in her hand. Wancheesa had leaned and lifted her head, and she, Feuille, had drunk. Then she had fallen back, bewildered and frightened and agonized, searching her mind for a reason for what had occurred.

It was the snuffbox, she told herself; for his face changed as soon as he saw it. Can he think it too valuable for a bond servant to own? Can he think that I lied when I told him about it? Can he even think that I *stole* it?

Wancheesa's sleeping potion took over at that point. But when Feuille woke in the next dawn, realization swept over her in a wave colder and more bitter than the draft.

If I could only have explained, she kept reminding herself. If he thinks me a thief he cannot believe anything I said, and he cannot possibly love me. Perhaps he thinks that I stole the snuffbox from Alf and made up the story that Alf attacked me. If Troyes thinks that, he thinks me no better than Husk or Spy. He must have all this time been mistrustful of me in his heart and ready to believe me a criminal. In that case there is no use ever to try to explain. He does not really love me, and sooner or later he would let something turn him against me again.

But in spite of that flare of pride, she beat the bed with small clenched fists and sobbed. If only she could have talked with him and discovered what changed him so suddenly and made him look at her with loathing instead of love! She had asked him, and had clung to him until he threw her off. She recalled that physical repulse, and the look of repugnance in his eyes. His bracelets were still upon her wrists, and she could not help believing that he had loved her when he clasped them there. But there was abhorrence on his face when he cried out *"Do not touch me!"*

Wancheesa came, soundless and wordless, to bathe her face with cold water. Later the door opened, and Camille entered with a cup of breakfast chocolate. Feuille only shook her head, with tears running down her face and her eyes imploring.

Camille answered their question. "Pierre has not yet found him. But we will find him. Do not fear!"

What use to find him? Feuille thought, as she lay with closed eyes on her bed. He does not love me, he hates me; and he will not return until I go away. I am only seventeen, and for the third time in my life I am being driven out from a place I hoped was my home. But this time is the bitterest, because it is his home and he had offered it to me along with himself. I must go at once, no matter where I go. All other places will be the same: strange and lonely and sad after this.

The house servants were unhappy for her, and they tried all day long to show their sympathy. She opened her eyes to find Jane leaning over her and regarding her with a frightened, mournful gaze. At noon Juba brought a tray, and she showed distress when Feuille refused it.

"Please, *Maduba,* to eat this here vittle. Tee Val tell me if I come back in his kitchen without makin' you eat, he goin' to pin the dishrag on me."

But even that strange and ultimate threat, which the Negro cooks reserved for the worst offenders, failed to make Feuille taste the food. At this meal she and Troyes should have been eating together—on their way to Jamestown—perhaps already married. Why had he made her love him and promised her safety and happiness, only to change his mind and repudiate her? She had had no thought of love for him until he made the first approach. It was he who had shown passion and begged her for a return. Why, in spite of that pretense, had he promised her everything and then cast her aside? Was it possible that God would lend her courage enough for this?

"Take the food away," she wailed, to Juba's grief and terror. "Tell Tee Val that I thank him, but that it would choke me to death!"

She unfastened the bracelets which she had worn all night, and as she did so tears burned her eyes again. All left to show for them were dull deep marks on her wrists. She told herself, all I shall ever have in my life to remember Troyes will be a dull deep scar in my heart.

Wancheesa took them and laid them upon the chest of drawers. "Let me dress you now," she said. "Ree waiting outside to talk to you."

Feuille's heart jumped at the name. Ree had not yet come to her as the other Negroes had done, so she had reason to suspect that he had been with Troyes. His face was grave and compassionate as he came through the door, but he did not look frightened as the maids had looked.

"Little Missy," he said gently. "I got a letter for you from Mas Troy."

She tore it open. Her eyes swept its few scrawled lines and then darkened with a great disappointment.

> *Stay at Bois Bleu. I shall give you the house and enough income to keep it. Tell Ree of anything you need; but do not try to see me—or even write to me.*

With desperation in her eyes, she raised them to the kind strong face of the Mandingo.

"Why does he treat me this way, Ree? Do you know what is the cause?"

"I do not know, little Missy. I tried to find out what was wrong. I have been his man for ten years, and he has never before raised his hand against me. But, when I asked him yesterday, he raised it and threatened to strike me. He said: 'God has set upon me a load more heavy than I can bear. Do not dare to speak of it! Only do as I tell you.'"

"I cannot understand," she said. "Ree, I did nothing wrong."

"That is what I told him, little Missy. I said, 'Mas Troy, she is good as a young leaf with dew on it.' I said, 'She has done nothing wrong. If there is fault, it must be yours.'"

"What did he say then? Did he blame me?"

Ree frowned as he tried to find words to describe a situation which he could not understand any more than she could.

"He did not say that he blamed you; but he said, 'What I cannot understand is why I did not realize when my mother told me on her deathbed!'"

So, she thought, it is something that happened before and not during that last interview. It made her even surer that he thought she had stolen the snuffbox. He thought that the ill mother whom he idolized had been tended by a thief and a criminal; possibly by a murderer if Alf Riggs was dead. It must be either that, she thought, or that he had been driven mad by his mother's death and the grief which he referred to. But she knew him too well to accept that alternative. He had known that his mother was dying and that she was willing to go. He was a Huguenot and believed deeply and certainly in his God. No, she thought, there is some misunderstanding—some mistake awful enough to account for his behavior. He has told me to stay in the house. Although I know he abhors me and only offers me that to make restitution for what he has done to me, I will remain a few weeks. I will finish the indigo harvest, as I undertook to do. That will give me enough time to decide where I will go—and enough time to make sure that Troyes has left me forever.

She had wondered repeatedly where he was. Now she asked Ree the question.

"He staying in the new cabin Injun Sam got half-built. He tell me to bring his clothes."

She lifted her wedding gifts from the chest.

"Take these to him with the clothes. Tell him I will stay at *Bois Bleu* long enough to make my plans and to harvest the indigo. Tell him I will then go on and earn my living elsewhere. Tell him he need not be afraid that I will ever write to him or come to him."

The Mandingo took the turquoise jewelry in a hand made hard by work. But neither work nor slavery had been able to harden his heart. He was closer to nature and his God than were the people he served.

"I will give it to him and tell him what you say. But I tell you to stay at *Bois Bleu*, little Missy. I do not know what has happened, but I know he loves you still."

She turned disconsolately to busy herself in the room, tidying its disorder and looking for the old blue cotton which she wore to the indigo field. I will work along with the women, she planned. Perhaps if I rake and hoe all day long, I may earn the mercy of forgetfulness in sleep.

Ree had gone to the kitchen, where Tee Val awaited him in a fury of impatience and curiosity. Not being Troyes' body servant, the old cook gave his loyalty to the family at large, and he had espoused Feuille's cause with violence.

"Why you can't talk sense in Mas Troy head?" he demanded. "You his man. You gotta right. He gotta lissen to you—lessen he gone clean crazy."

Ree only shook his head. To him Troyes held rank even above Feuille. Tee Val saw the trinkets and he understood. To return a gift to a faithless lover was the kind of fool thing white folks would do. In wrath he raised his cleaver, and brought it down with all his force on the leg of beef on his block. Drops of blood spattered his white coat and rained on the brick floor and the whitewashed walls. Jane and Juba, who were eating breakfast by the huge chimney, screamed aloud. He whirled and rushed at them, brandishing the bloody knife, and they dashed from the kitchen into the yard.

"Git way from me, you lazy nyung gal!" he shouted. "Don't you come back in here till I say you kin!"

But as he turned and viewed his bespattered kitchen, he yelled an afterthought.

"And when I say you kin come back I mean for you to scrub this place!"

Having somewhat relieved his feelings by attacking the innocent house maids, he continued his complaint to Ree.

"Most all wite folks crazy. Balonga say so. Balonga say some cunjur man musta putta spell on Mas Troy, an he doin' all he kin to take it off. If you was any count, you big Mandingo, you'd make Mas Troy come back an take care Missy. Balonga tell me strange wite man been hidin' in the abenue last night, an he turn an run like he been fixin' to steal something."

He stopped to scratch his head and think up other threats or persuasions.

"Sides that, a squinch owl come up close to this house an chuckle to heself all last night. I hear him, an I know trouble on the way when a squinch owl act like that."

Ree believed in neither conjures nor screech owls. He was thinking about the reported prowler. His mind went to the tinker. He knew all about that, but he had never let fall a word upon the subject.

"I'll tell Saraka to watch out," he reassured Tee Val.

And he reassured himself, Here's something to tell Mas Troy which will scare him enough to bring him home—if he still loves her.

As he left the basement, the last thing he heard was the angry roaring of Tee Val: "You, Juba! You, Jane! You good-for-nothin' nyung gal! You bes' come clean up this kitchen, or I takes this same knife an cuts your th'oat from year to year!"

In the rice field Troyes left his hands clearing a clogged drainage ditch and moved aside to listen to Ree. As he did so he too thought of the tinker. According to Ree, the glimpse

Balonga had caught of the trespasser had revealed a murderous countenance and the flash of a long knife.

Gypsies are revengeful, Troyes was thinking, and I gave this one cause to want revenge. This is just the time of year for a tinker to come. He is probably camped in the pinewood outside the gate. His wife and his ox will wait for him there, while he sneaks in through the dark avenue and sets fire to the house.

His brain told him that the sensible thing to do was to take his six best men from the work at that moment, and deploy them to find and scare the marauder away. But Troyes Saint Lys was not just then thinking along sensible lines. He was recalling with a cruel pleasure the lashing he had given the tinker. To use such physical force against another man might, he thought, ease the torture of this crossfire lashing of my desires and my conscience. To hear the sound of a whip upon flesh and a scream torn from resultant agony might in some dark way soothe my own agony of mind and body.

He recalled he had promised the tinker forty lashes if he ever came back, and he felt a definite urge to keep the promise. The man was branded a thief by his cropped ear; he had done two dastardly deeds when he took the girl away and at the same time betrayed her; since he had returned to commit arson, no punishment was too severe for him.

Ree thought: At least it has waked him up. Until now he looked like a dead man who comes from his grave and walks. He listened with silent approval to his master's orders.

"There is no danger until tonight. Until it is dark he will not dare even try to approach. I do not wish to scare him off, but to find out what he intends and catch him in the act. So we need not move until we knock off work."

He paused to shape his scheme, and Ree saw him smile very faintly.

"When the hands start home, you must go along with them to the Quarters. Tell Balonga to creep into the avenue from that side and find and follow the man, and cut him off from the gate. Only Balonga can do that, for he hunts more silently than any Indian. Tell Saraka to climb into the oak east of the piazza, and you hide in the box bushes upon the other side. When he comes only watch him until he begins his mischief. You are there to guard the house and the people in it. But do not make a move unless I call, or unless he strikes."

"I understand, Master. But where will you be?"

"I shall approach the house from the back, after night has fallen, and I shall hide myself somewhere inside."

The field hands were coming in from the rice when Feuille stopped work at sunset. Her women hurried eagerly to their cabins in the Street, but she had no eagerness to reach the Big House. For she pictured Madame Saint Lys' room empty and darkened and the door of Troyes' office closed blindly upon the hall. The deRossets were kind but were as bewildered as she was. Camille kept hinting that she, Feuille, must have done something to change Troyes, and Pierre merely gazed at her with hopeless sympathy. She would far rather have been left alone with the servants, but she knew these two friends would stand by—would stand by until the last hope was gone and she closed the house and started northward alone.

Early in the evening she asked them to excuse her, saying that she was tired from work. Fully dressed she waited in her room until she heard them retire to theirs on the floor above, and then she went to sit in darkness on the front piazza steps. From the oak tree on her left Saraka could see her. Ree was watching from the hedge on the other side. Both knew that Balonga must be by now at the far end of the avenue and the prowler must be surrounded. All three were enjoying the game. They recalled other occasions when tramps had come to *Bois Bleu* and had been attended to much more simply. Troyes had at those times merely taken Saraka with him and had caught them and tied them and sent them on a mule to Monsieur Noë Serrée, High Sheriff of Craven County. But this capture had grown to be a game of such proportions that four of them were taking part in it.

Hearing a sound behind him, Ree turned and saw Tee Val come out of the basement, look around him, and then start for the Quarters. He recalled that the cook knew nothing of what was going on. Although he had no right to leave without permission, perhaps it was best to have him out of the way.

In the avenue the strange man was advancing from tree to tree, with Balonga moving like a shadow behind him. When he reached the last oak his eyes were accustomed to the darkness, and across the lawn he could see the house with the small figure on its steps. He paused before he ventured into the open space. He had been frightened away the night before by a black man who was squatting and digging something from the ground; but he still imagined himself unseen because the man had not turned his head or made any sign. He had no idea that Balonga's jungle-taught eyes had learned every detail of his appearance, and that when he retreated Balonga had followed him back to his hide-out in the pineland.

Now, although nervous, he told himself that he had come too far to forgo either the pleasure of revenge or the gain he had come for. He was sure it was the girl on the steps. She was alone and she was to blame for his injury. As he left the last tree he crouched low and began to cross the lawn swiftly.

Feuille had turned her head because she heard a faint noise in the house. It sounds almost like a step in Troyes' bedroom, she told herself. That was the front room across the hall from his mother's room, and like hers its windows opened on the front piazza. But those windows were now dark, and their shutters were bolted. It might be Wancheesa going to bed. She always moved quietly. It must be that, Feuille told herself; because Troyes' room is as empty as my heart is.

She sighed and turned her head again—and sprang to her feet as she saw the man coming up the steps.

From his bedroom window which opened on the piazza, Troyes could both see and hear. Things had happened faster than he had expected, and for a second he was unsure what to do. He had not expected the tinker to act as this man was acting, and this man loomed immense alongside the girl. As she moved to escape, he reached out and seized her arm and laughed jeeringly.

Troyes' hand was on the shutter bolt to open it and jump through when the man's words stopped him where he was.

"It's little Johnny Sevens at last," the man mocked in Cockney English. "But she don't seem half glad to see her old chum Alf Riggs."

He was twisting her arm, but Feuille felt no pain. All she felt was utter hopelessness and despair.

Troyes has left me, she told herself, because he believes I injured and robbed this man in a low dockside quarrel. Now this man has found me, and he will expose me and cause my arrest.

She wrenched her arm from his grasp, but he was between her and the house door. She backed then against the banister rail, as she had retreated against the window in the London room; but this time there was no weapon for her reaching hands. She heard herself saying the same words which she had said to him there:

"Don't you touch me, Alfie Riggs!"

He laughed with pleasure at being able to frighten her.

"Same little fighting nipper you are! Wouldn't have me touch you then, won't have me touch you now. Hit me with my own rum bottle because I tried to give you what any other girl would have been glad to get. But all your fighting don't help you now. I've found you, and I've got you just where I want you."

"Why did you come?" she asked him faintly.

"Didn't I always want to come to America? Wasn't I the one put the idea in your head? All along I wanted to come—and I wanted to find you."

"Why did you want to find me? What do you want, Alfie?"

"What do you want, Alfie?" he jeered. "Well, I'll tell you what. I want what's owing me from little Johnny Sevens."

"I do not owe you anything!"

"Oh, yes you do, my girl! You owe me for your passage, and you owe me for breaking my head and laying me up for a month."

"You never paid for my passage. I worked it out at this place. The man who bought my covenant would tell you—if he were here."

She caught herself, but he pounced on it.

"So the master's away and you're alone with a bunch of blacks? So much the better, my girl. We can settle accounts in private."

"The Negroes are good and will help me! They are my friends. If I scream—"

Troyes heard her voice rising with threatened hysteria. It was hard for him to hold back, but he knew he must let Alf Riggs talk and convict himself.

"If I scream," she threatened Alf, "they will come to my help. They will come to my help, and they will go for the master."

He stepped closer to her, hiding her from Saint Lys' gaze.

"But you don't want that, my girl, do you? You don't want the master, or anyone else, to find out. You don't want to be turned over to the police for attempted murder. The police are on the lookout for you now. Ma was the one told 'em. Proper scared she was when they brought me in as limp as a boiled fish. She told 'em a French girl had been with me and she was the one as had done it. She had the paper with those three names that looked like 'Fool Johnny Sevens.' She told 'em, too, how you stole that gold box the little girl had. Ma seen her showin' it to you, and planned to get it for herself. But you were too smart for her."

"Alfie, I didn't take it! It was *given to me.*"

"What if it was?" he asked roughly. "You and the little girl was so thick that I don't doubt she gave it to you. But unless you turn it over now, and plenty more along with it, I'll go straight to the police in Charles Town. I came in there with a shipload of workmen two weeks ago, and I found out all I needed to know before I started for this here Boy Blue."

"How did you know I was in this province?"

"Everybody in London knows what happened to the *Eagle*, and that her covenant servants were sold in Charles Town. As soon as I got there I went to the judges' court—"

Troyes heard her gasp: "Did you tell the judge about me?"

"Not yet, I didn't—and I won't if you treat me right. A man on the ship who knew about law told me I had a right to go and look at records of the court. It's written there that a planter named Saint Liss from a place called Boy Blue took up the covenant of a woman named Johnny Sevens."

He slapped his fat hip with a gesture she remembered.

"Alfie's the one gave you that name, and you liked it enough to keep it."

Although he had learned little yet, Saint Lys' heart turned over at the sadness in her voice.

"I didn't like it. I hated it—and hated you for calling me so. But I thought the police would be hunting me for hitting you with the bottle, and I was afraid to use my real name of Feuille Joany from the Cévennes."

"You better be afraid," he warned her brutally. "You better take your choice right now of handing the gold box over to me, along with what money you've earned from this Saint Liss, or of my turning you over to the police."

Saint Lys heard her sobbing, but he held himself back still. The Cockney voice continued: "I can squeeze him dry too with the papers Ma and I got out of the little girl's doll. He'd probably give me Boy Blue to know what became of his sister."

"Alfie, you devil! Was Fleurette his sister?"

"She was his sister, all right. That's why I kept his address. I was going to cut you in when I found him and told him. But you were too smart for me. You took the letter and came to him."

"I *didn't* come to him! You know that I sailed for Virginia. Pirates took the *Eagle* and brought her to Charles Town. I happened to fall into the hands of a Frenchman who knew

Monsieur Saint Lys and knew he needed someone to take care of his mother. But I tried not to work for him, because I was afraid—afraid that sooner or later you would come. I didn't know your reason. You said only that he was a man who would help you."

"He'll help me all right," Alf said with certainty. "Maybe he'll be helping you too, if you do as I tell you. Maybe I'll let you go along with me, if you go in the house now and bring me the box and the money."

"I'm going," she told him. "But I won't go with you."

"Oh, yes, you will! I've got you now just where I want you. On one hand I can tell the police that you tried to murder me. On the other this Saint Liss will kick you out in a hurry if I say you only came here to help me clean him out—"

She interrupted him with a cry. "I didn't! I'd die before I did that!"

"Then come along with me now. I still like you, Johnny."

"Alfie, I'll give you all I have if you only go away! You know in your heart that Fleurette gave me the snuffbox. All she could recall of it was that she called her brother Boum-Boum—"

But at that second someone took Alf Riggs by the collar and threw him violently down the stairs. He lost his balance and rolled the flight of sixteen steps to the ground. Before he could pick himself up, he was seized upon either side by a black man just as tall if not as stout as he. He heard one of these two speak softly but longingly.

"*Mahaba*, you want we should tie this wite man and haul him to the High Sheriff?"

Then, bruised and dusty, Alf raised his eyes to the piazza, unable to believe his ears. For the man who had thrown him, and who now stood with both arms around Johnny Sevens, was speaking with only good will in his tones.

"Turn the scoundrel loose," he said. "Give him all he wants to eat and a bed for the night in the basement. Tomorrow I'll see that he's sent on out of the county."

He paused, then added: "He ought to be hanged, but no

good could come of that. All I can think of—my darling I nearly lost!—is that he's proved to me you're not my sister."

Camille and Pierre had run downstairs, disheveled and apprehensive. But Troyes seemed unable to do anything except sit holding Feuille's hands and gazing at her while she explained.

"Do you not remember, Troyes, when down in the indigo field you said *leaf* was the loveliest word in the French language? Do you not recall that I told you later you would like my real name because you loved flowers and fruit and leaves?"

"I remember perfectly. It was another reason for me to think you my little lost sister Violette. That was her baptismal name and her little love name was Fleurette."

"If I had only known in time to tell your mother that I loved Fleurette and was holding her hand when she died!"

He groaned aloud and dropped his face into her hands.

"But Troyes, how could you imagine that I was your sister and that your mother would not have recognized me?"

He raised his face. "Feuille, have you forgotten that my mother called you 'daughter' just before she died?"

Her fingers tightened on his. She could see it now. He was going on.

"There were so many other things. Violette had big blue eyes. They were darker than yours, but time changes us. From babyhood she loved music and sang. More than once Camille has remarked that you were enough like me to be my own sister."

"I am more like you than your own sister was. She was gentle and timorous, while I fight back—as you do. Had I not come from a stony land I could not have lived through Silk Throsters Lane. Its horror destroyed Violette's memory, and in the end it killed her."

His mouth twisted as if in pain. "The loss of memory too. I construed your words to mean you were speaking of yourself. When I looked down and saw my own snuffbox in my hands, it came over me like a wave and I felt I was drowning."

She held his hands tighter, for she longed to comfort him even more than she longed for his comfort and caresses.

"Try not to grieve, my Troyes. Violette is safe now. Tell me how it was that you lost her. All she could tell me was that the brother she called Boum-Boum gave her the musical box when she wept at parting and said she must go by another road but that he would find her."

"I had to make the choice of taking with me either my mother or Violette. I was then only seventeen years old; but I was the man of the family and decision was upon my shoulders. A young man and his mother are a pair of travelers usual enough not to incur suspicion. But a young man of seventeen with a child of five is not. I had to consider all that, because I knew that the Saint Lys family was proscribed and a description of its every member published. I took my mother north and overland to Holland. We had agreed that Violette's governess, Madame Charles, disguise herself as a peasant woman with a peasant grandchild and take ship at Boulogne-sur-Mer and meet us in Holland. If I failed to meet the ship at Gravenhage, she was to come on to Middleburg and wait there for six months. In case we still missed each other, she had funds and instructions to sail for Charles Town and go to the home of the deRossets. She must have sewn them inside Violette's doll before she died."

"So that is how Alf got your address—and the money he used to spend. That is why you came to America."

"That is why we came. When our time at Middleburg expired we took ship for Charles Town, praying to find them here. I had no reason to think they had not embarked from Boulogne on the ship which sailed every week for Holland. But upon the voyage to America the captain told us of a recent outrage by the arch-pirate Bartholomew Roberts. Operating in the North Sea, he had captured a French-Hollandish ship. Although a devil incarnate as all pirates are, he was said to have certain rules about sparing women and children. In fact, some of the women passengers from the captured ship were found to have been set ashore on the northern coast of France. That is why for the last ten years I have employed a lawyer in Holland to continue attempts to trace my sister in Europe. Mr. Allein in Charles Town has been working with him."

"Did they not look for her in England?"

"Both they and I wrote to Threadneedle Church, and to every other refuge for Huguenots. But we asked for Violette Heloïse Antoinette Saint Lys, and for a middle-aged lady by name of Madame Charles."

Feuille told him of her own escape from France.

"If Madame Charles found herself under suspicion when she reached the port, she would have embarked on any boat she could get aboard."

"I realize that. I tried to think ahead of time of everything that could possibly happen. But it never occurred to me that Madame had died suddenly and that little Violette had lost her memory from the shock and terror. I knew Madame as both intelligent and resourceful. I had given her more than sufficient money."

His face was so sad that Feuille changed the subject.

"Will not Alf Riggs now go to the police and make trouble for both you and me?"

He laughed shortly and shook his head.

"Early tomorrow Riggs will start, guarded by Saraka, for the sheriff's office on the Winyah. But Sam will be riding ahead of them with a letter from me. In that letter I shall explain to my friend Noë Serrée, High Sheriff of Craven County, that the prisoner is an undesirable character whom I caught trespassing on my property. I shall write that I am willing not to charge him with the misdemeanor if he leaves this province and never returns. I know that Serrée will set him on his way to the Albemarle—and I know that is the last we will hear or see of Riggs."

She knew it too. She knew that when it came to teasing Fleurette or frightening her, Alf was a loud-mouthed bully, but that he was a coward when he faced a determined man.

She sighed with happiness as she reached out and picked up the snuffbox. As she did so, Troyes drew from his pocket the turquoise ornaments which Ree had taken to him. Camille came into the room, and her husband followed her.

"Where have you been while I did all the work, my useless Pierre?" she scolded. "I have been down in the basement to wake up the maids and tell them to make hot chocolate for us."

"I've been outside in the hall," he replied, "peeping through the door and listening to all that Troyes and Feuille said."

He smoothed his still-tousled hair and grinned at them; but they only smiled back at him, too happy to care.

"And here is the chocolate," added Camille. "As soon as we drink it we will go to bed and rest for tomorrow's journey."

Troyes reached out and clutched Feuille, as if to hold her against all the past.

"I will not go to bed," he told Camille determinedly. "So if you insist upon chaperoning us, you may make up your mind to spend the rest of the night in this drawing room. I shall hold Feuille here in my arms until day begins to break and Ree comes with the coach to drive us to Jamestown."